GONE
IN THE
NIGHT

BOOKS BY HELEN PHIFER

DETECTIVE LUCY HARWIN SERIES

Dark House

Dying Breath

Last Light

BETH ADAMS SERIES

The Girl in the Grave

The Girls in the Lake

DETECTIVE MORGAN BROOKES SERIES

One Left Alive

The Killer's Girl

The Hiding Place

First Girl to Die

Find the Girl

Sleeping Dolls

Silent Angel

Their Burning Graves

Hold Your Breath

Stolen Darlings

Save Her Twice

Poison Memories

Two Broken Girls

Their Dying Embrace

Twisted Bones

Standalones

Lakeview House

The Vanishing Bookstore

GONE
IN THE
NIGHT

HELEN PHIFER

bookouture

Published by Bookouture in 2025

An imprint of Storyfire Ltd.
Carmelite House
50 Victoria Embankment
London EC4Y 0DZ

www.bookouture.com

The authorised representative in the EEA is Hachette Ireland
8 Castlecourt Centre
Dublin 15 D15 XTP3
Ireland
(email: info@hbgi.ie)

ISBN: 978-1-80550-284-5
eBook ISBN: 978-1-80550-285-2

For my utterly brilliant editor, Jennifer Hunt, this one is for you. Xx

ONE

Lydia Williams could not finish work soon enough. Her eyes kept glancing at the tiny clock in the right-hand corner of her computer screen. Every minute was taking forever, and if the office hadn't been full of her coworkers, she would have grabbed her backpack and strode out thirty minutes ago, as if she'd already been given permission to finish early. Her cheeks flushed red at the indignity of a thirty-nine-year-old woman having to ask permission to do anything. This job was the worst she'd ever had. Justin, her 'boss' (she always said his job title with inverted commas), was an idiot; an arrogant, slimy, brown-nosing idiot who made her skin crawl just looking at his smarmy face through the huge glass windows of his office. How many times a day had she fantasised about pushing him through those windows? Far too many to be healthy, that was for sure.

She glanced at the clock again.

Three minutes, that was all she had to wait.

You can do this, three minutes and you can go home, grab Barney and get out of here.

Two minutes, she began to tidy her desk.

One minute, she felt her shoulders relax for the first time in hours; it was almost freedom, she could taste the fresh air.

'Lydia.'

His voice made her shoulders stiffen, and she tried to not ball up her fists. Unclenching her fingers, she turned to see Justin leaning against the doorway of his office. The top three buttons on his shirt unfastened, his tie loosened, his dark hair, which was thinning on top, looked as if he'd stuck his finger into an electrical socket. 'Have you got a minute?'

She looked at the clock and watched it hit four. *No, I haven't. I'm out of work's time now and on my own, so leave me alone.*

'Yes.'

As she stood up, the voice inside her head swore loudly at her for not telling him to sod off. Everyone around her was scrambling to grab coats, backpacks, lunch bags and get the hell out of this too small office before he could say any of their names. But he wouldn't, he never did. It had been the same for the last four Fridays. She inhaled deeply through her nose before picking up her bag and throwing her jacket across her arm. She headed into his office that smelled of coffee and stale perspiration.

'I know it's Friday and you're keen to get away, so I'm sorry to keep you.'

Lydia stared into his eyes; he wasn't sorry at all. The way his top lip curled up at the sides told her he was enjoying this.

'What do you want, Justin? I need to get home.'

'Oh, do you have pressing plans?'

'Yes, I do.' She didn't embellish on them or tell him that the most important thing in her life was her dog, Barney. She didn't want him to know anything about her personal life outside of work.

'Are they exciting?'

'What do you want?' She'd had enough now; her freedom was so close she could almost reach out and touch it.

'I wondered if we could discuss the Ryerson account over a drink or two, maybe grab a bite to eat. All on company expenses, of course.'

He was too tight to even pay for after-work drinks for her.

'I can't, sorry, I'm sure we can discuss it on Monday.'

A look of anger flashed across his face, and his cheeks burned a little redder than they already were. 'What is so important that you'd decline my invitation for drinks and supper? You've turned me down the last three Fridays in a row. It's not as if you have any better offers. You're single, you live with a dog and you're almost forty, with no partner or kids, no real ambitions. I would have thought you'd jump at the chance for a date with me.'

She stared at him, was he really that oblivious to how obnoxious he was and how much of a creep? Plus, how did he know all this stuff about her? She never told him, she hardly spoke to anyone in this office – they were all kids except for Karen. He must have been looking through her Instagram, she realised, which infuriated her because that was the only social media platform she was active on. She used it to keep a record of what she'd been doing. Those photos were precious memories that one day she could look back on. She knew she was going to regret this, yet somehow, she felt no qualms about doing it. Taking a deep breath, a feeling of peace washed over her – this was long overdue.

'And you're a married man, who perpetually smells of stale body odour, are about as attractive as my ninety-year-old neighbour and have as much charm as a corpse; my dog's breath smells better than you do. I might be almost forty, but I have a great life, and you know what, Justin, it's just improved way beyond anything I could comprehend because I quit. You can take the Ryerson account and shove it where the sun doesn't shine, and whilst you're at it don't even think about not paying me this month, because I'm friends with your wife on Facebook.'

She heard his sharp intake of breath and turned away before he could see the smile on her face. She would rather beg on street corners than have to spend another minute working for him. As she hoisted her backpack onto her shoulder and walked out of the door, she muttered, 'What an arsehole.' She wasn't friends with his wife because she didn't have a Facebook account, but he wasn't to know that.

Smiling to herself, Lydia didn't take the lift in case he ran down the stairs and was waiting at the bottom for her. She wasn't sure how Justin would take this kind of rejection, but she didn't care. Lydia Williams finally felt free for the first time in her life. She knew that when the euphoria wore off and reality hit her, she would panic about what she'd just done, but for now she didn't care one little bit.

She was driving with Barney to the most scenic wild camping site she'd discovered in the Lake District, and she would spend the next few days sleeping in her roof tent, staring up at the stars, drinking hot chocolate and reading. She didn't need a man to make her life complete; she was quite capable of doing that herself.

Lydia had decided against taking her little Suzuki Jimny jeep up the narrow track to the spot she'd seen one of the other wild campers she followed on Instagram rave about. As she'd followed the road that led to the narrower coffin road, she'd had a change of mind. She didn't want to intrude on Shazza's pitch because, as far as she knew from her last post, she was still up there. Although it would be great to meet her in person, she wasn't quite brave enough to introduce herself, which was stupid considering they both had a lot in common. They both had 4x4s with roof tents, both loved the outdoors and both seemed to prefer their own company than being with others, which was why she didn't want to turn up unannounced. Instead, she'd gone to an official wild camping site where there was only one other tent pitched and decided it was near enough; and because the only amenity was a toilet block with a single shower that ran freezing cold, it was almost as good as being on her own. At least it was dog friendly, and she had been able to walk Barney for miles and hadn't met another single person.

Another couple of weeks and this place would be heaving with people camping, once the weather had improved, but she didn't mind the chill in the air of an evening. She loved being snuggled with Barney in her tent, reading, or they'd watch something on her iPad. This cold weather meant the night skies were usually clear, and the stars would paint a pretty picture for her to watch before bed.

As she walked back along the footpath that reached the campsite, she saw the other tent that had been pitched had now gone. The couple who had been camping had been so lovely and had shared their burgers with her last night, after she'd commented how good they smelled. They'd started following her on Instagram, and she had followed them, so they could keep in touch, which was very sweet, and they'd even asked her if she wanted to move on to the next campsite with them. Lydia had declined; she really did love her own company even if it did get a little spooky at night sometimes. Having this place to herself was worth the eeriness of being completely alone in a remote place.

Barney was in heaven. He'd never left her side since she'd gone home and packed their stuff, after she'd told Justin to shove his job. She lay reading, her eyes getting heavy. She was tired, as she'd walked miles this afternoon, contemplating what she was going to do with her life now she was a free woman.

Suddenly she heard the crunching of tyres crawling along the gravel track that led to the site. It was late. Whoever it was they were going to have to pitch their tent in the dark, unless they had a roof tent too. Her roof tent was amazing; within minutes she had a warm, cosy place to sleep without any of the usual hassle of pitching and struggling against the wind to get the pegs in the ground and secure it before it blew away. She thought about offering to help the person, but Barney was snoring next to her, and she was warm and cosy. It wasn't up to her, for all they knew she might be asleep.

Snapping a quick photo of herself and Barney tucked up in her sleeping bag, she tried to post it to Instagram, but the signal wasn't too good up here. Putting her phone under her pillow, she closed her eyes, pulling the hood of the sleeping bag over her head to muffle any noise her new neighbours might make, and began to breathe deeply in through her nose and out through her mouth, listening to the calming sound of the wind fluttering leaves in the trees in the distance.

She always used this little meditation to help her fall asleep and it did the trick. Before long she was drifting off unaware of anything that was happening around her. She didn't pick up on the fact that whoever had arrived in their car hadn't even got out of it. There were no sounds for the next hour except Lydia's and Barney's gentle snores that seemed to be in complete synchronicity with each other. They masked the sound of the footsteps getting closer to her tent and creeping around in the dark.

TWO

Joss Graham had been farming the land around here since he could walk. His father had taken over from his grandfather, it was truly a family affair. Although it was getting harder now, and he was struggling the older he was getting. His son didn't want to be a farmer, he hated it and had trained in computers, which Joss didn't understand. What was the attraction of being cooped up inside when he could be out here in the beautiful Lake District, working the fells and fields? The arguments that decision had caused. Until his wife, Ann, told him to let it go, because he was pushing him even further away and it was breaking her heart. He loved Ann more than anything and had stopped immediately, realising that all good things must come to an end. Who was he to dictate to their son what to do with his life? Maybe it was time for them to think about selling the farm, retiring and taking it easy. That was why he had gone up to the most desolate parcel of land he owned last week; he wanted time on his own to think about their future.

He spotted the Land Rover was still parked near to the entrance gate. He'd been shocked by the pure purpleness of it against the backdrop of the greenery of the fields and the beauty of the Skiddaw mountain range when he'd spoken to the woman, who wasn't some kid like he'd been expecting. She'd looked older; maybe in her thirties. She was friendly and had asked his permission to park near to the entrance to the field that was edged by Skiddaw Forest. He hadn't had a problem with her pitching there. Lucky for her, by the time he'd reached the field he had been in a grand mood and he'd agreed she could park there for one night. He had decided he was retiring, it was time to let someone else take over the farm, and tomorrow they were going down to Wales to visit his new baby grandson, and he couldn't wait to tell his son his plans. He usually told those wild campers no, to find somewhere else, but the woman had looked tired, a little sad and he'd been feeling a bit on the soft side, so he'd said yes.

He didn't use this field much, it was too high up, too rocky and not much good for anything other than the beautiful views it gave of Blencathra mountain and the very tip of the forest. How she'd discovered this was beyond him. It was way off the beaten track, but she had been so grateful to him and had promised not to leave any trace she'd ever been here. That was a week ago. After a wonderful time with his family, he'd come home and gone straight to bed with the flu; it had taken him off his feet and wiped him out. When he finally felt better, he remembered about the woman and hoped she'd moved on without leaving rubbish strewn everywhere. This morning, he had come to check if she had been true to her word and was mildly annoyed to find her Land Rover still here. As he drove the quad bike nearer, he realised he was more than annoyed; his fingers were clenched around the handlebars, and he was angry because she'd taken advantage of his good nature.

He revved the quad bike to alert her to his presence and waited for her to come out of the tent, but there was no sign of any movement.

Turning off the engine he strode towards the 4x4.

'Hey, hello, are you there?'

There were no sounds coming from the direction of the vehicle, and he wondered if she'd taken ill or had an accident of some kind. He had a sinking feeling in his stomach as he stood within touching distance of the narrow metal ladder that led up to the tent. It was making him queasy. He checked around the car to see if she'd left a note on the windscreen – maybe she'd broken down. There was no way any vehicle except a 4x4 could get up here to rescue her. What if she'd been waiting for him to turn up? Joss went through a whole host of questions in his mind, unsure what to do. He stared up at the tent then reached forward and knocked on the passenger window as hard as he could. 'Hey, are you up there?'

His voice fell flat as he waited for a reply, and it was then, as a breeze blew in his direction, that he caught a whiff of something dead. He'd dealt with death all of his farming life, cows and sheep getting caught up in fencing, their sometimes diseased and rotting bodies decomposing. He knew he should take a look inside the tent, but he also knew that smell. The girl was beyond any help he could offer, and he didn't want to touch anything and get himself in trouble.

Damn it, woman, if you came up here to end your life that's mighty sad and I am never going to forgive myself for leaving you to do it.

Joss took his baseball cap off his head and swiped a hand across his forehead. Taking out his phone, he doubted he would have a signal, and he was right. Nothing. Pushing his mobile back into the pocket of his checked shirt, he whispered, 'I'm going to get you some help, be back as soon as I can.'

He backed away, got on his quad bike and sped back to the farmhouse to call the police.

THREE

Detective Morgan Brookes hadn't stopped smiling since returning from New York. It was her first day back in work, but just thinking about how amazing the break had been made her heart so happy. She and Ben had wandered around Times Square, marvelling at the sights. They'd strolled across the Brooklyn Bridge, gone to the very top of the observation decks on both the Empire State Building and the Rockefeller Centre, drank cocktails on rooftop bars and shopped on Fifth Avenue. Saks had been amazing, but she'd preferred spending more time in the huge Barnes & Noble. She'd also visited as many small, independent bookshops as she could in the little time they had on the five-day trip. When they had stepped off the boat at Liberty Island and stared up at the Statue of Liberty, Morgan had tears in her eyes. It had been everything she had dreamed of and more. Rydal Falls was beautiful, but New York City had opened her eyes to a different way of life, and she couldn't stop thinking about it.

Ben had been called into Marc's office before they'd even taken two steps out of the lift, and she'd left him to it. As she walked into their office, she grinned at Amy who was smiling back at her, nodding her head in the direction of Des's old desk. Morgan glanced that way and stopped in her tracks. Sitting there was a guy in his late thirties, if she had to guess. He was chatting on the phone, so not paying her any attention, but he was pretty hot, his collar-length, dark brown hair looked as if it had been freshly styled by a hairdresser, and his tanned, stubbled face was handsome. She turned back to Amy and fanned her hand in front of her face, which made Amy spit the mouthful of Diet Coke she'd just taken all down the front of her shirt. Amy stood up, and grabbing Morgan's arm, practically dragged her out of the office down to the ladies' loos.

'Who is that?'

'My replacement.'

'What? Where are you going?'

Amy laughed and pointed to her rather swollen stomach. 'I have a date with this dude in four weeks. As much as I'd love to give birth on Ben's desk and carry on working, it's not happening. I have high blood pressure, and the doctor said I need to take my maternity leave now because of the nature of our job, and the fact that I got abducted and stabbed someone in my third trimester didn't help matters at all.'

Morgan couldn't help it and snorted with laughter. 'Oh, Lord. Yes, you did. Are you okay? Is high blood pressure dangerous for the baby? And how are you going to give birth in only four weeks? It's come around so fast.'

'So many questions, Morgan, slow down. It's part of the deal, you know, when you get pregnant you have to actually have the baby when it's due. And high blood pressure can be dangerous, which is why I'm finishing tomorrow and why Marc brought in a replacement.'

'Oh, I never thought this day would come. I'm going to miss you, Amy.'

'You liar, you think he's hot. I saw that look on your face.'

'I do not, I'm happily settled with Ben. But he is a bit

though; there's no harm in admiring what's in front of your eyes even if you're not interested, which I'm definitely not. What did Cain say about him arriving?'

'Spat his dummy out. I don't know whether he's a bit jealous or whether he's worried he'll replace him too.'

'Poor Cain, nobody could replace him. He's one of a kind.'

'I told him that, he's been my lifesaver these past few months. Anyway, I just wanted to give you the lowdown on the new start.'

'Where's he from? What's his name?'

'Tristan Carter, and he's from up the coast. St Bees. It's all posh up there. He's been a detective for four years apparently. I didn't ask too much because I didn't want to upset Cain. This is only his second shift. He spent most of yesterday with Marc who showed him around.'

Hammering on the door made them both jump, and Amy threw it open to see Cain standing there, towering over them, blocking out the light from the corridor.

'What's this private conflab, you didn't invite me?'

'Missed you, Cain.'

He grinned at her, opened his arms and scooped her in for one of his famous bear hugs. She sighed.

'I missed you too, Morgan, can't wait to hear all about The Big Apple, but the boss, boss is looking for you. Did you not hear that log come in?'

Morgan hadn't even switched her radio on, and she shook her head.

'Some farmer has found a body in one of those tent box things and it's all kicking off, welcome home, Brookes.'

'Are you winding me up?'

'Nope and guess what, you have the new boy to take with you; Ben and Marc are already en route to the scene.'

'Where are you going? Can't you come with us?' Morgan

didn't want to be paired up with Tristan already when she hadn't even said hello to him.

'Been demoted, haven't I?'

'What?'

'Boss, boss wants Tristan on scene.'

Morgan grimaced. 'Holy crap, it's been what, ten minutes since I walked into this place, you're definitely winding me up, Cain.'

Cain was shaking his head. 'I hate to tell you this, Morgan, but you truly are an angel of death. Those fishnet tights under those cropped trousers are not fooling anyone.'

Amy punched him in the arm.

'Ouch, too much violence.'

'If you think that hurts, just you wait until I'm in labour, and give her a break, Cain, stop feeling sorry for yourself. I thought you'd be glad to get out of going to a crime scene for hours.'

He held up his hands. 'You're right, sorry, Morgan. That was not very nice of me.'

'You're forgiven, just.'

She strode off to the office, where Tristan was shrugging on a jacket. He looked at Morgan and smiled.

'You must be Morgan; I'm Tristan but everyone calls me Stan.' He held out his hand, and she took it, smiling at him.

'I am, how did you guess?' she replied, bristling at the name Stan. Her dad's name. She felt the familiar wave of sadness wash over her at the reminder of her dad and wasn't sure how she'd feel calling someone else Stan, even though it was inconsequential. She'd have to get over it; he couldn't help his name.

He pointed to her boots. 'Cain said that I'd know you anywhere because you always wear black and your Docs are welded to your feet.'

'Did he now?'

Tristan smiled.

'Come on, we have to go. Have you got the details of the location for the crime scene?'

He waved a piece of A4 paper in the air. 'Even better, I printed out the log.'

'Great.'

She unhooked a set of keys off the board and threw her handbag onto her desk. Striding towards the stairs, a little shocked that a log had come in so soon, she was walking so fast Tristan had to hurry to keep up with her.

FOUR

Ben had managed to get keys for one of the off-road vehicles owned by the force. The farmer had made it clear when he'd phoned in that they wouldn't get up to the scene without one. As they'd driven towards the location, Marc had done nothing but talk about how good this new detective was he'd brought in from up west. Apparently, his track record was unblemished. Ben knew he was trying to defuse the situation because he'd arranged Amy's replacement without even consulting him, which pissed him off big time. Marc should have waited to speak to him first. He'd only been off work for a week and what a crappy start to their first day back. He was deep breathing and doing his best to keep calm, but it was a lot harder than he anticipated.

'So, are you okay with Tristan coming in then? I thought it would be best to get him introduced whilst Amy is still here, and you know how busy the team has been the last couple of months. I didn't want to leave you a woman down.'

'I have no choice but to be okay with him. It's not as if you consulted me first.'

'I guess we all thought Amy would carry on working until she went into labour.'

Ben had to give it to him, they had been so overwhelmed with the number of cases that he had let his duty to Amy slip in more ways than one, and he was going to feel bad about that forever. In all fairness to Amy, she had proved herself even tougher than she came across. She could have gone sick after the trauma of being held hostage by Gordon Wells, but she hadn't. She'd taken a couple of days off and then strolled back into work, as if she hadn't just been through the most traumatic experience of her life. He wasn't sure what he'd done to have such an amazing team of detectives working for him, who also happened to be the loveliest of human beings too.

'It's fine, it really is. Just a bit of a surprise that's all. As long as he's going to fit in and not cause major problems, that's all I'm concerned about.'

'He's a great guy, very sincere, not full of himself. I don't know how much experience he's had with murder cases, but I guess what he's lacking on that front he'll soon make up because you know what this place is like.'

The narrow lane that led to the old coffin road was bumpy; Ben wasn't sure that Morgan would get this far in a normal div car.

There was a quad bike parked a little further along the road, with a guy on it who waved at them.

'Must be the farmer who rang it in.'

Ben had to stop his eyes from rolling in Marc's direction. It was obviously the guy who'd rung it in. He gave himself a shake; he needed to get his act together and stop acting like a sulky sixteen-year-old; he knew he wasn't being the most professional. Ben stopped the 4x4 and jumped out. As he got closer to the quad bike, he noticed that the guy was completely grey, and his weathered skin was tanned; he had the look of someone who had spent his entire life working outdoors. As he walked to meet Ben, he estimated that the guy must be at least in his late sixties.

'DS Ben Matthews and DI Marc Howard.'

The guy held out his huge, calloused hand. 'Joss Graham, sorry to have to call you out like this.'

Ben shook his hand; Marc did the same.

'It said on the log you didn't see a body, but think there is one. Can you explain that a little more?' asked Ben.

'I'm a fourth-generation farmer, was born on a farm and spend just about every day on it, except for the holiday we just had to visit our new grandson. I know the smell of death, when something is decomposing, and before you ask, no I don't have experience with dead bodies, but a lot of dead animals over the years. It's that sickly sweet rotting smell that you can't get out of your sinuses no matter how hard you inhale on a Vicks cold and flu stick.'

Ben smiled at him; the guy wasn't wrong. 'Is it far?'

He shook his head. 'Half a mile further up, but the road gets bumpy. Glad you brought a suitable vehicle, or you'd be walking up there.'

'I just need to hang on for my colleague who shouldn't be too—' He didn't finish his sentence because the white Ford Focus Morgan was driving rounded the bend. He waved at her, while looking intently at the guy in the passenger seat. Both of them got out of the car.

Ben didn't know Tristan, had never worked with him, but he felt a twinge of something deep inside his gut at just how good-looking the guy was. He looked as if he'd just stepped out of a magazine photoshoot. He put Marc to shame. Ben couldn't help glancing at Morgan, wondering if she was overly impressed.

Marc nodded at them.

'Jump in, you're not going to be able to get up there in that.'

'Yes, boss,' said Tristan, and he smiled at Ben.

Ben smiled back.

'Tristan, this is Ben, your new DS, we'll do some proper introductions later.'

The farmer had already set off, and Ben was keen to follow him. Luckily, both he and Morgan had recently completed their off-road course that allowed them to drive four-wheel drive vehicles over rugged terrain. Marc would no doubt sign up to do his after this, and he wondered if Tristan had his off-road driving authority.

The purple Land Rover came into view with its roof tent up. Set against the dramatic background of Blencathra, it looked as if it could have been an Instagram advertisement for wild camping. Ben stored that thought. He would ask Morgan to check out Instagram and Facebook; damn it, Amy usually did this kind of stuff. He was going to miss having her to rely on.

Morgan leaned forward.

'That looks amazing, what a great place to camp. Especially with one of those, you don't even have to mess around putting a tent up. It's a genius idea whoever thought of it.'

'Car tents have actually been around since the fifties, but they didn't really take off back then. You wouldn't catch me up here camping on my own. It's too far away from civilisation.' Tristan was shaking his head.

She turned to him. 'Where would you rather be, in a busy campsite?'

He laughed. 'In a five-star hotel, with a soft bed, lots of pillows and room service. Camping is not my thing at all; I'm not one for the great outdoors full stop.'

Ben stopped the car and all four of them got out. 'I don't know if we have any kit in the back of this. Sorry, I didn't think to check.'

Tristan pulled a pair of gloves out of his pocket and held them up. 'I have these.'

Morgan opened the rear door of their vehicle and began

rooting around in a box of stuff. Pulling out several packets, she let out a sigh so deep Ben knew what it meant.

'They are all size small, what a surprise.'

The farmer stood to one side, while the rest of them watched her.

Ben said, 'Sorry.'

She didn't reply but began to tear open the packet with the white crime-scene suit inside it. Everyone turned away even though she was tugging it on top of the clothes she was wearing. She put bootees over her Docs and pulled gloves out of the almost empty box.

'If you kind of walk around the not obvious route to the ladder it might help preserve any forensics.'

She glared at Ben, and he shut up. Morgan knew better than any of them the correct way to approach a crime scene.

'How do we even know there's a body in there?'

'Joss said he knows the smell of decomp, so let's assume the worst.'

The sun was warm, and Ben couldn't help thinking that it would be awful if whoever was inside the tent had perished all alone.

Morgan reached the 4x4 and turned to look at him.

'I can't reach unless I use the ladder, I'm not tall enough.'

Marc shouted, 'Stop.'

Everyone looked at him.

'What if there are prints on the ladder? We could be jeopardising everything.'

Morgan caught a whiff of decay carried on the breeze and felt her stomach muscles clench tight. The smell was emanating from the tent. It didn't matter how many times she was faced with the stench of death, it had the same effect on her.

'Well, I think Joss is right. Something dead is up there, so how are we going to determine who it is and what they died of, if we're standing here all day twiddling our thumbs?'

'What if I drive the quad bike as near as possible and you stand on that?' offered Joss.

Ben looked at the large bike that would surely mess up the scene even more than Morgan.

'Thanks, Joss, but it's okay. Morgan, you're going to have to climb up and we'll deal with the consequences later.'

Marc shook his head. 'By consequences you mean Wendy.'

Ben shrugged. 'Same thing.'

Morgan stood on the ladder, only going as far up as she could reach the zipper to the tent.

Ben watched, not realising he was holding his breath until she tugged it down and a cloud of decomp and bluebottles filled the air, making Morgan almost lose her balance. Tristan cupped a hand across his mouth.

Morgan clung on to the side of the narrow aluminium ladder and turned on the torch she'd tugged from her pocket, staring into the blackness inside then nodding emphatically.

She climbed back down.

'There's a body in there. A woman, red hair, a lot of insects.' She was far enough away from the Land Rover to bend over and suck in a deep breath of fresh air to try and rid her lungs of the smell.

'Could you make out how she died?' Ben asked, his voice almost hesitant, as if not sure he wanted to know the answer.

'Knife through her chest. There's blood inside that's dried up. She's been there a while.'

'How do you know that?' asked Tristan.

'Because most of her face has been eaten away by the maggots.'

Tristan's tanned complexion turned a deathly pale colour as he turned away from her and jogged a short distance, his hand still cupped over his mouth, and vomited into a gorse bush.

Ben thought about all the ways he could have spent his first day back in work after his glorious trip to NYC. He'd envisioned catching up on a multitude of emails and being filled in by Cain on all the station gossip he'd missed. Murder was not even remotely on that list.

'Thanks, Morgan, right, let's do this.'

Ben's heart sank as he tugged the radio out of his pocket and began to request CSI and a pathologist, as well as officers to come guard the track up to the scene. This was going to be a nightmare; they had no way of knowing how long she'd been dead until the post-mortem. There was not a single house in sight, and it was so off the beaten track he didn't know if anyone used the road apart from the odd fell walker or mountain biker. He could feel a migraine about to descend upon him, and he heard Morgan whisper in his ear, 'Here we go again, welcome back, boss, it's like we never even left.'

FIVE

The man counted on his fingers how many days it had been since he'd killed the woman. Six days of her lying and fermenting inside that tent. He wondered if she was mummified? He thought that there was an excellent chance she could be with the warm weather and the dry air inside of the tent.

As a child he'd been obsessed with the ancient Egyptians and their mummification process. He had gone on a year six school trip to the British Museum, to see an exhibition all about Tutankhamun. He had been as enthralled as a ten-year-old boy could be with the whole thing, they even had a couple of mummies on display, which had totally blown his young mind. When they were allowed in the gift shop at the end of the tour, he had picked up a book he had enough pocket money for, which was all about the pharaohs, and clutched it to his chest the rest of the day, excited for the train journey home so he could read it and look at the photographs. So began his life's work.

He would have loved to have worked in a museum, but he wasn't clever enough for university, and his mum had made him promise not to leave her when she was so ill. He hadn't known back then that her illness was self-inflicted; she chose to drink neat vodka for breakfast, lunch and tea, then stay in bed wallowing. His dad had walked out years before, and although he didn't blame him for not being able to cope with his wife, he never forgave him for abandoning him and leaving him with a drunk who didn't care about anything but herself. As he got old enough, he'd realised that she'd probably pickled her own internal organs without any help, similar to what the Egyptians did. Instead of leaving her like he should have and going away to university, he'd stayed out of his duty towards the woman who had given birth to him and not much else. He wasn't very fond of change and preferred familiarity which was why he was still here and why he had opted for a job that was local. He'd found his mother dead in her bed a month ago and cried for hours, not over losing her but at the relief he'd felt of being finally free of her.

It wasn't that he disliked his job, in fact it was the opposite – he rather enjoyed it – but he still wished he could have gone to university. Maybe one day he would, it was never too late to follow your dreams. Wasn't that what all those bloody awful inspirational speakers on Instagram and such were always blathering on about?

He'd known as he'd crept up on the woman inside the tent that if he did this it was going to change his life forever. If he got caught there was not a chance he could follow his dreams, but the compulsion to do it had been so strong, so intense, so all-consuming inside of him he knew that he wouldn't satiate it until he'd stabbed her through her heart.

He'd been thinking about it for months – if he was honest, it was more like years – but he'd never had the perfect opportunity or the freedom until now, and it was foolish to give it up so easily. He may never get the chance again.

He had given up waiting for the police to knock on his door after the first forty-eight hours, had even managed to relax and carry on as normal. He hadn't stopped thinking about her, and the temptation to go back and see what her corpse looked like after all this time had been far greater than he'd anticipated. He'd managed to hold off, though and wondered if anyone had found her yet.

He knew from all the true crime documentaries that the killers who went back to the scene were more likely to get caught. He sat back, drained his can of lager and pressed play on *Mindhunter*, his favourite Netflix show. He was gutted they had never made another series; it was by far the best programme on serial killers he'd ever watched, and he secretly wondered if he would ever have the notoriety that Kemper, Bundy, Gacy and Nielsen had, or was that a thing of the past? All the women had a thing for the US killers, and he wondered why that was. He spent hours trying to figure out why they seemed so much more appealing than any of the UK killers. He got that everyone portrayed Bundy as a charismatic, handsome guy, but he wasn't any of that. He was like any other killer, like him, and that made them both sick, twisted, evil men. He was well aware that harbouring any kind of internal feeling to take another person's life had nothing remotely charming about it. It crossed the line between good and evil, and up until he killed that woman, he had been able to stop those intrusive thoughts, but they had finally won over. Now, he wondered if he was forever going to be chasing the high that it had given him, or would he chalk it down to been there, done that and now walking around in the T-shirt?

He didn't know where his story would end, but it would never be turned into an episode of *Mindhunter*, which was a real shame.

SIX

The scene was difficult to manage purely because of the access issues with vehicles. Declan owned an Audi 4x4 and he had managed to get a blow-out when he'd hit the sharp, jutting edge of a huge rock, causing his tyre to explode with such force it made everyone duck thinking someone had thrown an explosive at them. Morgan had walked down to meet him, and she radioed Ben to come and collect the pair of them. She had tried not to laugh, it wasn't funny, but Declan was fuming about it and his expression was so serious it was hard to contain it.

'For feck's sake, what's the point of this car being a 4x4 if the tyres are going to pop like a balloon at a kid's birthday party for no good reason?'

'I think that rock was a pretty good reason, Declan. It's massive and has very sharp edges.'

He glared at her for a moment, then looked at the rock and began to laugh. 'Mary, mother of Jesus, how did I hit that? Do you think I need some driving glasses?'

She shrugged, trying not to grin, not wanting to antagonise him as they watched Ben driving slowly down towards them. Declan had got suited and booted whilst waiting for him to arrive. He got into the front seat of the car, Morgan into the rear. He held up his hand towards Ben and spoke.

'Don't even ask.'

Ben glanced at the blown-out tyre. 'I wouldn't even.'

'Can you not get me a body somewhere decent for once? You know, if there is a remote location that even Bear Grylls would struggle to find, I can guarantee you or Morgan will come up trumps.'

Ben glanced at Morgan in the rear-view mirror. She was grinning, and she looked as if she knew he was struggling not to laugh.

'I hate to break this to you, mate, but it literally has nothing to do with either of us where we find the bodies.'

Declan let out a sigh. 'I suppose not. What's happened then, who took first look at it?'

'Me, but I'm not saying anything because I don't want you to shout at me.'

He whisked his head around to face her. 'Would I shout at you? Never would I do such a thing, Morgan. Why are you saying that?'

'You're in a bad mood.'

'I'm annoyed about my tyre, but I'm annoyed with myself not you or Ben.'

'Good. You need to see for yourself anyway because I don't know what's going on. There's a lot. I can tell you one thing though, it's enough to put you off camping in one of those tent things for all the money in the world.'

'I wouldn't camp for love or money. The last time we had to deal with bodies missing from tents was enough to put me off for life.'

As Ben reached the scene, Declan leaned forward. 'This is beautiful, look at the mountains, it's framed like a picture post-card. No wonder she picked this spot to camp; but why was she up here alone and how did she find this spot because it's completely off the beaten track?'

Morgan nodded. 'I'm going to try and find out through her Instagram or her friends once we identify her. Maybe she posted on the internet where she was camping and someone who knew this area decided to come pay her a visit.'

Ben smiled. 'That's an excellent idea. Hopefully, we'll find identification with a name inside the tent. Could you do that as soon as you can, and maybe we will see who commented or liked the posts, if there are any.'

'Unless some random walker saw her and took the opportunity to kill her.'

Declan shrugged. 'Nothing surprises me anymore; it would not even make me question that, Morgan. You know what this whole area is like, I'm convinced there is something in the air around these hills and mountains that takes a relatively sane person and turns them into monsters.'

'Me too, I think the land was cursed centuries ago.'

Ben rolled his eyes. 'Well, when the pair of you have finished scaring the crap out of each other can we focus on the here and now?'

Declan waved a hand in Ben's direction. 'I'm on it. Is permission granted to take a look? I can't see Wendy anywhere.'

'Wendy has been and recorded it; she went back to the station to get some gear whilst we were waiting for you to arrive. You're good.'

Declan arched an eyebrow at Morgan. 'Ah, that's a shame, I'm sad I missed her. I kind of like being told off by Wendy. She's like the mother I never had.'

Morgan had to stifle the laughter; he was such a bad influence on her. Whenever she was with Declan, she reverted back to her fifteen-year-old self who on the rare occasion in school used to get the most inappropriate giggles and would always do what

Brad, her best friend back then, would tell her to do, even though more often than not it got them both into trouble. She closed her eyes momentarily, picturing Brad, missing him more than ever.

Ben walked away to go and speak with Marc, and Declan whispered, 'Who is that?' His gaze was in Stan's direction.

'Amy's replacement. Stan.'

'He's hot, but don't tell Theo I said that.'

'I know, don't tell Ben I agreed with you.' She winked at him. 'He hasn't got much of a stomach for this kind of thing though; he puked when I described the state the body is in.'

'Did he now, that's a shame. It takes away from that manly ruggedness.'

'Do you plan on looking at the body or are you two just here for the gossip?'

Ben had walked back towards them whilst they were whispering to each other, and Morgan felt her cheeks burn, hoping he hadn't heard them.

They both straightened up, and Declan smiled at him. 'Just getting ready. My, he's tetchy today, isn't he? Did you get up on the wrong side of the bed this morning?'

'First day back, I'm jet-lagged and wasn't expecting this.'

Declan clapped his hands. 'Of course, how was New York? Did you love it, did anything exciting happen?'

Ben's eyebrows were scrunched up that tight Declan grimaced. 'Never mind, you two can fill me in on everything later.'

Ben's phone began vibrating in his pocket, and he answered it as Declan lifted up Morgan's left hand to feel her ring finger underneath her gloves. She wondered what he was doing and then as his eyes went wide she realised: he was looking for a ring. She shook her head at him, and it was his turn to scowl. Shaking his head, he rolled his eyes in Ben's direction and then walked along the metal foot plates that Wendy had placed to give him a direct route to the vehicle without compromising any possible evidence.

Everyone had stopped to watch Declan who was at the foot of the small ladder. He was almost tall enough to peer into the tent without climbing it and only had to step on the first rung. As he unzipped the tent, Morgan watched as he took in the sight before him. He didn't flinch.

'Morgan, I'm going to need you to pass me some things from my case.'

She hurried along the temporary path towards him, still thinking about Declan's reaction to Ben not giving her a ring. She hadn't even thought about getting married. They were happy as they were, weren't they? She didn't need a ring from Ben to prove he loved her. She knew he did without that kind of commitment.

'Paper bags for her hands, please, and elastic bands. I want to preserve them in case she managed to put up a fight and get me some lovely DNA.'

Declan's voice stirred her out of her thoughts and into action as she prayed that the victim had. Ben was watching. There was nobody around, the whole area was silent except for the occasional bleating of sheep in the field behind the Land Rover. There were no crowds, no onlookers and Morgan thought that at least it was peaceful. The farmer had been sent home, and Cain had gone to take his statement. She envied Cain, no doubt he'd managed to get himself a cup of tea and was sat in a cosy farmhouse kitchen whilst she was dealing with the horrors of what had happened here.

'We have a possible ID for her,' Ben's voice called out. 'The car is registered to a Sharon Montgomery. Can you see if there's anything in the tent with her ID on, Declan?'

Declan was busy collecting samples of maggots and pupae that were left on her face. He passed the collection pots to

Morgan, who wrote on them before putting them into his case. Ben wouldn't normally be shouting out private details about victims, but they were so remote there wasn't anybody to hear. While she waited on Declan's next pot, she watched as Ben began talking to Stan who was nodding his head a little bit too emphatically, and then Stan turned and began to walk down the narrow track. She turned back to see that Declan was watching him go.

'Well, if your new boy didn't just get a gift from the Gods. Why didn't Ben send you to follow up on enquiries and let him do the donkey work?'

'Because I trust Morgan with my life, and I have no idea what Stan the man is capable of. I've sent him to go and check the isolated houses that are dotted around the roads up to this point, to see if they have any doorbell cameras or CCTV.'

Declan had the decency to look embarrassed, and Morgan felt bad for him.

'You need to stop creeping up on us today, Ben, you're freaking me out and at some point you might overhear stuff that wasn't for your ears.'

'I can hardly creep up on you, we're on the side of a fell, out in the open.'

He lowered his voice. 'Morgan, it's not that I want to make you do all the work, you know that, don't you?'

She nodded, she did know that and despite the horrors that her job often brought, she wouldn't change it for the world, because nobody would work harder than she would, and she was good at finding the sick killers who thought they were invincible and bringing them to justice.

SEVEN

'Where's Cain?' Ben asked.

'Taking the farmer's statement, isn't he?' Morgan replied.

'Yes, sorry. Brain dead. Can you ring him and tell him we're going to need him? I'm thinking that we're going to have to get that tent off the roof of the car in order to move the body. It's going to be really awkward trying to get it out of there, and we're probably going to need mountain rescue to get it down the fell to a waiting hearse.'

Declan was standing with his arms crossed. 'You could drive the jeep down with her still inside of it. Get Wendy to process inside the driver's side, and Morgan could drive it down.'

Morgan knew her mouth had fallen open; this was by far the most extreme suggestion she'd ever heard. 'Won't she roll around in there and ruin the forensics?'

'I think it will be okay. There's not a lot of room to manoeuvre in there, and she's pretty secure in that sleeping bag. Once she's out of the tent, the car can be driven down to the road ready for her body to be lifted.'

Ben looked as horrified as she did. 'I don't think the boss is going to go for that, but it's a good idea.'

She glared at him. 'You're not seriously thinking about that, are you? What if she falls out? It's a bumpy track down there.'

'We could tie some rope around her. Look, no matter what you do it's going to be difficult. I'm just proposing the easiest option for you. I'm confident that it will be okay. She's not going to fall out, especially if we zip the tent up and Morgan takes it easy.'

Ben was looking around for Marc and spotted him at the far end of the field in front of the car, pacing down towards the end.

He cupped his hands around his mouth. 'Boss.'

Marc turned to look at him and waved, then carried on. All three of them watched him until he came to an abrupt stop and turned, walking back towards them.

'Strange,' whispered Declan.

'Very,' agreed Morgan.

'Actually, I think he's making sure there's no way the killer could have gone that way. It could be an escape route.'

Marc was out of breath as he came towards them. 'I didn't realise how much of an incline there was coming back this way. It's a steep drop at the end, very rocky, not suitable for a vehicle except maybe a quad bike and even then it's doubtful. It looks like whoever did this either walked up here and took their chance, or maybe they were in a similar car to that.' He was pointing at the 4x4.

'Wouldn't Sharon have heard another vehicle approaching, even if she was asleep? You must be able to hear everything through the thin tent fabric. She looks as if she was completely caught off guard. I think whoever did this walked up here. I also think they knew she was here and that means it's someone who knew her that she'd told her plans to or...' Morgan turned to stare at the purple Land Rover, it was so unusual and very photogenic.

'Or?' Ben prompted.

'Or she posted her location on Instagram or Snapchat. I think she may have had a stalker.'

'Why kill her up here if she had a stalker? Why not kill her at home?'

'Why not? It's perfect, well apart from the difficulty getting here. There's nobody around, no witnesses, nobody to hear any screams for help; she was so isolated and off the beaten track that whoever it was could take their time and know there was zero chance of them being disturbed. When we find whoever did this, and we will, I wouldn't be surprised if they have pictures of the crime scene.'

Nobody said a word; they stared at the scene in front of them. Morgan couldn't get the image of Sharon's decomposing face out of her mind. The fear she must have felt would have been off the scale. She thought she was safe, loving life and spending time doing what she enjoyed only for someone to come along and decide that it was time for Sharon Montgomery to die, and Morgan felt a blackness inside of her that was turning into a red mist of fury at the injustice of it all. How dare someone do this to her. She hadn't deserved this, nobody deserved to die all alone, terrified and in pain.

'Boss, Declan suggested driving the car down to the main road so the body can be transferred directly to the hearse when the undertakers get here. We can shut the road in both directions so nobody sees what's happening whilst we get her out of there, or we can call mountain rescue out to assist. That could take some time though, what do you think?'

Morgan, Ben and Declan watched Marc screw his eyes up as he looked at the 4x4 with the roof tent up.

'Can you drive with that thing up like that though? Won't it blow off or fall off?' asked Marc.

'It's quite weighted down,' Ben replied.

Marc nodded. 'Who's driving?'

Declan and Ben both pointed in Morgan's direction.

'Are you happy to do this, Morgan?'

She sighed. 'I'll give it a go, but do not blame me if it falls off. Hang on, do we even have the keys?'

'Damn it, they must be in the tent with Sharon. Where would you put them if you were sleeping in that?'

'Well not in my pocket, they'd dig in. Under the pillow probably.'

'Go have a look then, Morgan.' Marc was being serious. 'I mean you've already climbed the ladder and touched stuff; you're going to be driving it down the side of the fell, so there's no point me or Ben adding our DNA to everything as well as yours and Declan's.'

Morgan felt as if she was in some bad dream that was going from ridiculous to worse and she'd wake up any moment now.

Declan leaned towards her and whispered into her ear, 'Sorry.'

She couldn't even look at him, she was so annoyed about this whole situation, and strode off along the metal plates, her Docs making them vibrate under the stomping of her boots until she reached the ladder. Climbing up, she shone her torch around, trying hard not to stare at Sharon's poor face, but finding it impossible not to. Lifting the corner of the pillow, the beam glinted off a metal ring and she thanked the universe for making this easier than she'd imagined. Reaching out her gloved hand, she plucked the key ring, losing her balance a little, and her hand brushed against Sharon's face, making her squeal to herself as she leaned too far back, losing her balance. She tried to stop herself, but it was too late, she was falling backwards to the sound of all three men shouting her name, and then landed with a loud thump on the metal plates that sent a shock all the way up from her backside up her spine.

Mortified, she jumped up. 'I'm good.'

Declan arched an eyebrow in her direction. 'I doubt that, you're going to have a bruise the size of England on your bottom. Would you like me to take a look at it for you?'

Not thinking her cheeks could burn any brighter, at his suggestion they absolutely did because they were positively glowing, and she shook her head. Ben was standing there shaking his head.

Marc walked towards her. 'Blimey, Morgan, are you sure you're okay? That must have hurt.'

'I'm good,' she growled at him, and he stepped back. 'Let's get this over with, shall we? Because if that tent falls off and sends the victim sprawling, I am not taking any responsibility, is that understood?'

All three men nodded.

'Good. This is ridiculous, but I'll meet you at the bottom of the track; the recovery vehicle can take it from there.'

She strode to the telescopic ladders, fiddling with them until she managed to push them up enough so she could drive without ripping them and the tent off the roof of the car. Opening the driver's door, she took a quick look inside to ensure there was no obvious evidence, and then she got in and slammed the door shut.

'She's pissed,' Declan said to Ben.

Ben nodded. 'Can't say I blame her. What the hell are we doing here? This was your suggestion, it had nothing to do with me.'

They watched as the engine roared into life and Morgan began to slowly navigate the Land Rover until it was facing the right way.

Ben held up a hand to her and shouted, 'I'll go in front; Marc will walk behind and keep an eye on it.'

Then they slowly made their way down the steep side of the fell, the strangest procession that had ever made its way down there in possibly hundreds of years, when the old coffin road was in use by the locals who lived in this remote area, to carry their dead down to the church.

EIGHT

Unbelievably, Declan's plan worked without any hitches, and Morgan carefully navigated the 4x4 down to the wider road, which had been closed off to the public. It wasn't a busy road anyway, but it was still eerily quiet when she climbed out of the Land Rover. There was a silver Ford Transporter with blacked-out windows slowly crawling its way up towards them, and she recognised the undertaker's van.

'Well done, Morgan, you made it.' Marc's praise wasn't lost on her, and she could hear the pure relief in his voice that the tent hadn't toppled off, spilling its contents all over the side of the fell.

'You guys can take it from here; I've done my part.'

Ben smiled at her and nodded. 'Do you want to get Cain to come pick you up and you can both get back to the station, get those social media checks and background checks started on the victim?'

She didn't need asking twice and sent Cain a quick message.

Hey, come rescue me now. I need to get back to the station.

Three dots appeared immediately.

On my way.

She sighed as she walked down the road towards the officer who was standing all alone like a fish out of water with a crime-scene logbook in her hands. She took it off her and smiled.

'I think they might release the scene as soon as the body is recovered from the tent.'

'Oh my God, there's a body inside of that tent. How did you manage to drive it down without it toppling over?'

'Very slowly.'

'Well done, that's really impressive.'

'Thanks, I can add that to my list of ever-expanding skills on my CV.'

The student officer, who looked even younger than she did, giggled, and Morgan smiled at her then carried on walking down the road before anyone could change their mind and call her back. She'd done her part. It could take hours before they managed to get the Land Rover recovered for a full forensic lift. They were lucky the entire crime scene had been contained inside of that small tent, with possible forensic traces outside and surrounding the vehicle. She saw the white car Cain had been driving heading their way and carried on walking towards him, not sure why but desperately wanting to get away from this scene. Maybe it was the contrast of the beautiful surroundings with the desolation of the crime combined with the absolute horror she felt inside her stomach at what had happened. How had the killer found Sharon Montgomery? It was weighing heavy on her mind. As far as she was concerned there were three options: it was an opportunistic kill carried out by someone who just happened to be passing and had a sudden urge to commit murder; it was someone Sharon knew, someone she had told where she was going to be and they had followed her up here planning to kill her. Or thirdly, it was someone unknown to Sharon who knew her, someone who had been closely monitoring her social media accounts.

Morgan got into the car, and Cain nodded at her.

'That poor guy, I feel bad for him. He's not been well and now this happening right on his doorstep.'

'I feel even worse for Sharon. She didn't ask to be murdered in a tent whilst she slept.'

'Well, when you put it like that.'

'What is the world coming to, Cain? I always thought that living around here we were a safe bet far from all the horrors that happen on a daily basis in the big cities, but it seems as if there's a chance we're in more danger than ever before. Every violent weirdo is flocking to this part of the Lake District as if it's some kind of challenge.'

He shrugged. 'Or maybe it's always been this way, but we didn't realise because we were too young and the murders happened before we joined the police.'

That gave Morgan pause for thought. Had it always been this way? Maybe it had and she hadn't been aware of it until she'd become a detective. She sighed. 'I'm going to look into it one day, when I get a minute.'

'I bet if you gave it a good old google you'd be horrified. I also don't think you help matters much.'

She snapped her head in his direction. 'What do you mean?'

'Well, don't take this personally but—' He stopped and looked as if he'd changed his mind about what he was going to say.

'But?'

'I keep telling you, the weirdos are coming here because of you. They want to be the killer that the famous Detective

Brookes couldn't catch. I'm pretty sure there's a secret club they're all members of and they get to take a turn to see if they can try and outwit the one and only Morgan Brookes.'

'Rubbish.'

'Maybe, but you've made quite an impression on the media, and look at that detective from Birmingham who said he'd heard of you.'

'Gulfam, how do you know about that?'

'Ben said.'

Morgan wondered what else Ben said about her when she wasn't around, but she knew it would never be anything bad. He wasn't the kind of guy to talk about her that way, and besides, as much as they had the occasional argument and disagreement, they were still as in love as when they first got together, even though he hadn't proposed to her. *Damn it, Declan, why did you have to go and put that idea in my head? I had never even considered it until you brought it up.*

They drove back to the station in silence, Morgan too consumed with the task of finding out all about the victim and wondering if Ben was as madly in love with her as she was with him.

―――――

The office was empty when Morgan walked in, and she breathed a long sigh of relief; occasionally it was nice to have a bit of time to think. Amy had been about to go grab lunch and Cain had gone with her, giving Morgan free rein. She logged on to the computer and then signed herself into Instagram to see if she could find Sharon Montgomery's account. It popped up straight away.

There was a picture of the distinctive purple 4x4 parked in the same position they had found it a couple of hours earlier. She sighed; this was too easy. Almost anyone could find out the location – all they had to do was right click on the picture, select information or properties and see if the GPS coordinates appeared, then it was a simple case of typing them into Google Maps to find out the exact location. Morgan knew that not everyone would be aware of this, but it was a straightforward way to try and find a location. However, because Sharon had added her exact location to her photograph with an Instagram tag, she may as well have tied a flag to the top of her tent to alert people exactly where she was and how to come find her.

Morgan sat back in her chair. People did this all the time, especially when they were on holiday or doing something remotely exciting. They had no idea that it could be dangerous if the wrong person was following their account. She clicked on the post to see how many people had liked it and was shocked to discover she had over a thousand likes just on that one post. This made her scroll up to her bio to see she had almost five thousand followers. Her bio said she loved wild camping in and around the Lake District. Morgan began to read the comments below the pictures, looking for usernames that commented a lot or made odd remarks.

By the time Cain and Amy came back from lunch she had compiled a list of thirty-six names that usually commented on almost all of Sharon's posts. It was a lot; she was going to have cross-reference them to determine if they were Sharon's friends in real life or whether they knew her from social media, and also try to find where they lived in relation to Sharon and the Lake District. Morgan felt deflated, as none of the many comments were helpful to the investigation, they were all comments like 'I love this'; 'So perfect'; 'Have fun.' And there were so many purple heart emojis on posts she couldn't get any kind of information from them except the usernames, clicking on those took her to their profile pages but it really was looking for a needle in a haystack. It wasn't going to be as easy as she'd hoped to find this killer.

Cain handed her a latte, and she sighed. 'I needed this, how did you know?'

'You always need coffee, Morgan, and it looks like that is a complete shit show. Have you come across any Michael Myers kind of stalkers on there yet?'

'Nope, they don't tend to post pictures of themselves in navy blue boiler suits wearing a mask and waving a huge knife around, there is nothing obvious at all. Just a lot of love for Sharon's solo adventures. You know what I'm so angry about this whole case? The fact that she was out there doing what she loved, causing no harm or upset to anyone, and some sick bastard thought they had the right to take it all away from her. For what reason? What was the point? She wasn't hurting anyone. She was literally camping on her own, living her life and, from what it looks like on her Instagram page, sharing her adventures online to inspire other women to do the same.'

Amy was tearing apart the cheese savoury baguette and dropping crumbs all over her. She nodded. 'Have you checked YouTube? I bet she's got a channel on there, too. Most of these solo adventurers like to vlog their trips and expeditions.'

Morgan groaned. 'Christ, how many hours before you finish?'

Amy looked at her watch. 'Four, give or take depending upon what kind of mood the boss is in. Would you like me to make a start on it?'

Morgan paused, she felt bad. Amy should be having a relaxing last afternoon, packing her stuff, saying goodbye to everyone – and then she realised that none of them had even organised a leaving do for her and that was downright disgraceful.

'I, erm. You don't have to, I'm just feeling sorry for myself.'

Amy grinned at her. 'It's allowed, occasionally. I don't mind; I'm not doing anything else.'

Cain stood up, taking his coffee with him. 'Got to go speak to Madds, be back soon.'

He left them to it, and Morgan sent Ben a quick message:

We need to organise gifts and a cake for Amy. Why did we not organise this sooner?

Then she began the painstaking job of clicking the user-name of each person on her list to check out their bio.

NINE

Morgan had cleaned off the whiteboard and then stuck up a sheet of paper with a selfie of the victim, which she'd copied and printed from Instagram. Beneath it, she added a list of twelve names from Sharon's Instagram followers. The photo showed Sharon smiling and clearly loving life; it was taken at some point when she'd first set up camp outside the entrance to the field. The sun had been setting behind the mountain, sending bright orange rays through the clouds that covered them like an exotic blanket of light.

Beneath the names, Morgan also added the name of the farmer who had found Sharon's decomposing body.

Joss Graham 60 + years old – last person to speak to Sharon that we are aware of.

Cain had come back into the office ten minutes earlier, with a smile on his face that had both Morgan and Amy rolling their eyes at each other. The new boy was nowhere to be found, though none of them were too bothered about looking that hard, as it was nice to spend time together as a team before Amy finished. Morgan hadn't realised how much she was going to miss Amy's sarcasm and sense of humour; things were going to be a lot different around here without her.

Marc pushed the door open too hard, as always, and it swung inwards with a loud clump as it hit the wall, knocking yet another chunk of plaster off it – that wall had more holes in it than Morgan's fishnet tights. Ben was behind him.

'Everyone okay? Briefing in the blue room in ten minutes?' said Ben, before disappearing into his office with Marc behind him.

Cain went from smiling to positively beaming to himself. Amy stared at him.

'Are you okay over there? You're not having some kind of medical episode, are you? Because you know that nobody ever has the right to look as happy as you do whilst at work.'

He shrugged. 'Never been better.'

'Weirdo,' muttered Amy, and Morgan stifled a laugh.

Cain ignored them and walked out again, leaving Amy staring after him.

'What's with him? He's acting so shifty.'

Morgan shrugged. 'Who knows? Maybe he's happy in his work.'

Amy laughed. 'Glad someone is, I'm going to miss this place. It's like some fucked-up family unit that I can't get enough of; but I'm not going to miss sitting in these uncomfortable chairs and having permanent backache.'

'We're going to miss you too; it won't be the same.'

'Ah, but at least the new guy is better looking.' She winked at Morgan who felt her cheeks begin to burn.

Marc and Ben came back out of Ben's office; Ben had an all-too-familiar blue folder tucked underneath his arm. In it he would keep a detailed record of the ongoing murder investigation. All four headed to the blue room, where Tristan was hovering outside.

'I wasn't sure where the blue room was. I saw Cain go in, but he told me to keep out until it was time for the briefing.'

Marc arched an eyebrow at Ben. 'He did? No idea why.'

He pushed the door handle down and stepped inside to a sea of pink and blue balloons, banners, cakes, confetti and bunting. Cain was literally beaming from ear to ear, and Amy, who looked almost as shocked as Marc, burst into tears. Ben was looking confused, and he shrugged at Morgan and mouthed, 'What's happening?'

Cain stepped towards Amy, wrapping his huge arms around her and hugging her. He yelled, 'Surprise! Do you like it? It's your baby shower; there's no need to cry about it, Amy, you could at least look happy.'

Amy buried her head deeper into his chest and sobbed. Cain looked at Morgan, a grimace on his face as he whispered, 'Too much?'

At this Amy began to laugh. Pulling herself away from him, she slapped his arm and wiped the tears on her cheeks with her sleeve. 'No, it was just the shock. Nobody has ever done anything like this for me before and my hormones are all over the place. It's just so lovely.' She sniffed and blinked a couple of times.

'Phew, thank God you're okay. Don't go into early labour or anything before we've eaten the cakes. I wasn't sure whether you had decided if it was a girl or a boy, so I went for both.'

Morgan and Ben laughed, but Marc looked horrified.

'Wasn't sure if she'd decided? Cain, you don't get to choose. It's a girl or it's a boy, end of story,' he said.

'You know what I mean. She won't tell us what she's having so I went for the safest bet.'

'I don't know what I'm having, that's why. I didn't want to know; I want it to be a surprise.'

'Same thing, anyway, congratulations, Amy. You'll soon be pushing that watermelon out of—'

'Enough,' yelled Ben who had both his hands in the air. 'We're going to miss you, Amy, but I bet you're going to be glad of a break from him.' He pointed at Cain, and she shook her head.

'I don't know what I'd do without him; he's been my life-saver the last few months.'

'Aww,' said Tristan. 'How lovely, congratulations to you both, how exciting.'

Nobody bothered to correct him because they were all too busy diving to grab cakes and sandwiches. The door opened and in sauntered Al and three task force officers along with Wendy, Joe, and Madds who didn't miss any chance to eat cake. He grabbed a cupcake and pointed to Marc. 'Thought this was a briefing?'

'Slight change of plan. After this there's a briefing so you may as well stick around.'

'Not me, I just came for the cake. I've got a meeting at Kendal town hall to attend. Congratulations, Amy. I hope it goes well.'

She smiled at Madds. 'Thanks, me too.'

He disappeared along with a paper plate of sandwiches and another cake; everyone sat down and soon there was nothing left on the plates but crumbs. Amy hadn't stopped smiling, and Morgan realised that Cain had just saved all of them. They would thank him later. She had no idea he could be so thought-ful, and she wondered if Angela had pushed him in the right direction.

Eventually Ben stood up. 'I'm sorry to bring your celebra-tion to a rather abrupt end, Amy, and I hope you don't mind but we really need to crack on with this briefing. Are you okay with that?'

She nodded, and he smiled at her. 'You're welcome to finish for the day now. I don't want to spoil your lovely afternoon with the case in hand.'

Amy stood up. 'Are you sure you don't need me for anything? I'm happy to stay now I've been fed.'

Morgan knew the answer was a resounding yes, they did need her, but Ben shook his head.

'Absolutely not, you get yourself home and take it easy. We'll catch up with you soon. Keep us updated, won't you? And let us know if you need anything at all.'

Then he walked towards Amy and hugged her. Morgan stood up and hugged her too when Ben let go. Marc looked like a fish out of water – he shook her hand, and Tristan who didn't know any of them, smiled at her.

Amy blew a kiss to Cain. 'Thanks, Cain, I'll speak to you later and thank Angela for me too.'

She winked, and Cain laughed. 'It wasn't all her idea.'

Amy waved a hand at him. 'Yeah right, of course it wasn't.'

She left the room, closing the door softly behind her.

Morgan looked at Cain. 'You did good, we'll all chip in to cover the cost. Thank you, it completely slipped my mind, and you just made us all look like we're not complete arseholes.'

'I couldn't let her just walk out with nothing. It would have been terrible, she deserves better, and you're welcome.'

Ben stood up. 'Yes, thanks, Cain. We'll all contribute towards this, well done. Are we okay to get started with the briefing?'

Everyone nodded.

'Good, what do we have up to now? The victim, Sharon Montgomery, do we have an age for her yet?'

Morgan nodded. 'Thirty-six, according to her Instagram profile, although not sure if that's a hundred per cent accurate. I haven't started the Intel checks yet, as there's been a lot going on.'

Ben smiled at her. 'It's certainly been busy. Tristan, did you manage to get the Intel checks started?'

All eyes fell onto the new guy, who nodded. 'I can confirm

she is thirty-six; there are three reports on the system for her. She was a victim of domestic violence back in 2022.'

'That's interesting, were there any after 2022?'

'No, I guess she kicked the boyfriend to the kerb.'

'Who was it? Did they get arrested, are they known to us?'

Tristan looked down at his notebook. 'Eddy Lightburn.'

Just about everyone in the room let out a groan, and he looked up at them wide-eyed. 'Known to you all then?'

'Unfortunately. He's a little weasel. Handy with his fists, fancies himself as an amateur boxer with his current woman his sparring partner, but I'm pretty sure he's inside. He got locked up for a whole multitude of crimes, breaking in, theft, assault by battery, handling stolen goods,' said Cain.

'Tristan, can you do a full check on Eddy? I want to know where he is and if he's been within a two-mile radius of Sharon at all. Did he get locked up for his last assault on her or was it someone else?'

Tristan shrugged. 'Sorry, I didn't get time to do a deep dive into him, but I will as soon as this is finished.'

Marc smiled at him. 'Good, at least we have a possible suspect. I want everyone focused on finding out where Eddy Lightburn is and if he's been in contact with the victim.'

Morgan glanced in Cain's direction, and he caught it, rolling his eyes in Tristan's direction. He was thinking the same as she was. What had Tristan been doing all this time? It would have taken him ten minutes tops to search Eddy's name and find out who he was.

TEN

Morgan raised her hand. 'Sharon was very active on Instagram, and her posts on that platform also got carried over to Facebook and were shared on there. I haven't even started looking at her posts and activity on Facebook yet. It's going to take some time, but meantime I have a list of twelve names that I put together of people who keep commenting and liking her stuff on social media, we could see if any of them own or have access to 4x4s if they drove up to where she was camping they would need a four-wheel drive. Or if they didn't and walked up they would need to be pretty fit, it's a bit of a hike up there.'

'That's a start, anyone on there who is known to us, or is that asking too much?' Ben looked hopeful, and she sighed before she crushed him completely.

'Not that I'm aware of, at least no one that jumps out as familiar. Obviously, I need to run them through the system in case. I mean they could live anywhere in the UK, even the US or Europe. We also have a bit of a problem which makes finding suitable suspects even harder, unfortunately for Sharon and for us, on her last post she gave her location away.'

Marc's eyes almost popped out of his sockets they widened so much. Morgan wondered if he would go blind.

'She did what?'

'She posted her exact location, well she added it to the post of her 4x4 with the roof tent up, outside the gate to the field.'

He was shaking his head. 'She was on her own, camping; she took a photo of where she was then added the location for good measure, so that any weirdo in the UK could track her down?'

'Basically, yes.'

'Dear God, why would she do that?'

Ben looked shocked, not quite as shocked as Marc but almost; he looked as if he was struggling to get his head around it. 'She clearly wasn't scared that someone might do that, so that tells me she had no prior problems with anyone stalking her or making her feel uncomfortable. Especially not if she was posting everything for the world to see.'

Morgan nodded in agreement. 'I think this was a stranger or someone who knew of Sharon, but she didn't know about them, or if she did, she clearly didn't see them as a threat. She wouldn't be inviting the world to come and pay her a visit when she was on her own in such an isolated area.'

'I don't know what to say.' Marc stared at the picture of her on the whiteboard. 'She clearly looks like an intelligent woman, smart enough to know that what she was doing could be dangerous, so why act so irresponsibly?'

Morgan felt her fingers curl and clench into tight fists, and she pushed them under the table so Cain couldn't see. She was unable to stop the words that came spilling from her mouth even if she had wanted to.

'If she had no one to be scared of and no worries about anyone wanting to hurt her or follow her, then that doesn't mean she was irresponsible. Would you be saying that if it was a guy who we'd found slaughtered in his tent who was camping on his own? No, you would not, and you know that. It makes me so mad that women are always blamed for the stuff that happens to them. You're talking as if she posted an open invitation for some maniac to come and kill her. It's disgusting that we are still having to live this way. This is not Sharon Montgomery's fault, in no way, shape or form. Judging by her photos she was experienced at wild camping and going on solo adventures. It's always some dickhead who has to come along and think they know better and can do what they want to any woman who is on their own, living their life and having fun without relying on a man.'

Everyone was listening to Morgan who had managed to keep her feistiness under control for quite some time, but Marc had clearly pushed her too far and the anger was bubbling inside of her chest like hot lava.

He held his hands in the air, palms facing towards her in a *keep calm* gesture that made her feel even worse as she glared at him.

'I'm not blaming her, that came out wrong and you're right, Morgan, of course you are. Women should not have to live in fear, they should be free to do whatever the hell they want. But you and I know by the countless cases that have come into this department that unfortunately some men, and occasionally women too, will always think they can live outside of the law and do what they want to women with no regard for them as human beings. It doesn't mean I'm blaming her.' He shut up and sat down as if realising he wasn't helping.

Morgan was seething and she couldn't even look in Ben's direction because she knew he was staring at her, and she didn't want to lose her cool with him, too, in front of everyone. She pushed herself away from the table and stood up. 'If it's okay with you, boss, I'm going to carry on with the enquiries into the list of names I've come up with.'

Marc nodded, he looked relieved she was leaving but before

she walked out of the cramped, stuffy room she turned around. 'Who is delivering the death message to her parents? Has that even been done?'

This time Ben did groan. 'Oh Christ, what a shit show.'

Morgan walked out, a small smile on her lips at Ben's last comment that she didn't want Ben or anyone else to see. This had indeed turned into a shit show, and it was getting worse by the minute.

———

As she sat writing down the info on each name she had, and cross-checking it against Sharon's Facebook posts, she didn't look up when the office door opened softly.

'Is it safe to come in?'

Cain's voice was tinged with caution, and this time she did look up at him.

'Don't you dare start.'

'I'm not. Christ, if that hadn't been true what you'd said, it would have been funny. Did you see the boss's face?' Cain was smiling at her. 'Honestly, you almost gave him a coronary, and Stan the man looked as if he was going to die of shame. I bet he rings in sick tomorrow; he won't be able to cope with you on a bad day. Good on you, Brookes, I think they'd forgotten what a seething pot of anger you have burning inside of that beautiful exterior. Tell me, is it because you is a ginger?'

Morgan snorted with laughter. 'Sod off, I don't know anyone who has a death wish like you do, Cain, and no, being ginger has nothing to do with my inner anger. It's ignorance and stupid statements that tip me over the edge. It's so unfair, I couldn't stand to hear him judging her for doing nothing wrong. It's always the same, always has been.'

Cain dragged his chair over to where she was sitting and

patted her arm. 'I know. Ben has asked if we can go deliver the death message before her parents find out off social media.'

She shook her head. 'Is he trying to get me out of the way?'

'No, I think he genuinely feels you'd do a better job than anyone else. Come on, let's blow this joint before the misogynists come back in. I may be a lot of things, but I don't look down on any woman or treat them any differently to how I'd treat male colleagues.'

Morgan smiled at him. 'I know you don't. Yeah, let's get out of here, even if it is to do the worst job there is.'

She grabbed her jacket and coffee that was now more iced than hot, but it didn't matter – she was used to drinking her coffee cold; it was the nature of the job. 'Where are we going?'

'Windermere. It looks like Sharon grew up in the area, and her parents still live in a nice house by the lakeside.'

Morgan felt sad. They were about to go and shatter their world with the worst news that anyone could ever receive. Today, she was feeling no love for her job at all. It had been nothing but heartache since she'd started this morning, when they got called out to that secluded place where Sharon Montgomery had been so happy spending time until her killer had found her.

ELEVEN

The house had security gates that were taller than Cain, and he had to press the intercom to ask if they could be let in. As they watched the gates opening, he whistled. 'Those gates cost more than our annual salary.'

Morgan shrugged. 'All the money in the world isn't going to make any difference to what we're about to tell them.'

'I suppose not.'

The house was fairly new, all slate and beechwood with huge floor-to-ceiling windows on the ground and first floor. Through the windows, they could see that the huge chandelier that hung down from the open-plan first floor was the most beautiful cut glass, the droplets the size of the palm of Morgan's hand.

They got out of the car, and Cain whispered, 'I don't think I can do it.'

She tried not to glare at him. Smoothing down the non-existent creases in her three-quarter, black trousers she straightened up. The front door swung open and a woman in an actual maid's uniform was standing there, giving them the once-over.

'Don't speak, Cain, it's safer for us both this way.'

He didn't disagree. They walked towards the open door, boots crunching on the gravel drive. The maid looked mildly annoyed at being inconvenienced, and she was still glaring at them.

'Hi, we're Detectives Brookes and Robson from Rydal Falls police station. Are Mr and Mrs Montgomery home?'

Morgan spied the Porsche 4x4 and the Mercedes convertible out of the corner of one eye.

'Yes, what do you want with them? Have you any ID?'

Morgan tugged her lanyard out of her jacket and showed the woman her warrant card. Cain was fumbling in his pockets for his. He looked at Morgan with a mild hint of panic in his eyes and then he pulled out the small white plastic card with his picture on it and thrust it towards the woman. She studied first the warrant cards and then their faces, scrutinising them.

'I've got better looking since they took that. You could say I've aged well.'

Morgan couldn't even look in his direction and thought if she could have punched him in the arm to shut him up, she would have. Thankfully, the maid was trying not to smile at him, and Cain grinned at her.

'Marie, what are you doing? Who is that at the door?' a man's voice called down the hallway.

'Sorry, sir, I was just checking these visitors were who they claimed they were.'

Footsteps echoed off the polished black and gold flecked marble tiles, and Morgan sucked in a breath as the man who was peering over Marie's shoulder smiled at her. She smiled back.

'Who are you?'

'We're detectives, is it okay to come in and speak to you?' Before she'd even spoken, she'd run through a list of words that were suitable, *chat* and *talk* didn't give off how serious their visit was.

The guy she assumed was Sharon's dad arched an eyebrow at her, a bit like Ben did at times when he was winding her up.

'Am I in trouble? Did I drive too fast through the village? Was my music too loud when we were out sailing on the lake? Don't tell me the neighbours have complained about the noise from the barbeque we had at the weekend.' His smile was infectious, and his brilliant white teeth were perfect, definitely not Turkey teeth. These were expensive veneers. He was wearing faded denim jeans and a black linen shirt.

Morgan liked him and this made her feel even worse for what she was about to do.

'I'm afraid not, can we come inside?'

'Oh, this is serious then. Yes, of course, come in.'

Marie stepped backwards to let them in, and he turned to walk down the huge, long entrance. He pushed open a door which led into a stunning home office, which made her feel more than a little envious of the lifestyle the Montgomerys led. The bookshelves were floor to ceiling and the desk filled an entire wall. There was a huge black suede sofa, and he pointed to it.

'Please, take a seat. Can I get you guys a drink?'

Morgan shook her head. 'No, thanks. Is Mrs Montgomery here? It would be best if we could speak to you both at the same time.'

He smiled at her, turned around and said, 'Just a moment.' He took out his phone and dialled his wife, who answered immediately.

'*Make your own lunch or better still get Marie to do something useful for once.*'

'The police are here; they want to talk to us both.'

There was a slight pause.

'*Oh, okay I'll be right in.*'

The line went dead.

'She's out in the garden; it's her baby. She spends all her

spare time out there, won't have a gardener for love or money. She reckons it keeps her fit and busy.'

'Yes, it does, and it saves money too.' The voice was clearly a lot less well-spoken than her husband's. Mrs Montgomery was wearing a pair of khaki cargo pants, a white T-shirt that had mud stains on the front and a belt around her waist with an assortment of gardening tools tucked into it. She stood next to her husband and looked at them on the sofa.

'Are we in trouble?' She reached out her hand and shook both Morgan's then Cain's. 'I'm Beth Montgomery and the funny guy is Stefan, my husband and part-time comedy act.'

Morgan shook her head. 'Absolutely not. Are you Sharon Montgomery's parents?'

The woman glanced at Stefan, a quick side eye, then she looked at Morgan. 'Yes, we are. Is Sharon in trouble?'

Morgan wished an alien spacecraft would hover above the house and send a beam of light down to whisk her away from this uncomfortable situation.

'I'm afraid we have some terrible news for you. I'm so sorry to have to tell you this.'

Beth held up a hand to stop her from speaking. 'Don't say it, if you don't say it out loud then it isn't true.'

Stefan's arm had snaked around Beth's waist, and he was holding her tight. He nodded at Morgan to continue.

'A body was discovered this morning in a roof tent that was parked up on the top of the narrow coffin road that leads up to Southern Fell, did Sharon mention she may be doing this?'

Beth was shaking her head. 'She never mentioned it.'

Morgan took out her phone and showed Beth a picture of the Land Rover.

'Is this Sharon's?'

'Yes, it is. I don't understand why you're here though.'

Morgan tried to keep her voice gentle. 'We believe the body we found inside of the tent is Sharon. I'm so, so sorry.'

Beth's legs seemed to give way, and she slumped onto the leather desk chair next to her.

Stefan looked as dazed as Beth did. 'How do you know it's Sharon?'

Morgan looked down at her notebook then read out the registration number of the purple Land Rover. 'Sharon's driving licence was under her pillow. I also checked her Instagram account.'

Beth looked up at Stefan, her eyes wide and brimming with tears that were about to fall. She opened her mouth to speak, but nothing came out.

'How did she die, assuming this woman is our daughter?'

Morgan wished she hadn't told Cain to keep quiet now. As if sensing her distress, he softly pushed his knee into hers then said, 'I'm afraid she was murdered.' He paused, letting the information sink in.

Stefan was shaking his head. 'No, sorry. This is just not possible. Why would someone murder her? Are you sure you have the right woman? Show me a picture, please, and we can tell you if you've made a mistake. I mean it happens all the time, doesn't it? I'm not saying you're both incompetent, but mistakes do get made like this.'

Morgan agreed. 'Yes, on the rare occasion they do. Which is why we would like one or both of you to go to the mortuary to identify the woman we believe is Sharon. I'm so, so, sorry.'

'Why can't you show us a photo of her face now?'

Beth stood up and almost snarled at him. 'Because it must be too bad, that's why. How did she die? What did they do to her?'

'It was violent. She was stabbed multiple times.'

Beth let out a sob, this time bending over double as if all the air had been sucked out of her lungs. Stefan carried on shaking his head. Morgan looked at Cain, then back at the Montgomerys.

'I'm sorry. Are you able to come to the mortuary with us, now?'

The only sound in the room was Beth's gentle sobs. She managed to whisper, 'Yes.'

'I'll let them know you're on the way,' Morgan said.

Cain excused himself and went outside to phone the mortuary, to tell them they were setting off. Morgan thought that the Montgomerys had every reason to hope and pray that they'd got it wrong, that they hadn't come to tell them the most terrible news of their lives.

There was a small niggle of doubt about them though. Were they as happy as they made out? Almost everyone had secrets, and she wondered if they did too.

TWELVE

The silence was golden, as the saying went. He was enjoying the alone time before it was broken. He let out a huge yawn. He'd stayed up far too late last night and had walked for miles, but oh how it had been worth it. Too wary to use a torch, he'd had to walk the paths that led to the campsite relying on the little light from the crescent moon.

It had been a relief the sky wasn't cloudy; he'd even managed to catch a glimpse of the aurora borealis when an alert had flashed up on his phone. He'd taken out his phone, put it onto night mode and spent five minutes staring at the muted colours of purple, pink and green through the camera on the screen. He had been tempted to snap a couple of pictures, but he knew that was stupid. If the police ever caught him, the first thing they would do is take his phone and send it off to get everything scrutinised. If there were photos of the aura in this location, with a date and time stamp on them, he would be screwed. It would literally be game over without even a confession, because he had no legitimate reason to be out here except... he could state he was chasing the aurora; it could also work in his defence, he realised.

It was quite something standing on the little uneven path, alone, at midnight watching the night sky putting on a show of utter beauty. He wondered how many people got to die under the beauty of the Northern Lights; it was a pity he'd never be able to talk about it. It was even sadder that the woman would never know. When he'd finally reached the campsite she was staying at, and she had taken her last breath, he'd wondered: would her soul see them when it left her body?

He smiled to himself, so many questions that he'd never be able to answer, and unless he could find an authentic psychic medium to ask her, it was impossible.

He'd reached the campsite an hour later than he'd liked. It had been further than he'd anticipated, but thankfully there were only two cars parked up. One with a tent was parked some way down the fell, a good distance from the car with the roof tent he was after. He was going to need to be quick, not to mention silent. The element of surprise was going to be difficult with this one because if her dog started to bark it would wake everyone up.

Taking the plastic sandwich bag of sausages out of his pocket, he unzipped it, wafting it outside of the roof tent. He heard the dog stirring, snuffling about, and carefully standing on the bottom rung of the ladder, he reached up and unzipped the tent enough to let the dog out. A wet nose poked out through the gap as he wafted a sausage in front of it. He was holding his breath, more than a little nervous. He was aware that this could all go horribly wrong at any moment. If the dog began to bark, he'd have to leg it out of there. He held the sausage out, and the dog took a bite. Then it pushed itself out of the gap in the zip, and he swiftly grabbed it with both hands, dropping the sausages. He put the dog down and it completely ignored him as it began to eat the chopped-up sausage and dog treats he'd thrown on the ground.

The dog taken care of, he'd withdrawn the knife in his belt

and slid it from the sheath. From inside the tent, he heard the woman murmur and some movement as she turned over. He didn't hesitate. He unzipped the opening more fully and leaned in and drew the knife across her throat. It was dark inside of the tent, and he couldn't see what was going on, but he felt the warm blood as it sprayed over his gloved hands and heard a wet gurgling sound that came from her mouth. Her eyes had flown wide open, but the cut was a good one; he had cut deep and had severed the jugular. She was bleeding out and didn't even know what had happened to her.

The dog was sniffing around on the ground completely oblivious.

A full body shiver of delight ran through his veins, and he smiled to himself.

He was clever enough to know that if he went on to do more killing, he might not be so lucky and could lose the anonymity he currently had. He also thought that by mixing up the MOs in the next one it could cause the police to go into a serious meltdown of confusion.

Pushing the knife back into the sheath, he tucked it back into his belt. His gloves were bloody, but he tugged the zip back up before he ripped them off and stuffed those into his pocket. Looking around, he watched the tent at the far side of the site; but there was no sound or movement. Finally, he looked down at the dog that was staring up at him with huge eyes, waiting for more treats.

He shrugged, bent down to rub behind its ears and whispered, 'Sorry, bud, got nothing left.' Then straightened up and hurried back the way he'd come, leaving the dog staring after him.

It realised it was free and began sniffing around the wheels of the car, not in the least bit bothered that its owner had just bled to death in the zipped-up tent above him and now it couldn't get back up there. It carried on doing what dogs do and began to mooch around in the dark.

As he scurried back down the path, he hoped the dog wouldn't follow him. The last thing he needed was a dead woman's pet dog. He could say he found it wandering around on the fell, but that would be an added complication he didn't need and cause so many questions. He didn't know how to look after a dog; it was better that it stayed where it was. Someone would take it in, but as he hurried away, he felt a sensation of guilt about the animal that he'd never encountered before. It was alien to him – he hadn't felt guilty about his parents' deaths, and he certainly felt no remorse for the woman he'd just killed inside the tent. So, why was he feeling bad for a scruffy looking dog?

He almost got halfway down the path before he heard it scrabbling along behind him. He swore then turned around, wishing he'd not given it the sausages. It was probably not used to such a rich treat and now it was never going to leave him alone. He stood still, hoping it would neither sense nor smell him, but he was wrong on so many levels as it came padding towards him, tail wagging as if he was its new best friend.

'Go, get away from here. Go back to your owner.' He waved his hands in its direction, and it just wagged its tail faster then sat down on the path.

'Oh, for fuck's sake, dog. I just killed your favourite person, bite me or chase me but do not think I'm taking you home, you stupid mutt.'

The dog stared at him with its big brown eyes. Christ, he shook his head, ignored it and carried on walking.

He didn't turn around, but he could hear it trotting along behind him, and he didn't know what the hell he was going to do about it.

THIRTEEN

The Montgomerys had insisted on driving themselves to the mortuary at the Royal Lancaster Infirmary, and Morgan couldn't say she blamed them. The div car Cain was driving was a small white Ford Focus. Not much room in the rear, especially with Cain's seat being pushed all the way back to accommodate his long legs. Their Porsche Cayenne looked like a much better option. Morgan had asked if they were okay to drive, and Stefan had nodded, glassy eyed in shock, but still with the belief that Morgan and Cain were a couple of bumbling idiots who had made the gravest mistake of their careers, and she didn't blame him really. If it was her, she'd want to believe it was all some huge error because the reality was far too painful.

They led the way, with Stefan following behind, but as soon as they reached the dual carriageway on the A5284, he overtook them swiftly and far too fast for the speed limit.

'What an arsehole, I'd thought he was okay, but it seems as if he's not,' Cain muttered. 'What's he going to do, demand to be let in before we even arrive?'

She nodded. 'Probably.'

'Why though, what's the point?'

'He's clearly used to doing things his way, Cain. He doesn't think it's his daughter and wants to get it over with. I kind of understand that.'

'Yeah, well I've a good mind to do him for speeding over the limit.'

Morgan chuckled. 'Don't be a dick, you're just jealous of his Porsche.'

Cain grinned at her. 'Okay maybe a little, it's just people who think they're above the law because they have more money than most of us really do my head in.'

'Give him a break, he seemed like an okay guy before we tore his world apart.'

'Yeah, I suppose he was. What did you think about the mum? She didn't seem as posh as him.'

'Maybe not, Sharon's not exactly an upper-class name either, is it? What is wrong with you today? You are being so judgy. They might have started off poor as the rest of us and worked their way up to the position they're currently in.'

'Maybe.'

They drove the rest of the way in silence, with Cain exceeding the speed limit to try and keep up with the Montgomerys.

They found Stefan's car abandoned on the double yellow lines outside the mortuary building, being eyed up by a parking warden. Morgan jumped out to go and talk to the warden.

'Hey, could you like give the guy a little time? He's just been told his daughter is dead.'

The parking attendant looked her dead in the eye. 'Doesn't mean he can leave the car there.'

Cain sauntered over and flashed his warrant card at him. 'Give us ten minutes, we'll get it moved.'

The parking attendant, who was the same height as Morgan, looked up at Cain who towered above them. 'Whatever, I'm going on my break now anyway.'

He strode away, and Cain whispered, 'What a nice guy.'

Morgan grinned at him. 'Takes a special person.'

They headed into the mortuary and straight to the viewing room, to see Susie and her peacock blue and green hair trying to pacify the Montgomerys, who were arguing with each other until Beth turned on Susie and began arguing with her. Declan was rushing up the corridor to go help Susie and waved to them.

By the time all six of them were crammed into the viewing room there wasn't much time to manoeuvre.

Declan raised his voice.

'Hello, I'm Doctor Donnelly, the forensic pathologist. Could we please take a moment to breathe and just try to bring it down a little? I know you're both very anxious about this and I completely understand how scared and upset you're feeling.'

'Do you, do you really? Because it's just another day for you lot, isn't it? This isn't your life that's in tatters.'

Beth spat the words with such venom that Declan took a step back.

He nodded. 'I have been doing this for a very long time; I have been in the position you're in when I lost my father in a pointless pub brawl. Please, we want to help you, but we can't if you're shouting and being aggressive towards my staff. It's not helping anyone, least of all your daughter.'

Stefan took hold of Beth's arm. 'He's right, you need to calm down, Beth, it's not helping Sharon.'

At that moment Beth looked as if she was going to cause Stefan serious injury. '*My* daughter, and you weren't even talking to her, so I don't know what you're being so upset about.'

Morgan felt Cain's eyes glaring into the back of her head, but she didn't turn around. All was not as they'd first thought about the couple in front of them.

'That's uncalled for, Beth, of course I'm upset. I love Sharon deeply.'

Beth stopped whatever was about to tumble from her lips and nodded. She turned to stare at Declan. 'I'm sorry, can we just get this over with.'

She was clutching her phone in one hand and a beep of the voicemail message ending was heard in the room. Morgan realised Beth had been phoning Sharon, and God forbid if this wasn't her daughter on the gurney in the viewing room, then she'd just left her the most awful of voicemails, begging her daughter to phone her now because she was about to look at someone's corpse.

'Would you like us to show you a photograph of her on the screen, or do you want to see her in person?'

'In person.' Beth didn't pause. 'Can I go in with her to take a look?'

'I'm afraid not, we can't let you touch her at the moment and I'm terribly sorry. We need to do a thorough forensic examination to find as much evidence as possible so we can find the perpetrator. We've covered part of her face. I'm sorry to say that there is some decomposition and it's not nice. If you'd like, maybe you could identify her by the clothes she was wearing or her hair.'

Stefan held up his hand. 'No, we need to see her, don't we? To make sure you guys haven't made a huge error.' Then he reached out for Beth's hand, who clasped his fingers, despite her venomous attack on her husband.

Susie left the room, a look of relief across her face at the chance to escape.

'We're ready,' said Beth.

Morgan felt her heart break for the woman because she was not and never would be ready for what she was about to see. The curtains were drawn back and Beth gasped. Sharon's waxy face with her eyes open and dried blood was even more horrific with the cloth covering the half of her face that had been eaten away by insects. The white sheet was tucked under her chin to hide the rest of the wounds on her body.

Declan spoke softly. 'Take your time, we understand that it might not look like your daughter, how you remember her.'

Stefan nodded his head. 'Christ almighty, it's her, it's Sharon. Shut those damn curtains, we've seen enough. I mean how long has she been dead to look like that? Do you even know?'

Declan waved to Susie; Stefan was staring at his daughter until she was no longer visible. 'My rough estimation would be anything from four days to a week. I won't be able to give you a definitive answer until I've conducted the post-mortem.'

Stefan gulped. 'Now what? Do you even know who did this?' He was glaring at Morgan.

'We've already begun our investigation; we have some questions that we need to ask you about Sharon. Would you like to do this here or back at your house?'

'Can you get it over with here? No offence, but I don't want you back in my house.'

Cain looked mildly offended by that statement, but she got it and would probably feel the same.

'Can I get you some tea or coffee?' Susie was hovering at the doorway.

Declan nodded. 'Tea would be good, Susie, thank you.'

She hurried away; Declan turned to Beth. 'I'll let you speak with my lovely colleagues and then I can talk you through what the next steps are.'

He left them to it, smiling at Morgan as he left, and she wanted to follow him out of this too hot, too small room, but instead she sat on a chair opposite the Montgomerys and took out her notebook.

FOURTEEN

Ben had taken Stan with him to track down Eddy Lightburn, Sharon's ex-boyfriend. He'd considered sending patrol officers to pick him up, but he thought it might be a good chance to get to know Stan a little bit. Stan was clutching a sheet of paper with a list of addresses for Eddy and associate addresses.

'So, which is his current address that's on his prison release for probation?'

Stan studied the sheet of paper. 'It's at twenty-three A Sandy Lane Avenue, Kendal.'

Ben nodded; he knew the area well. He'd grown up not far away from there.

Ben drove to Sandy Lane Avenue and parked a little way up the street.

'Eddy is all mouth and no trousers, except for when it comes to how he treats his women,' he told Stan.

Ben got out of the car, and Stan followed him. Knocking on the flat door, Ben could hear the beat of some awful music from inside and felt bad for whoever lived above. The door opened, Eddy took one look at Ben and slammed it shut.

'Nice guy,' whispered Stan.

'Oh, he's just the best,' replied Ben. He twisted the handle and shoved it open before Eddy could lock it.

'Long time no see. That was a bit rude, Eddy.'

Eddy had a shaved head and a tattoo of a spider on his neck. He was over six foot tall and twice as broad as both Ben and Stan. He looked ripped in his too-tight vest. He also looked as if he'd just let a couple of Jehovah's Witnesses into his flat by mistake. 'Fuck off,' he said.

Ben, who wasn't in the least bit threatened by Eddy, turned to Stan. 'How rude.'

He turned back to Eddy. 'I just need a quick chat with you about Sharon Montgomery.'

The music was louder inside, and Ben strode past Eddy into his small kitchen, where the speaker that was almost as tall as the guy who owned it was pulsating with the awful sound, and he yanked the plug out of the wall. The silence was wonderful.

'You can't come in here and do that. Have you got a warrant?'

Ben shook his head. 'I don't need one. Are you still on parole?'

'Yeah.'

'Then you know that part of your licence conditions is that police officers can enter your property to make sure you are complying with that licence.'

'What do you want? I haven't seen Sharon for years. So, if she's made up some bullshit story that I've been to her address harassing her it's a load of crap.'

Ben looked around the flat which was surprisingly neat. 'Have you been to Sharon's address?'

Eddy looked uncomfortable. 'Well, yeah, when I first came out, I thought I'd go see her.'

'How did that go?'

'It didn't, she didn't answer the door, so I left. End of story.'

'Why did you go see her? I mean you didn't end on the best of terms.'

He shrugged. 'I liked her, and she's loaded, her parents are rich. I thought she might be able to help me out with a bit of cash to tide me over.'

Stan was staring at Eddy with a look of disgust on his face. 'You beat the woman up, got sent down for it and thought she'd want to help you when you came out of prison?'

'What can I say, it was a misunderstanding that's all.'

Ben spoke before Stan could. 'So, you went to her house. How long ago was that?'

'Last week, look I didn't do anything, so why are you here?'

'Because we found Sharon's body earlier this morning and, unfortunately for you, you're top of my suspect list. Eddy Lightburn, I'm arresting you on suspicion of murder. You do not have to say anything. But it may harm your defence if you do not mention when questioned something which you later rely on in court. Anything you do say may be given in evidence. Do you understand?'

He nodded his head. 'Sharon is really dead?'

'Yes, I'm sorry.'

The blood had drained from Eddy's face. 'I didn't do it.'

'Save it for interview.'

Eddy stared at the floor. Stan took out his handcuffs, but Ben shook his head.

'Eddy, are you going to behave yourself or do I need to let my colleague cuff you and walk you out of here?'

'Yes, I mean no. I mean I'm not going to kick off. What's the point? I haven't done this.'

'Good, walk yourself out to the car like a good citizen then and we can get this over with as quickly as possible. If you had nothing to do with Sharon's murder, we could get you processed and back here before you know it.'

Ben walked in front, Eddy in the middle and Stan behind.

Stan locked the door and pocketed the key to the flat. Ben knew he should probably have waited until they had more evidence, but Eddy had admitted to going to Sharon's house. He wanted him booked in, forensically examined and interviewed to make sure he didn't have anything to hide.

They didn't have time to waste. It would be a refreshing change to have Sharon Montgomery's killer behind bars in record time.

FIFTEEN

Susie carried in a tray with four mugs of tea and a sugar bowl on it. Cain took a mug, heaping two spoons of sugar into it and stirring. Beth and Stefan declined, and Morgan felt too queasy to drink tea but thanked Susie, who left them to it.

'Do you know of anyone who might want to hurt Sharon?'

Beth was having a hard time looking away from the viewing window, even though she could no longer see her daughter's mutilated body. She shook her head. Stefan nodded.

'That idiot Eddy Lightburn is out of prison. Have you spoken to him, arrested him yet? I'm assuming you know he beat the shit out of her.'

'Yes, we have officers looking for him as we speak.'

'Good because he's a vile man.'

Beth finally tore her gaze away from the window and looked at Morgan.

'I don't think it was him.'

Stefan's head snapped in his wife's direction, so fast Morgan wondered if he'd given himself whiplash. 'What, are you being serious?'

Beth ignored him. 'He's handy with his fists, loud mouthed,

likes to drink, I just don't think he's the kind of man with the brains to find out where Sharon was and go and do this to her.'

Stefan looked at Morgan. 'Beth isn't a very good judge of character; you can disregard that.'

Beth glared at him. 'Clearly, I'm not a very good judge of character because I'm still married to you. How dare you tell them to disregard my opinion? Where were you last night because you weren't home? You were arguing with Sharon only last week.'

The tension in the room was so fraught the air was practically crackling with the energy.

'What are you saying, Beth, that I snuck out of the house and stabbed our daughter to death? I may not be her biological dad, but I'm the one who has been there since she began to walk. I've always treated her as if she was my own child, so don't throw that in my face, especially not now of all the times.'

Cain was staring at Morgan, but she couldn't look in his direction; she was trying to figure out where to go from here. There had been some important revelations in the last couple of minutes that she couldn't disregard.

'Cain, do you want to see if Declan will let you take a statement from Stefan in his office, whilst I take one from Beth? It might be easier that way.'

Beth was back staring at the small window again. 'Yes, I think that would be best. I would like to talk to you without being criticised by my husband who can't lie straight in bed.'

Cain stood up. 'Come on, we'll go somewhere else.'

Stefan walked towards the door, but not before he turned and glowered at Beth. Cain ushered him out, closing the door behind him.

Beth waited a minute then began to talk. 'I'm sorry about that, but I'm devastated and I'm furious that someone has hurt my little girl. I'm never going to talk to her again and tell her I'm sorry.'

'Sorry about what?'

'About not sticking up for her last week when Stefan threw her out of the house and told her to never come back. I turned up mid-argument and stood there with my head bowed, too afraid to argue with him because I wanted an easy life, but he's a liar. He's always been a liar. He's always been unfaithful too, but I love having a life where I never have to worry whether I can afford to eat out for lunch. I'm disgusted with myself that I put up with him for all this time, all his lies, deceit and unfaithfulness just to have an easy time. I watched my daughter walk out of my life and didn't even try to stop her. I'm never going to be able to tell her I'm sorry and I'm furious with myself, but even more so with him. Lord help me because I'm so angry with him I think I might stab him myself.'

Morgan stopped writing. 'I get that you must be devastated and angry, but please don't say that in front of anyone else, Beth. Do you really think Stefan could have done this to Sharon?'

Beth paused; her eyes downcast. She shrugged. 'I don't know, I'm lashing out because I'm so mad.'

'Has he ever been violent towards you or Sharon?'

'No, not ever.'

'Does he have anger issues?'

'Only when he's caught out in his web of lies.'

'Can you tell me what happened between him and Sharon? What did they argue over?'

'Sharon has been telling me for years that he sleeps around. I told her it was none of her business and to leave it be. She did until last week when she caught him sleeping with her friend whilst I had been away for a couple of days, visiting my oldest friend in York. Sharon came to the house to borrow a dress.'

'She doesn't live with you both?'

'No, she has a beautiful little cottage where she works from home. YouTubing has turned into a full-time job for her, which is, was, nice.'

'Sorry, she came to borrow a dress?'

Beth nodded. 'I'd told her to help herself, that I was on my way home and would see her there. I hoped we could have a bit of a catch-up. Lately she's been too busy vlogging and solo camping to come around much, and I miss her. She has the code to the gates, the keys to the house, so she let herself in and went upstairs to get a dress for the wedding she has this weekend.' Beth paused, struggling to breathe, and Morgan reached out for her hand.

'It's okay, you're doing really well. I know this must be so hard for you.'

Beth nodded. 'Her friend Leah walked out of the bathroom wearing nothing but a towel. She'd clearly been in the shower. Sharon said Leah was horrified but not as horrified as Sharon was. She told her to get out of the house now, wouldn't even let her get her clothes, pushed her out of the front door and locked her out. The girl was standing in the driveway in nothing but a towel, with wet hair and no shoes.'

'Sharon told you this?'

She shook her head. 'Marie. I also watched the camera footage that Marie downloaded before Stefan could delete it.'

'What did she do? Leah, I mean.'

'Marie stepped in and did what she always does, took her into the garage and gave her clothes, called her a taxi and sent her on her way.'

'You must have been so upset about this.'

'Angry, degraded, yes. I wasn't upset about Stefan because he's always been this way, but I felt terrible for Sharon. I mean, she knew he was a player, but that was too much for her. He slept with her best friend just because he could. She then confronted Stefan who told her to get out and keep her nose out of his business. Sharon lost it. Marie had to stop her from attacking Stefan, who wasn't bothered at all by any of it. Not even when she threatened to tell me. I'd walked into absolute carnage in time to hear him tell her he was finished with her, she could get the hell out and never come back. They were done, no more money, no holidays or handouts – and Sharon told him to go fuck himself. I've never been so proud of my baby; she had the courage to do what I should have done myself years ago, and now she's not here for me to tell her that. I know what I must do now; I'm not going home with him. It's over, it has been for a long time, this just brought it all home.'

Beth buried her head in her hands and sobbed. Morgan moved next to her and did the only thing she could. She rubbed her back gently, all the time wondering if Stefan had killed his stepdaughter.

SIXTEEN

Amy had walked home with a smile on her face and a feeling of peace inside of her heart that she had never known before. Cain had made her cry with her leaving party and it had melted her heart beyond what she'd ever known. The fact that he'd cared enough to do all of that for her meant the world to her, and she was truly thankful to have such good friends. A slight twinge in her stomach made her pause. It wasn't enough to take her breath away, but it was a little uncomfortable. The midwife had told her she may have Braxton Hicks contractions in the last month, so this must be what it was because she still had three weeks left to go.

The image of the woman who'd been murdered in her tent filled her mind and she couldn't let it go; it was so horrifying. Ben had told her she could finish so she wouldn't have to even think about this case, but she'd seen the photos and now they were stuck in her head. She thought about Gordon Wells, that could have been her, stabbed to death, or even worse kept captive in a tiny room with no windows or escape. What if she'd had her baby in that tiny concrete cell? She shuddered and stopped walking, whispering to herself, *no more, Amy, it didn't happen. You can't keep thinking like this, you have to concentrate on the baby.*

As she reached Cain's house, where she was now officially renting because he'd moved in with Angela, she saw a familiar figure sitting on the front doorstep and did a double take. Jack looked awful, his complexion was pale, his normally clean-shaven face was covered in dark stubble, and he had big, purple circles under his eyes.

He stood up when he saw her and smiled. 'Hey, long time no see.'

She stared at him, furious that he'd turned up now when she'd been in such a great mood. She wasn't in the right frame of mind to argue with him; he'd shown his true colours when she'd told him about the baby.

'What do you want, Jack?'

'Blimey, Amy. No need to sound so happy to see me.'

'I'm not happy, why are you here, tainting my doorstep with all your bad vibes?'

Jack looked at her. 'Your doorstep, I thought this was Cain's house.'

'It is, but I'm renting it from him so technically it's mine, and you're making the place look untidy.'

'Can I come in?'

She didn't even need to think about it. 'No.'

His mouth dropped open; and she realised he hadn't been expecting such a blunt reply.

'I guess I deserve all of this hostility.'

She nodded.

'How are you? How's the baby?'

'We were doing just fine until I saw you. I want you to leave. I have nothing to say to you. I gave you a chance and you blew it, so don't bother to come around here asking if we're okay because you and I both know that you don't give a crap about either of us. All you've ever cared about is yourself.'

'Ouch.'

'Does the truth hurt? Actually, don't answer because I really, honestly do not care one little bit.'

'I'm in a bit of a mess.'

She paused, he looked a mess, and he also looked sadder than she'd ever seen him since she met him.

'Can I talk to you? I really need to talk to someone.'

Amy sighed, she wanted to tell him to fuck off out of her life, but she hadn't ever seen him looking so dishevelled and down. The last thing she needed on her conscience was for him to go off and do something stupid because she wouldn't talk to him.

'Five minutes. You raise your voice at me and I'm calling the cops. I mean it, I'm not in the mood for your bullshit, Jack.'

He nodded. 'Thanks, Amy, I appreciate it, best behaviour. I promise that I'm not here to give you any grief or cause any trouble for you.'

She opened the door, and he followed her inside, but she didn't lock it. She took her phone out of her pocket and placed it on the breakfast bar in the kitchen in front of her, where she made sure it was charged enough that she could phone 999 if he kicked off. He was a copper; he was supposed to stick to the code of conduct in and out of work, but up to now he'd had a hard time controlling his emotions when it came to the subject of her and their baby. She pointed to a stool. 'Sit down.'

He did as she told him.

'Do you want a drink?'

'I'd love a coffee if you have any.'

She made him a coffee, a lemon and ginger tea for herself, thinking about how she was going to have the world's largest latte after she'd given birth because she missed it so much. After she managed to get herself and her extra-large bump onto a stool and they were sitting facing each other, she asked him, 'So what kind of mess are you in, and why do you think I care about that?'

He flinched at her harsh words, but she didn't care. He hadn't cared about the way he'd spoken to her, telling her to get an abortion when she'd told him she was having a baby, their baby.

'You look great, being pregnant really suits you.'

'Does it? Not sure why you'd care, Jack.'

'I'm sorry I was such a dick to you, Amy. I get why you're mad at me, I do, and I deserve it. I shouldn't have spoken to you the way I did, it was cruel and I messed up big time.'

'What do you want?'

'I've been drinking too much, got into playing online poker and I'm going to lose the flat if I don't sort myself out, but that's not what I'm here about. The woman I've been seeing.'

'I knew you were seeing someone, Jack, nothing is ever a secret in the station and you should know that. What about the girl you were seeing? She's realised you're a complete loser and gave you the brush-off?'

'She's dead.'

Amy sat up as straight as she could. 'What do you mean she's dead?'

'I heard the log come in as I was finishing work, and I didn't think anything of it, but there's a picture of a purple Land Rover with one of those roof tents on it posted all over Facebook, saying they found a body inside of it. I was seeing her, I mean we weren't serious or anything, but if it's true and Sharon is dead, then my prints will be all over the place. I didn't do it. I wouldn't do something like that.'

Amy couldn't believe what she was hearing. 'You were going out with the woman who was found murdered this morning?'

Jack's eyes filled with tears as he nodded.

'Holy crap, did you kill her, Jack?' She had to ask, needed to know.

'No,' he shouted across the breakfast bar at her, making Amy shrink back a little.

She looked around the room at the knife block, it was within reach, and at the same time thinking *this isn't happening, please God this can't happen again.*

'No, I didn't, I would never.' His voice was much softer this time. The tears in his eyes and the pain as his voice cracked made her believe him. He was a dick, an idiot and selfish, but he wasn't a killer.

'You have to speak to Ben, tell him what you just told me because when they go to her house and search it, then print the car and the tent, your fingerprints will flag up on the database in seconds.'

Jack buried his head in his hands. 'I can't.'

'Well, if you don't, they're going to come and arrest you, and I'm telling you now it will look much better if you go speak to Ben first and tell him what you just told me, instead of letting them discover it themselves. You can't worm your way out of this, Jack.'

'I didn't kill her, Amy. I wouldn't kill anyone.'

Amy sighed. 'Do you want me to ring Ben and tell him?'

Jack shrugged. 'I don't know what to do.'

'Yes, you do. You tell the truth; you're a police officer, you're one of the good guys not a killer. You speak with Ben, get interviewed, and make sure you have a brief with you. You be open and honest, no lying, no withholding anything that you think makes you look guilty because in the long run it never works, and we both know that. If you didn't do anything it will all be okay, but you're going to have to face up to speaking with Ben whether you want to or not.'

'But you know what the gossips are like in the station, it will be all around that I did it. I'll get suspended whilst I'm investigated, and PSD will get involved. My career will be over. If I'm lucky, I'll get put in an office working the crappiest crimes on the system if or when they ever let me go back.'

'And if you don't, you're going to look as guilty as sin anyway. Either way you're going to have to come clean because you've already told me and I'm not withholding any evidence for you. So either you phone Ben or I will. For once in your life do the right thing, Jack.'

She brought Ben's phone number up and passed him her phone. He took it from her and called it.

SEVENTEEN

Cain couldn't quite believe what he was hearing coming from Stefan's mouth and was listening with his jaw slack and eyes wide, despite trying his best not to look or sound judgemental.

'So, let me recap. You slept with Sharon's best friend; she caught the pair of you, and you had a massive argument where you told her to get out of your house, and you didn't want anything to do with her and at this point your wife walked in mid-argument?'

'Yeah, not my best moment.'

Cain shook his head. 'Okay, then what happened?'

'Sharon said she hated me, had always hated me, which was a bit of a shock because you know I've treated her like my own kid since she came into my life. She's never wanted for anything, her mortgage, bills, clothes, car, insurance, I pay for it all so a little gratitude would have been nice.'

'How did Beth take this?'

'Like Beth always does, keeps out of it. Doesn't get involved because she knows which side her bread is buttered on. Beth likes the lifestyle I give her, so she turns a blind eye to my extra-marital flings.'

'Beth didn't get mad at you at all? You slept with her daughter's friend in your house and then threw her daughter out. I find it hard to believe she didn't get angry with you over that, pal.'

He shrugged. 'Nope, maybe if she had lost it with me over the years, I'd have stopped but she is literally like a doormat. As long as she has access to my money, she keeps her mouth shut.'

Cain could feel the anger welling up inside him at the guy sitting opposite. His total lack of respect for his wife was appalling.

'Did you know where Sharon was camping on this trip? Where have you been this past week or so? At home each evening?'

'Are you accusing me of killing Sharon?'

'No, I'm trying to establish the facts. If I was accusing you, I'd have read you your rights and we'd be in an interview room down at the station.'

Stefan nodded. 'I've been meeting Leah at her place. I wasn't bringing her home again. I've been seeing her a lot especially last week before I broke it off with her, it was coming to an end... I wanted to make the most of it.'

'And Leah can verify this?'

He nodded. 'She can.'

'Leah, what's her second name?'

'Leah King, she lives in a flat above the rock shop in Ambleside.'

Cain knew the shop so didn't need anything else.

'What's going to happen now?'

'Obviously I'm going to have to speak to Leah to make sure you're telling me the truth, and if she confirms your alibi, then nothing.'

Stefan was getting angry; Cain could tell by the way he kept clenching his fists then unclenching them.

'I didn't kill Sharon, I'm devastated, I'm angry that someone has done this to her. I love her, she's the closest thing to a daughter I've got. Her biological dad is a waste of space. He didn't want to know when Beth told him she was pregnant. He's never had anything to do with Sharon. It was me from the moment I fell in love with Beth, and now she's gone, I'll never see her again. Don't you think I feel bad about how I talked to her, how much of an arsehole I was to her? I was angry with her because she caught me with her friend, but it didn't mean I'd want her out of my life for good. It was just a temporary glitch. We'd have got over it in a couple of weeks and everything would have been back to normal.'

'Even though you told her that you wanted her out of your life?'

'It was all words. Are you telling me you've never said stuff you didn't mean and regret?'

Cain did, almost every day but he wasn't telling Stefan. He shrugged.

'Oh, fuck off,' was Stefan's reply, and Cain thought how much he'd like to lean across and punch the arrogant bastard right between the eyes.

'I'm not saying another word unless I have a solicitor.'

'Good, I don't think you should either and I'm finished anyway for now.'

Cain let the *for now* hang in the air. He stood up and pointed to the door. Stefan followed him outside, where Declan and Susie were both hovering, trying to look as if they hadn't just heard the last few minutes of conversation.

'Thanks, Declan, we're finished now.'

'Anytime.'

———

Cain knocked on the viewing room door.

'Come in,' Morgan's voice called out.

Morgan looked a lot more relaxed than he felt. Beth was sitting there, her eyes red, dabbing at the corners of them, and he realised that Stefan hadn't had to wipe his eyes once.

Morgan stood up. 'Beth is going home to pack some things then going to stop at a friend's house for a couple of days, Stefan. I've got a family liaison officer coming to drive her there, and if Cain has finished taking your statement, you're free to go.'

Stefan was glaring at Beth. 'For real, you're leaving me now?'

Beth didn't even make eye contact with him.

'We should be together for Sharon, to help each other through this. You're not thinking straight, we need to plan the funeral.'

Beth stood up. 'I am thinking straight, for the first time in twenty years I'm thinking straighter than I ever have before. You can take your house and money and—'

'Hello, I'm Caroline, the FLO. I'm so sorry about your daughter, it's devastating, I'm here to help you with anything you need, and to drive you home, Beth. Stefan, a colleague of mine from Barrow is on their way to give you the same support.'

Stefan shook his head. 'I don't want anyone interfering, I can manage on my own.'

'You might feel different when you get home.'

'I said no, I want you all to leave me the hell alone. I don't want some soppy copper hanging around my house when I'm grieving.'

Caroline nodded then stepped into the room, defusing the situation, and Beth looked at her.

'Come on, flower, let's get you out of here. I'll answer any questions you may have on the drive home.'

Beth walked out with Caroline, and Cain, who barely knew the woman, felt proud of her for finally putting herself before her creep of a husband and the money in his bank account.

EIGHTEEN

Morgan and Cain arrived to find Ben in his office, phone clamped to his ear, scribbling notes on a piece of paper on his desk. Neither of them spoke, but Morgan picked up a marker pen and wrote Stefan Montgomery's name on the whiteboard, then turned to Cain.

'What was Leah's surname?'

'King, she lives in a flat above the rock shop in Ambleside.'

'I used to love that shop, it's so neat. I haven't been for years.'

She wrote underneath Stefan's name in brackets.

(*Leah King, Stefan's lover. Sharon's best friend.*)

'Well, now's your chance for a visit. What do you think is up with Ben? His face is a picture.'

Ben looked stressed beyond belief. The way he was scrubbing his hand across his face was a huge indicator that he was dealing with something off the scale. The door opened and in sauntered Stan who looked as if he hadn't a care in the world. He smiled at them.

'What are you and Ben on with?' Morgan didn't return his smile.

'Well, we found Eddy Lightburn, he's in custody. I don't know who Ben's talking to now though. I've just booked Eddy in.'

Stan was reading the whiteboard. 'Stefan Montgomery, is that the victim's dad?'

'Yes.'

'He's a viable suspect then?'

'He is until we can confirm where he was last night.'

Tristan whistled. 'What a mess this is, that's some weird relationships going on in that family.'

Ben was standing at the door to his office. 'It's just got even messier.'

'Why?' asked Morgan.

'Jack White was dating Sharon Montgomery.'

'Amy's ex Jack White?' asked Cain.

Ben nodded.

'He turned up at Amy's house, went to speak to her and tell her. She made him phone in. I'm on my way to speak with him.'

'He's seeing the victim?' muttered Tristan.

'*Was* seeing the victim,' corrected Morgan.

'You better add him to your ever-growing list, Morgan,' said Cain with a smile on his face.

'Stop gloating, Cain, it doesn't suit you.' Ben pointed to him, and Cain shrugged.

'Maybe not, but it serves him right the way he's treated Amy, not wanting anything to do with the baby or even being there for her the last few months, he deserves everything coming his way.'

'Boss, what do you want us to do?' Morgan was looking at Ben.

'I'm not even sure, someone is going to have to interview Eddy Lightburn. Cain and Stan, can you sort that out? Morgan, you come with me and do not utter a word of this, especially not to Madds or anyone on Jack's shift. This is strictly on a need-to-know basis until it's sorted out, so don't write his name on the board, okay?'

Everyone nodded, and Morgan followed him out.

———

When they were alone in the car Morgan breathed a sigh of relief. 'That was some death notification.'

Ben turned to her. 'Really, even worse than usual?'

She nodded. 'It wasn't the identification, although that was bad, it was the drama afterwards. We had to separate her parents to take statements. Cain had to take the dad, well step-dad, Stefan Montgomery, to Declan's office. The mum, Beth Montgomery, told me Sharon had found him cheating with Sharon's best friend, then Beth walked in mid-argument.'

'When was this?'

'Last week. Beth then decided in the middle of the interview that she was finally leaving Stefan. It was as if seeing her daughter's body made her realise that life really is too short to live the kind of life she was living. She also disclosed that Stefan wasn't home last night, hasn't been home much since the whole Leah incident.'

'Has he got an alibi? Do you think he did this? Oh, he couldn't have, Declan estimated time of death at least four days ago but that doesn't mean he still couldn't have killed her.'

She shrugged. 'He said he was at Sharon's friend's flat; we need to speak to her and get a statement about Stefan's movements the past seven days. He said Eddy Lightburn was responsible for Sharon's murder, but Beth didn't agree. She said he didn't have the balls, and I kind of got the impression she was trying to implicate Stefan without saying it outright.'

'I sort of agree with Beth. Eddy is a thug, but I don't think he's the sort to plan a murder of this level. Although he breached his licence conditions by going straight to Sharon's house, I think he's more the kind of bloke who would lash out in a fight or an argument. I just don't see him plotting to go find Sharon whilst she was camping, then getting himself up there with no vehicle. He doesn't have access to one. Stan checked it out, said he doesn't even own a bicycle.' He paused and then asked Morgan, 'Do you really think the stepdad is good for it?'

Morgan peered out of the window; they were almost at Amy's. 'I don't think so, but we still need to rule him out, don't we? Stan, how is he? I kind of find it hard to call him that.'

'Oh, Morgan. I'm sorry, it's not a common name, is it? I think he's okay, he seems on the level. Probably a bit keen, but he's trying to fit in. It's not easy coming into a team that's as close-knit as ours. We should probably cut him a little slack. I don't think he's the worst person Marc could have picked, although I would have liked to have been consulted first.'

'Yeah, I'm probably being a bit touchy about him. I'll try, okay, I'm not promising though. If he's an idiot, I'll tell him.'

'Good, because I wouldn't expect anything less.'

She closed her eyes and was there, strolling down Fifth Avenue, staring up at the Empire State Building. 'New York was amazing, wasn't it? But it feels like it was forever ago not a few days.'

'It really was. I don't know if I'd go back there though. Far too many people for my liking, but it was cool seeing all those famous landmarks. When do we go to Salem?'

'Three months and counting. I'm even more excited about finally going there than I was about NY.'

Ben laughed. 'I bet you are; you're going to fit right in, my little Goth girl.'

Morgan pulled down the flap on the sun visor to look in the mirror and made a face. 'Not so much of a girl anymore, this job is ageing me beyond my years with the constant stress. Botox should be a required bonus because much more of this and I'm going to need it.'

'You do not, you're still as beautiful as the day I dragged you into working for me.'

'Flattery will get you everywhere, Matthews.' She blew him a kiss, and he roared with laughter.

Morgan elbowed him in the ribs. 'Less of the laughter, Amy is standing on the doorstep looking as if she's going to commit murder.'

'Poor Amy, as if she needs Jack turning up and dumping his problems on her when he's been a total idiot with her.'

Morgan was pulling Amy in for a hug before Ben had even locked the car. She whispered, 'Do you want me to kick the shit out of him for you? I've been waiting for an excuse.'

Amy grinned at her and whispered back, 'If you get the opportunity, then please don't let me stop you. I have no idea why he turned up here to tell me this because I honestly don't care, but he looks a state and, against my better nature, I thought I should do the right thing, in case he went off and did something stupid.'

Morgan squeezed her again. 'You're a better person than he'll ever be.'

'Amy, I didn't think I'd see you again so soon. You're almost as bad as Morgan, can't keep away from us all.' Ben winked at her and Amy rolled her eyes.

'This is not through choice; Morgan is just a glutton for punishment.'

'Come on, let's get this over with so we can leave you in peace.'

Ben was being serious even though he smiled at her, and she led them into the house and down to the living room, where Jack was pacing up and down in front of the window like a tiger marking its territory.

NINETEEN

Cain sat opposite Eddy Lightburn in the small interview room. Eddy had demanded a solicitor, and the duty solicitor, Lucy O'Gara, was sitting next to him. Lucy had been down this road more times than any one of them. She smiled at Cain, who nodded at her. Stan could not tear his eyes away from her long blonde hair, sharp suit and warm smile. Cain could see him from the corner of his eye, and he gave him a side kick in the shin with his extra-large boot. Eddy looked bored, as if this was all a major inconvenience to him. After the introductions, Lucy looked up from her notepad.

'My client is happy to be open and honest with you; he has nothing to hide so will answer your questions as long as they are reasonable and pertinent to the case.'

'Thank you, Lucy. Eddy, that's good. We can get this over with if you're happy to comply.'

'I've got nothing to say, except I'm sorry to hear Sharon is dead. I know I treated her badly, but I'd never have killed her.'

Cain refrained from stating the obvious: that Eddy had beaten her so badly he'd gone to prison for it.

'When was the last time you spoke to Sharon?'

'The day I was released from prison, I went to her house.'

'Why?'

He shrugged. 'I had nowhere to go. Have you stayed in a bail hostel? They're full of nonces and weirdos.'

Cain shook his head. 'Can't say I have.'

'No, you're on the right side of the law.'

'What happened when you saw Sharon?'

'I said I was sorry, could we maybe start over.'

Stan let out a loud noise that was a mixture of disbelief and disgust, and Cain had to stop himself from kicking him again.

Stan asked, 'I thought you said Sharon didn't open the door to you when you knocked?'

Eddy shrugged. 'Wasn't going to admit to that, was I? But seeing as how I don't really have much choice, I'm being honest with you now.'

Cain continued. 'Well, we appreciate that, Eddy. I'm having a hard time understanding why you'd think that Sharon would want to see you again after you hurt her so badly the last time you were together. Did you not think to yourself that going to her house was a little messed up? Like you say, you didn't exactly treat her well. Don't your release conditions say you are not to even set foot on the same street as Sharon Montgomery?'

Eddy glanced at Lucy, who nodded. 'Yes, I just wanted to make things right. I thought she might forgive me; she was such a forgiving person. I've had a lot of time to think about stuff in prison. I'm getting tired of living the same shit life, go straight for a bit, then fall off the wagon and end up back inside. It's the drink, you see? Not me really. I wanted more and I'm not getting any younger. This time I've been looking after myself inside, working out and trying to focus on getting healthy, you know.'

'And you thought that Sharon could give you more?'

'Yes. She's loaded, or her parents are anyway.'

'How was Sharon with you? We have no log of her calling the police out to remove you.'

'She was a bit shocked, but she was polite. Told me she forgave me, but was struggling with a lot of personal stuff at the moment and wasn't looking for a relationship with anyone.'

'How did you take this?'

'I told her I respected that and left.'

'No shouting or arguing, no feeling angry enough to want to harm her?'

He shook his head. 'Check the neighbour's doorbell camera. It was lit up and recording the whole incident. I thanked her for being kind and honest, turned around and left, wishing that I hadn't screwed up the one good thing I ever had in my life with my drinking.'

Eddy looked genuinely sad, and against his better judgement, Cain felt a little sorry for him.

'You haven't seen Sharon since that night?'

'No.'

'You didn't go to where she was camping and kill her?'

Lucy opened her mouth to speak, but Eddy held up a hand.

'I swear to God, I didn't. I'm not being funny, mate. I'm broke, I have no car, I don't have a phone that connects to the internet without paying a fortune. I wouldn't have known where she was camping even if someone drove me up there and pointed her tent out to me, and I had no reason to kill her. Why would I do that?'

'Because she reported you to the police and you ended up doing three years inside. Because you know she loves camping, you know where she camps.'

'Mate, if I killed every person who reported me to the police over the years, you'd have a stack of bodies as high as Helvellyn. And the camping hobby started after me. It must have been something she started doing while I was inside.'

Lucy did interrupt this time. 'I think you have everything

you need. My client has admitted to speaking to the victim the day he was released. I suggest you check out the doorbell footage to confirm what he's told you. I don't think there is anything else for us here unless you have any evidence to suggest he was involved with the murder.'

Cain shook his head. 'We will do that. Thank you for your time, both of you.'

Eddy looked at Lucy, then turned to Cain. 'Is that it, you're not keeping me?'

'Not at the moment, the court will decide what to do about you breaching your conditions, but you're free to go. Eddy, keep out of trouble and don't leave town because I don't want to have to come looking for you.'

'I will, I mean I won't get in trouble. I'm done with it; I want an easy life.'

Cain stood up. 'My colleague will see you out.'

He left Stan with them and went to speak to Marc, who had offered to interview with him, but Cain had wanted to get a measure on Stan, and he'd certainly done that. In Cain's opinion he was a thug, and he wouldn't be surprised if Lucy, who Cain had worked with many times over the years, didn't put a complaint in about his leering at her. But he thought Eddy was telling the truth.

TWENTY

Jack looked dreadful, and Morgan did a double take. If she didn't know any better, she'd think he had some terrible secret he was hiding that was burning him up from the inside, but she didn't think he was a killer. Then again, she hadn't thought he'd treat Amy the way he had, so she wasn't a very good judge of his character at all. She didn't even try and speak to him; he looked at Ben then her.

'Can I talk to you on your own, Ben?' Jack asked.

Amy shook her head. 'Whatever you have to say, Jack, you say it in front of us all or you go to the station with Ben and tell him there. I didn't invite you here for this, you're in my home and I'm too tired to put up with you acting as if you can call the shots. You're up shit creek without a paddle. Take it or leave it.'

Jack pursed his lips but nodded.

Ben sat opposite him; Amy and Morgan squeezed on the sofa together.

'Should I tell you what I know or what's been happening?'

'Yes, please.' Ben's voice was calmer than Morgan's would have been.

'I started seeing Sharon about eight weeks ago, we went on a couple of dates. I met her when I arrested Eddy Lightburn for assaulting her a few years ago.' Jack kept his focus on Ben.

'Did you go out with her three years ago?'

'No, of course not. I liked her, we got on well and I felt sorry for her, but I was with Amy.'

Amy tutted; Jack turned to her. 'I have never cheated on you, Amy, I swear down.'

'Good, because God help you if I find out that you ever did, Jack.'

Ben interrupted. 'Go on, Jack, I'm busy and you know that you could get in trouble if you did have a relationship with her after you worked on her case when she was at her most vulnerable.'

'I know and I didn't. She popped up on my Instagram, so I followed her. This was only six months ago, and I commented on one of her camping posts about three months ago, we got talking and then I finally asked her out for a drink. She said yes and we began dating, just casually.'

'When did you last see her?'

'The night before she went on this camping trip. She picked me up from the pub and I went back to hers. I stayed the night; she was up bright and early to get ready for her trip. She's very good at vlogging and wanted to spend the day setting up camp and filming for her YouTube channel.'

'Did you not offer to go with her?'

He shook his head. 'Her channel is all about solo and wild camping adventures. I wish I had because she wouldn't be dead now if I'd been there. I feel so bad, it's horrible. I can't stop thinking about it.'

'Did Sharon mention if she had a stalker, any followers on her social media that gave her cause for concern?'

'She said there were a couple of creeps who liked everything and would send her DMs, but she didn't think they were anything to be scared of.'

'Would you know who they were?'

'No idea, you'd need to go through her account.'

Ben nodded. 'You didn't fall out with her before she went camping?'

Morgan didn't take her eyes off Jack; she was watching his body language for signs he was lying, but he was shaking his head emphatically.

'No.'

'Okay, what about Eddy Lightburn? He's admitted to visiting her the day he was released from prison. Did she ever mention him? Was she worried about him turning up?'

'She said he'd turned up, they had a civil conversation and he left. I asked her why she didn't ring the police, and she said she thought he was genuinely sorry and that everyone deserved a break. She didn't want to dwell on the past.'

'What about you, do you think he could have killed her?'

Jack paused. 'It would be easier for me to say yes, I think he did. But I have my doubts that he's even clever enough to find her and do something like that.'

'So everyone keeps saying,' murmured Ben. 'Look, Jack, you know that I'm going to have to write this up as a statement, and I'm also going to have to speak to Madds and let Professional Standards know. You need to speak to Davey, if he's still the FED rep, and tell him everything you told me because they're going to be looking into you from every angle. You were one of the last few people who saw Sharon alive, this is not something that can be brushed under the carpet and forgotten about. Are you good, do you need me to get you an urgent referral to a counsellor or a medical professional? If I were you, I'd go sick, so you don't have to worry about PSD marching into work and doing what they do in front of the whole station. But you didn't hear that from me, okay, this is me giving you some friendly advice. You don't have to take it.'

Jack was nodding. 'I'm okay, I'm sad not suicidal, and I'm

worried that they'll try and pin this on me, but I'll do that, thanks, Ben.'

'It's Amy you need to be thanking; I'm surprised she didn't kick your sorry arse out of the door. You do not deserve the respect she's given to you after the way you've treated her.'

Jack's eyes sparkled with unshed tears. He looked at Amy. 'I'm sorry, Amy, I really am.'

She shrugged. 'Thanks.'

Ben stood up. 'We are not going to try to pin anything on you, we are a team of professionals and only want the truth, so unless you've told me a pack of lies, I have no reason to disbelieve you. However, I suggest you go home, phone Madds and report sick. I'll do the rest. Do you need a lift back to your place?'

'No, I'll walk but thank you. I need to clear my head.'

'Do you have a key for Sharon's house?' Morgan asked.

'No, we weren't serious enough for me to have a key, like I said it was early days. We didn't tell anyone we were seeing each other, and I never met her friends or family, although she was raging about her stepdad getting it on with her friend. I gave her a lift to her parents' house once. It's one of those huge mansions by the lake. I waited in the car, they even have a maid, she was going into the garage, but she never even looked over at me.'

Morgan sighed. 'I guess we should have got one off her parents.'

'There's one on her car keys, that's where she kept it.'

'Thanks.' This time Morgan did give him a half smile; she wasn't sure if he was involved or what the hell was happening, but she did know that this complex case wasn't going to be solved before the end of her shift unless the killer walked into the station and handed themselves in.

TWENTY-ONE

Back in the car, Morgan was biting at the chipped nail varnish on her nails, and she announced, 'Stan was right, this is a shit show of the highest degree. Do you think Jack's telling the truth?'

Ben was watching Jack as he walked down Amy's street with his head hung low and his shoulders stooped. 'He's a waste of space and the way he treated Amy was unforgivable. I don't like him as a person, but this isn't about that. It's about whether Jack White has a moral compass we can trust.'

'Do you trust him? Because I kind of don't, not one little bit.'

Ben was still watching Jack, until he reached the corner and turned out of sight.

'Between you and me, no, I don't, and this puts me in a very awkward position regarding the investigation. We need to search Sharon's house, see if there are any leads or forensics in there.'

'Did you hear the way he said she picked him up? He's accounting for his prints being in her car and at her home address.'

'I noticed that. At least we have Stan who can interview him if needs be. However, I don't think it will come down to that. PSD are going to be all over this like a rash. It's not good publicity if an officer is involved in a high-profile murder investigation to the degree he is.'

'I keep thinking about Sarah Everard, that was horrific beyond all measure.'

'It was horrendous, that scumbag.' Ben stopped. 'I can't even put into words how I feel about that case. This is going to be high profile when the news breaks tomorrow. I mean all the murders we deal with are equally important, but the fact that she was a, what's the word they use for people who aren't famous except for on social media?'

'Influencer?'

'Yeah, that. She has a pretty big following, her parents are wealthy, she was dating a copper, and her ex beat her up and got sent to prison. The press will have a field day with all of that.'

Morgan sighed. 'Yeah, they love to focus on everything except what's important.'

Ben's phone began to vibrate, and he put it on speaker when he saw Declan's name on the screen.

'Ben, I thought I'd better let you know the post-mortem is scheduled for nine thirty tomorrow morning.'

'We'll be there, thanks, Declan. I believe it was a bit disorganised this afternoon.'

'It was certainly something. Morgan handled it very well. You should give her a pay rise for all the crap she puts up with.'

Morgan grinned at Ben. 'Thanks, Declan.'

'Ah, my sweet child. Praise where it's due, that was out of the blue and totally unexpected.'

Ben smiled back at her. 'See you tomorrow, today is getting worse by the hour.'

'Take care, guys.'

Declan hung up.

Morgan poked Ben in the ribs. 'I think he's right about the pay rise.'

'I would give you one and a huge bonus for every killer you catch. Unfortunately HR doesn't work that way. Come on, let's see if we can locate a key for Sharon's house and go have a ratch around in it. Who knows, we might get lucky and find a stack of correspondence from her killer.'

'Forever the optimist, I love that, Ben Matthews.'

Back at the station, Ben left Morgan to go and speak to Madds about Jack. She didn't know what she felt about Jack. How could you feel bad for someone like that? Although if he was telling the truth, his girlfriend had been brutally murdered. Morgan decided that all her time and sympathy would focus on Sharon Montgomery. She was the innocent victim in all of this. Jack was his own worst enemy, but how peculiar that he just happened to be dating their murder victim.

Cain and Stan were gossiping, a mug of something hot in their hands and a half-empty packet of biscuits on the desk between them. Morgan plucked one out of the packet. 'No cakes left?'

'I forgot about those, there might be. I need to go and clean up the blue room before the cleaner gets upset about the mess.'

She shook her head. 'I'll do it, least I can do.'

Taking another biscuit, she left them to go to the blue room, which looked as if a piñata had exploded everywhere. Picking up the wastepaper bin, she began scooping paper plates and crumbs into it. There were some curled-up cheese sandwiches on a paper plate that nobody had bothered to cover up, so she threw them in the bin as well. There were three cupcakes left and after making sure the only mess was on the floor, she sat down in one of the chairs and peeled back the wax wrapper on one of the cakes. Taking a huge bite, she sighed but her pleasure was short-lived when the door opened and Marc strode in.

'Aha, just in time, I see, to snag a cake.'

Morgan pointed at the plate, swallowed and said, 'There's some stale sandwiches in the bin if you're really hungry.'

Marc grimaced. 'No, I'm good, a cake will do. What's up then?'

She took another bite of her cake, asking herself if he really just asked her what's up. Marc sat down opposite her, managed to tear the cake apart and stuff half of it into his mouth.

'Wow, that was something.'

He grinned at her. 'It was, I'm starving. Are we going to eat food at some point? It seems like hours since we had Amy's tea party.'

'I guess we could order pizza or something.'

'Anything will do, as long as it's hot. Any updates for me?'

Morgan realised he didn't know about Jack because that was a huge update. Not sure if she should tell him or leave it to Ben. He leaned across the table on his elbows, shoved the rest of his cake in his mouth and sighed. When he'd finished chewing, he pointed at her.

'Come on, where did you and Ben disappear to? Cain and Stan have not long come out of interview with the delightful Eddy Lightburn, who by all accounts is a reformed character, which I think is a load of old tosh, but I guess we have to give him the benefit of the doubt until we find something that ties him to the crime scene.'

'You think he did it?'

'I don't think he one hundred per cent did it, but I'd give him a fifty per cent chance of being guilty.'

'We went to Amy's house because Jack turned up there.'

Marc's eyes were wide as he looked at her. 'Was he giving her grief?'

She shook her head. She'd done it now, she may as well tell

him the rest of it, and besides it would give Ben a bit of a breather if she took the flak for it.

'No, he went to confess something to her. He looked awful, really rough.'

'What? Come on, Morgan, you're worse than Cain when he's trying to make all the boring gossip he's retained sound interesting, just spit it out.'

'I don't really know if it's my place to say anything.'

He laughed. 'That's quite the understatement; you normally have no problem speaking your mind.'

She couldn't argue with him there; she'd given him what for at the briefing earlier. 'Jack was dating Sharon Montgomery; he slept at her house the night before she went camping, and Ben has gone to speak to Madds about it.'

'Oh Lord, for real? Jack, one of our officers, was dating the murder victim?'

'Sorry.'

Marc leaned back in the chair. 'Do you think he killed her?'

'No, he said she picked him up from the pub, he went back to her house with her and slept there. He left her the next morning to get her stuff ready; I was going to pull up his duties, but Madds will know if he turned in for work anyway.'

'He was giving a reason for his prints being in her vehicle and home.'

'That's what I said.'

'Wow, this is just not what I was expecting at all. What did Ben say?'

'His words were something along the lines of, "we need to figure out Jack's moral compass".'

Marc stood up. 'I have a headache.'

'Join the gang, so do the rest of us. Should I order pizza, or would you prefer a Chinese takeaway?'

'Pizza.' He took out his wallet and put two twenty-pound

notes on the table. 'My shout, to show my appreciation to you all for working late.'

Morgan picked the money up. She wasn't going to turn down free pizza and he knew it, none of them would. She took out her phone and scrolled through her apps until she reached the one for Gino's Pizzeria.

TWENTY-TWO

The pizza was good, too good, and Morgan was stuffed, wishing she'd not eaten the cake so she'd left room for more pizza, but that was life. She hadn't known Marc was going to buy them food, so she was never going to turn down the chance to eat anything when they were up to their necks in an investigation. Two officers had been sitting outside of Sharon Montgomery's address on scene guard in case her parents tried to get into her house, or anyone else who could have a key. Ben had told them all to get ready to do the search, and Cain had gone to look for the huge search bag where they kept all the evidence bags, protective clothing and anything else they may need. Task force had finished for the day, so it was them or nothing.

As they were walking out to the cars in the rear yard of the station, Marc stopped. 'We could leave this until tomorrow if you want. It's late, it's dark. As long as there's officers outside all night it should be good.'

Ben shook his head. 'No, boss. I think it needs to be searched now, especially knowing that Jack was one of the last people inside of the address with the victim. He's telling us that everything was hunky dory, but what if it wasn't? What if they were arguing and he somehow manages to get inside and clean up any evidence?'

'That's a lot of what if's. Ben,' said Marc.

'It is, but I need to be able to finish tonight with a clear conscience that he was telling me the truth.'

'Your call, Ben, I'm happy to do what you think. You know that PSD are going to storm in tomorrow and take over anyway, don't you?'

Ben nodded. 'That's exactly why I'd like to get a look before they kick us off this part of the investigation.'

Morgan wasn't sure if Ben was doing this because he still thought that Jack was one of them or if it was for Amy's sake. In Morgan's opinion, Jack had given up the right to be classed as one of them the moment he started being a dick to Amy, and whatever mess he'd got himself into was purely his own fault. She was tempted to tell Ben, but he knew, didn't he? Maybe he was hoping to find some damning evidence and get Jack locked up before anything else happened.

Sharon Montgomery lived in a pretty little cottage with a beautiful little front garden full of purple and white flowers. The front door was purple too and Morgan wondered if she was a witch. Her aunt Ettie had a purple front door. Morgan knew the lore that if a house had a purple door a witch lived inside, or was that just an Instagram lore? She didn't think it was; Ettie really was a kitchen witch. Sharon drove a purple 4x4, maybe it was her favourite colour, or could she be into witchcraft? Suddenly Morgan was keen to go inside and look around, see if she had shelves of books on witchcraft, plants and herbs on her windowsill and a crystal collection to be envious of. Morgan had quite a collection now; she had found a couple of trusted sellers that sourced the most beautiful, ethical crystals. Her latest was a beautiful clear quartz skull that Ben had bought her. One day, when things slowed down a little, she was going to spend time with her aunt who had promised to teach her everything she knew. That thought filled Morgan with a warmth that made her heart so happy. There was a lot more to this life than anyone could figure out, and she had always been drawn to the witchy side of it.

'So, Morgan, you take the upstairs with me; Cain and Marc, downstairs. Stan, you can check the rear garden, sheds, anything else.'

'Yes, boss.' Morgan snapped back to her current reality, pushing her thoughts of being the witch in the woods to one side. Oh, how she envied Ettie, she really was living the dream.

They all dressed in the white paper suits, boot covers and gloves, and Ben, who had retrieved the house key off Sharon's car key fob, opened the door. Stan had also been tasked with signing everyone in and out of the house, which he didn't look so happy about, but he was the new guy, he had to do the crappy jobs. God knows she'd done more than her fair share when she'd first joined Ben's team.

Ben pointed to the door for her to go inside first. She paused on the doorstep and inhaled, the scent of lavender lingered in the air – there was nothing bad. No underlying tinge of anything bad or decaying. She reached in and switched on the hall light. The cottage was bigger inside than it looked, and it was beautiful. The entrance was a dusky pink with gold framed pictures hanging on the wall, a huge mirror and pine flooring. On some floating shelves were stunning pink amethyst, rose quartz and clear quartz crystals. A crushing wave of sadness washed over Morgan for Sharon whose life had been so violently ended; she was never coming home to this beautiful cottage.

'I think we're good to go. Please, be careful, it's so pretty inside. Cain, no clumsy fumbling of anything you don't need to touch.' She wasn't in charge, but she felt that, out of respect for Sharon, she should ensure they didn't go in like bulls in a china shop and wreck the house more than they needed to.

She went upstairs, pausing to stare at the gallery wall of pictures, all of Sharon's camping trips, beautiful views of the fells, mountains and lakes of the area. Some of Sharon and her beloved 4x4, but mainly of the area surrounding her wild camping sites. There were three doors off the landing: the first one she opened was the bathroom and that was spotless; the second door led into a small guest room with a single bed and a tiny pine table with Sharon's MacBook on it. They would seize that and get it sent off to the tech guys at headquarters; there were bookshelves and Morgan stepped further inside to look at the spines. *The Crystal Year*, and *Affirmations and Crystals* by Claire Titmus, and *The Witch's Way Home* by Emma Griffin were just a few that Morgan had on her own bookshelves, and she smiled to herself – she was right, Sharon was into the witchy way of life. It also made her feel even sadder: who was going to take care of Sharon's beautiful crystals and books? She pulled open the small pine chest of drawers to look through it, but it was empty. She really didn't have much clutter, and Morgan respected that. Maybe her main bedroom would be messier.

'Anything?'

Ben's voice startled her, and she shook her head. 'Where have you looked?'

'Bathroom, it's clean, no blood spatters, or anything untoward.'

'I'll take Sharon's bedroom.' She walked towards the last door and opened it; this room was much bigger and a little more cluttered. Some of the drawers were half open, the bed was a little messy, there was a stack of books on the bedside table and an empty bottle of water. Over the back of a dark pink velvet chair was a pile of clothes. Morgan thought this was more like it. She said a silent apology to Sharon before she began pulling out each drawer and looking through it, then she checked the bedside drawers, and the books in here made her smile too. Sharon had a mixture of witchy fiction including *Weyward, The*

Lost Apothecary, *Practical Magic* and *The King's Witches* on her stack. Morgan had read and loved all these books too. There was a big, thick, black leather journal in the first drawer. Morgan took it out and flicked through it. Photos were taped inside, notes about books Sharon had enjoyed, places she wanted to go, a daily list of the three things she was most grateful for. No notes about her relationships with anyone, nothing about finding her stepdad with her best friend, no mention of Jack White, or Eddy Lightburn turning up at her house. Morgan continued looking around but found nothing else of interest to their investigation. She went downstairs to where Cain and Ben were in the kitchen chatting. Ben looked her way.

'Find anything?'

'Nothing, she lived a pretty lovely life.'

'Unless her friends tell us otherwise,' said Cain. 'I mean she can't be perfect, can she? None of us is. She must have had some faults.'

'Well, if she did, I'm not picking up on them. This house is beautiful. Her things are too, I reckon she was a good person with no dark secrets to hide. There's no secret diary with the ramblings of a maniac inside of it.'

Ben nodded. 'Where's all her camping stuff though? I mean this isn't a huge space, but it is a good-sized house for one person or a childless couple, but there's no camping stuff, no outdoor gear.'

Stan appeared at the door. 'It's all in the shed. I had a wander around the back and she's got a shed that I'd kill for.'

Morgan arched an eyebrow at him. 'What's that supposed to mean?'

'It's got all sorts of outdoor equipment, paddleboard, canoe, climbing gear, outdoor clothing, wetsuits, camping stoves, tables, tents, you name it she has it stacked out there and most of it is brand new.'

'Did Sharon have another job, or do you think the bank of mum and dad have paid for all of this?' asked Cain, and it was a legitimate question, but Morgan still found it a little rude.

'She's a YouTuber, some of them make a lot of money from the ads on their vlogs.'

Ben shrugged. 'I have no idea about that, but we need to speak to someone to find out more of her background.'

'Where is her camera stuff? Wouldn't she have that with her if she was wild camping and filming it? I didn't see it in that roof tent. Has the car been searched yet? Was it inside of there?'

Ben took out his phone. 'Hang on, let me ring Wendy.'

'Wendy, have you found any phone or cameras in the tent or car?'

He paused whilst she answered then replied. 'Nothing like that. Okay, thanks.' Pushing his phone back into his pocket, he said, 'The killer must have taken them.'

'There's only one reason they took her phone and equipment; she must have them on camera. So, she either knew who they were, or she caught them when she was filming and they're not taking any chances. Find the equipment and we've found the killer. We can get her phone number off her parents or Jack and run a cell site analysis.'

Marc came down the stairs with the MacBook in an evidence bag and the journal in another. He passed them to Cain. 'Yes, Morgan, get onto Jack or her parents, please, and get her number, then get that rolling. Stan, show me the shed. Is there any camera equipment out there?'

Stan shook his head. 'Not that I could find.'

Marc said, 'I think you're right; we find the camera we find the killer. I also think this is a very good point; we've made a great start. I would have liked to have had the suspect locked up by now, but this case has more complications than my grandad's heart bypass so let's finish up here, get the evidence booked in and call it a day. You're not going to be any good tomorrow if we keep on until the early hours, is that agreed?'

'Whatever you think, boss,' replied Ben.

Morgan went outside to phone Caroline, the FLO, and passed on what Marc had suggested. Caroline replied immediately and said she'd get the number from Beth who she was sitting with and get the cell site analysis started. Morgan leaned her forehead against the cool brick wall and sighed. She knew that they would keep on working all through the night if they had a definitive lead they could follow up on and have the killer in the cells, but Marc was right, there were far too many complications and different strands, and she was tired. Her head was banging with a lack of either caffeine or water, probably both. She was also on the verge of having a bit of a meltdown over everything because emotionally she felt wrecked and overwhelmed beyond belief. Not that she was going to go home and switch off, it just wasn't possible.

TWENTY-THREE

Morgan slept through Ben's alarm. It was only when he was standing at her side of the bed with a mug of coffee and plate of toast in his hands did she open her eyes.

'Argh, what time is it?'

'Seven.'

'How are you up so bright and early?'

'I didn't spend hours watching Sharon Montgomery's YouTube channel like someone I could mention.'

'True, I couldn't stop though, I just kind of got sucked in. She was good, really good, in fact she was a natural; she could have been a TV presenter. You know how some of those YouTubers are just awful, she wasn't and I'm not just saying that. Everything was really professional, the sound, the music, the camera work.'

'Did you find anything useful?'

'Unfortunately, no. I took screenshots of the comments under her most popular vlogs to check the names out with the ones on her Instagram account. I did find some beautiful spots to go wild camping though. She had some amazing recommendations.'

'And will you be going wild camping anytime soon, Morgan, that's the question?'

She paused, took the mug of coffee from him and sipped at it. 'Absolutely not, I'd be terrified after seeing her body in that tent yesterday.'

Ben smiled at her, then leaned down to kiss her forehead. 'Good, I thought that might have put you off. Let's stick to nice hotels in the States for now if that's okay with you. What's the one in Salem you booked us into?'

'The Hawthorne, it's a historic hotel and right in the heart of downtown. It has a tavern inside and it's all wooden panelling, it's beautiful. Oh, Ben, it looks so amazing. I can't wait to visit, and apparently it's haunted.'

'Is it? No campsites over there you want to try out?'

'Probably, but I'm more of a flushing toilet kind of gal anyway.'

He was smiling at her. 'Seriously though, we have a bit of a day ahead of us.'

'I know, what's different? Don't we always have a bit of a day ahead of us?'

'You're right, we do. I'm just making sure you're okay and not too tired.'

'You don't know the meaning of tiredness. For years I woke up at the same time and could never go back to sleep. It was only when I met you and found out about my crappy family history that the insomnia stopped.'

'I'm good.' He winked at her and walked out of the room to the sound of Morgan's laughter.

She finished her toast and drank half of the coffee before grabbing her outfit of the day. Black trousers, black T-shirt, black jacket, Doc Marten boots, always the same colour. Corporate Goth was a thing, she'd recently discovered on Instagram, only Morgan had been doing it for as long as she remembered.

·   ·   ·

It was strange walking into the office and not seeing Amy sitting at her desk. She was always early. Always the first one in. Morgan wondered how she was after Jack's untimely confession. She sent her a quick message to check in with her then began to gather the assortment of empty coffee mugs. She wondered what would happen if she didn't do this every single day. Would the guys just leave them fermenting on their desks until they ran out of clean cups in the brew cupboard? She was scared to answer that question because she knew they would. Cups scrubbed clean, kettle refilled and boiled, she made herself and Ben a coffee. There was still no sign of Cain or Stan, come to mention it there was no sign of Marc either, which was a bit strange. Were she and Ben early or late? She looked at her Apple Watch, no, they were on time.

Ben came out of the lift with a stack of papers under his arm.

'Where is everyone?'

'No idea, but let's enjoy the rare moment of peace before it gets spoiled.'

She passed a chipped mug to him and followed him back into the office. 'Well, there's not going to be much of a briefing at this rate if it's just us two.'

Wendy knocked on the door and walked in. 'I'm just on my way out, it's awful.'

Morgan felt a sinking feeling inside of her as her stomach dropped to her feet. 'What's awful?'

'Haven't you heard?'

Ben looked concerned. 'Heard what?'

'They found Jack White's body an hour ago. Joe is already on scene, but I said I'd give him a hand if he needed it.'

Morgan felt her fingers loosen their grip on the handle of the mug as it fell onto the floor and smashed all over the carpet tiles in an explosion of porcelain and hot liquid.

She cupped her mouth. 'No, no, that's not right.'

Wendy nodded. 'I'm afraid it is, sorry. I didn't know you were close.'

Ben intervened whilst Morgan tried to pull herself together. 'We're not, but we were speaking to him at Amy's yesterday afternoon. How did he die?'

'First officers on scene said it was suicide, but I said I can't see him doing that.'

'He was murdered?' Morgan's voice had a quiver to it that she didn't recognise.

'I don't know, Marc is on scene. Cain and Stan went there, and I think they sent Cain to speak to Amy. Madds and Stan are going to his parents' house to speak to them or at least that was what I think was happening. It was a bit hectic over the radio.'

Ben's expression was grim. 'Don't we always say that we never saw it coming though?'

Morgan knew Ben was talking from first-hand experience. His wife, Cindy, had taken her own life, and he'd truly never saw that coming.

Wendy shrugged. 'Yes, we do. Anyway, I'm off to the scene so thought you might want to make your way there too.'

'Where is the scene, his flat?'

'Nope, the poor farmer who found Sharon Montgomery found him slumped against the gate of the field where her 4x4 had been parked. Hanged himself from a tree next to the gate, but the rope snapped and he fell to the ground.'

Morgan turned to Ben, she didn't like this one bit. Wendy left them to it, and Ben waited until she was out of the door before saying, 'Guilty conscience or murdered by the same person who killed Sharon?'

'I don't like it, Ben, it's too much of a coincidence.'

'We need to get up there and see what's happening. Christ, is this ever going to get any better?'

Morgan shook her head. 'I don't think it could get much worse.'

Ben smiled at her, black humour at its best. She was trying to lighten the heaviness they were both feeling, but Ben's smile never reached his eyes, and she didn't think she would be able to push this to the back of her mind like she usually could.

TWENTY-FOUR

The scene was eerily quiet; nobody was speaking as they moved around with little noise. As they got there the undertakers were zipping Jack's body into a bag ready to move him. Ben went to find Marc who was talking to Madds.

'Terrible this is.' Madds was shaking his head. 'We're moving the body because we can't have him out in the open like this.'

Ben nodded, and as Madds walked away Ben turned to Marc. 'Are we sure it's not suspicious?'

'It's not, the lad had either a guilty conscience or was so heartbroken over Sharon that he didn't see any point in carrying on. We're giving him the dignity he deserves and getting him out of public view.'

Morgan moved closer to the scene. A frayed blue nylon rope like Sylvia her mum had for a washing line was dangling from the lowest branch of the tree, but it was still some height.

Ben joined her and she whispered, 'How did he get up there?' She pointed to the branch. 'Jack isn't very tall, even if he stood on the wall he wouldn't have reached. He'd need a ladder and what public view? There's nobody around except for us.'

Ben turned to Madds. 'Was there a ladder?'

He shook his head. 'No, he used the wall or balanced on the gate. He could have climbed the tree, he's fit. It's pretty clear. Whatever he had on his conscience unless he's left a note behind, we're never going to know.'

'I don't like this, Ben; they're moving too fast. We haven't even looked at the body in situ.' Not that Morgan wanted to look at Jack White's body, but if they were to get to the bottom of what happened here it would help if she could examine the scene before any forensics were destroyed.

'I agree with you, but I'll speak to them back at the station. It's too late now. They're not thinking about the fact that this could be staged.'

Morgan couldn't tear her gaze from the body bag that was lying on the floor as a shudder wracked her entire body. It was too hard to comprehend that Jack was inside of it. He was an idiot, but he didn't deserve to die like this, all alone in the exact place his girlfriend had been murdered. But she had the feeling deep inside of her gut that he hadn't been on his own when he'd taken his last breaths. That another person had been watching him take them and that person was the same one who'd violently killed Sharon Montgomery.

Morgan and Ben watched with heads slightly bowed as he was loaded into the back of the 4x4 that mountain rescue had driven up there. When it began to make its descent with the undertakers inside, to get them back to where they'd parked the private ambulance, Morgan whispered, 'How is it over so quickly?'

'We need to speak to Declan; they didn't even call him out.'

'I don't get it, I really don't.'

'Maybe we're seeing more to this than there is because we were only speaking to him yesterday. You know that we're too close. We're never going to be investigating Jack's death. PSD are going to interview us both and Amy.'

Morgan didn't care one little bit about PSD, what she cared about was the truth and there was something niggling away at the back of her mind.

'Should we go see Amy?'

Ben nodded and began the walk back down the path to where he'd abandoned his car, and Morgan followed him. The 4x4 had been driven up by Madds and Marc. Neither of them spoke until they reached his car and were sitting inside.

'Something weird is going on, it's like they're trying to cover it up, pretend it didn't happen,' said Morgan.

'Who is?'

She shrugged. 'Whoever authorised the removal of Jack's body before it had been properly documented and investigated. Whoever it is, they're involved at some level. I don't know how or why but they are.'

'Then we need to get a copy of the log and see who gave the orders.'

'It will be a closed log though; they always hide them when it involves coppers or police staff.'

'We have a legitimate reason to read it though; we're the investigating officers of a closely related murder.' Ben took out his phone and rang the control room inspector, requesting the log be sent to his email.

They agreed, which surprised Morgan, and he waited until it pinged through onto his smartphone, then he opened it and Morgan took photos of it, page by page, that they could enlarge and read later if for some reason it got deleted and Ben no longer had permission to view it. When they'd finished, he sighed.

'Marc gave the go ahead to move him. What the hell was he thinking? There's something off about this, I agree with you. Let's get to the mortuary and speak with Declan because we're supposed to be at Sharon Montgomery's post-mortem at nine thirty anyway.'

Morgan looked at the clock on the dash. 'We're fashionably late, and what about Amy?'

Ben grimaced. 'Can you ring Declan whilst I'm driving and explain what's going on? Tell him to triple check everything to do with Jack White's body when it gets booked in, and then ring Amy to see if she needs anything, tell her we're truly sorry and will come see her after we get back.'

Morgan spoke to Susie to pass on Ben's concerns. It was Cain's voice that echoed in her ear when Amy's phone was answered.

'Hey, she's not up to talking but said hi.'

'I bet she isn't, what a shock. I mean we only saw him yesterday. Does she need anything?'

'No, she's good. I'm here, tell Ben I'm sorry but I can't leave her like this. Where are you guys?'

'On the way to Sharon Montgomery's post-mortem.'

'What have they said about Jack?'

'Madds and Marc are adamant it's suicide; his body is on the way to the mortuary.'

'Already?'

'Yes, they wanted him out of public view.'

'What? Why couldn't they put a tent over him like we do with other people, and what bloody public? It's not like it's a tourist spot.'

'Exactly what me and Ben are thinking, it's all too neat.'

Cain sighed.

'Christ.'

'No point asking him, I don't think he knows what's going on either, speak to you both later.'

She hung up and let out a long, drawn-out sigh. They were no closer to finding out what had happened, and she didn't like being so out of control. Whatever happened today she was determined to find something that would help them make an arrest before Marc and Madds decided Jack had killed Sharon and closed the case.

TWENTY-FIVE

'*How much do you believe in the universe, or God, or whatever is the equivalent in your world?*' asked the woman on the screen. '*Manifesting is real whether you believe it or not, and I want you all to know that I manifested this beautiful life, this vlog, this YouTube channel being monetised, and if I can do it then so can you. Your life goals don't have to be pipe dreams; you have the power to make it happen.*'

He was enthralled, she was good, she was very good and he was sucked in already. Her voice, although distinctly northern, was not local like the other two, but it was soothing and easy to listen to. She was promising him that his dreams could become his reality if he believed they could.

A wet nose pushed at his hand, and he looked down to see the dead woman's dog staring up at him. He had never wanted a pet dog in his life, yet this one was different – the way it looked at him as if it knew what he'd done, but it didn't care as long as he was taking care of it, feeding it, taking it for walks and letting it lie on his sofa. It had become a problem because now he was responsible for it. He'd never been responsible for anyone or anything in his life, and he'd thought about taking it to the dog shelter, then he'd realised: first, he didn't know where the nearest one was and second, he'd have to fill in paperwork which would leave a trail. If someone recognised the dog, he'd be screwed; even if he gave false details they'd probably have CCTV and be able to show the police what he looked like.

A second nudge of that wet nose and he caved. 'Two treats, that's my best offer because I don't know if they are good for you or how many you should be eating.' The dog's tail began swiping the floor, and he stood up to go get a couple of the dried-up sausages out of the ziplock bag. He'd paid a small fortune for the sausages at the Booths supermarket because they were supposed to be made from all natural ingredients. He didn't want to dwell on what ingredients *not natural* contained, but if they didn't cost a fiver a bag, he would consider buying them. He stared down at the dog, it was some kind of terrier, at least he thought it was, he wasn't an expert on dogs so he couldn't be sure. He was too scared to google dog breeds in case it all linked back to him, although why he was bothered about that was beyond him, because anyone who knew the woman would know this was her missing dog.

He closed his eyes at the sharp pain behind them. He had caused himself far too many problems by letting it come home with him, and he knew he should have broken its neck back up at the campsite. Then he looked at it again and realised he wouldn't have been able to do that; how come he had been able to slice its owner to death with no regrets or worries yet be a sucker for her pet dog? That question was going to haunt him the rest of his life, however long that may be.

He went back to his laptop and pressed play. He didn't know anything about manifesting, he'd heard of it because the word got tossed around by every man and woman on social media these days, but he was completely mesmerised with the woman who did. She had the prettiest blonde hair, green eyes and when she did those yoga poses in front of her little car with the roof tent on it, with a view of Lake Windermere behind it, he knew that he had to find her. He paused the video again to write down her number plate. It wouldn't be too hard; she had already announced that she was going on a solo camping trip at the weekend to find herself and meditate under the new moon. He thought that by the end of this vlog or maybe the next she would give away the clues he needed to find her exact location, and this made him very happy.

The dog let out a gentle snore by his feet, and he hoped she didn't have any pets she took camping with her, or he was going to be running a rehoming centre for murder victims' pets, and what would happen to them if he got caught? When the video ended, he was careful not to like or subscribe to her channel because that could lead the cops right to his door. He knew they were good. He knew that red-haired woman was better than good, she was excellent, but he didn't think she'd be as good as he was. They were going to be all over the place when the next body was eventually discovered, and it had to be soon. Surely someone checked on that campsite, otherwise how would they know the people pitching their tents had paid? It was so tempting to go back up there to see if anyone else was camping, but he also knew by the killers back in the seventies and eighties he'd studied not to return to the scene of the crime. Everybody knew who Ted Bundy was, but he was obsessed with revisiting his crime scenes and the places he hid some of the bodies. All right, the guy was completely weird because he was into necrophilia which was disgusting. He paused and smiled to himself. Each to their own he supposed. Who was he to judge, when he could kill someone in the blink of an eye with no regrets?

At the end of the day, he was no better than Bundy, except for maybe his morals, he did have some of those, and as if to prove this the dog whimpered in its sleep on the floor next to him, and he smiled down at it.

TWENTY-SIX

Susie greeted Morgan and Ben with a sombre face. 'I'm so sorry it's one of your own, I can't imagine how hard this must be for you both having to work it as well as the murder case.' Then she reached forward and hugged Morgan, who hadn't been expecting it, but she hugged her back. Susie paused before hugging Ben, but he held his arms out and hugged her.

'Thank you, Susie, it means a lot.'

She let go of him and nodded. 'Can I get you guys a brew?'

'No, thank you, has Jack been booked in yet?'

A loud bell rang, and she pointed to the rear doors where the bodies were dropped off. 'He's just arrived. Declan's in his office; he said he'd have a chat with you first. I'll go get Jack booked in.'

They knew the way to Declan's office as well as they knew the way to their own, because the last couple of years they had spent almost as much time in it as they had the one at the station.

Ben knocked on the door.

'Come in.'

Declan was eating a sandwich, and seeing him doing something so normal and mundane made Morgan feel slightly better.

'How are you? Bit of a mess this one. Can I get you something to eat?'

They shook their heads in unison. 'No, thanks, we're good,' replied Morgan.

Ben sat down on the sofa where Declan spent a lot of time snoozing when he worked late. Morgan sat in a chair.

'What's gone on, do you know anything at all, did he leave a note? How was I not called out to an off-duty cop?'

'We literally know nothing. Marc and Madds were already at the scene by the time we got there, and he was bagged up and being moved. They're adamant it's suicide.'

'Yeah, I was a bit shocked when Susie came in to tell me the undertakers were on the way with an off-duty police officer. My heart was in my mouth, and I checked to see if either of you were online on Messenger; of course neither of you were because you're both rubbish at communicating. Then she told me it was a Jack White, and my pulse returned to normal. Do I know him?'

'Sorry to have worried you, but neither of us would die on purpose.' Morgan smiled at him, and he laughed.

'Are you sure about that, Morgan, because you seem to have a death wish. Have you seen they've made another *Final Destination*? They could make a film about all your near misses, Morgan, and I should shut up right now, shouldn't I?'

She nodded. 'Jack is Amy's ex-partner.'

'Our Amy?'

'Yes.'

'Oh Lord, did we like him or not? And how awful for her, isn't she almost due the baby?'

'We didn't like the way he was being with her since she found out she was pregnant, so unfortunately not a lot. It was her last day in work yesterday, and Jack turned up at her house last night and admitted to her that he was seeing Sharon Montgomery.'

Declan leaned forward, both elbows on the desk. 'The Sharon Montgomery who I'm about to do a post-mortem on?'

'The same one.'

'Holy mother of Mary, what is going on here? I mean this is wild even for us.'

Ben sighed. 'We'd be grateful if you could figure it out for us.'

'The pressure is on, are we ready for this and what do I do about Jack? Will his family need to identify him?'

Ben shook his head. 'I think he was identified by every officer at the scene, but his parents may want to view him. I'm concerned that Marc and Madds are going to want to brush this off as a murder-suicide.'

'They can try, but I won't be brushing anything off. I'll be doing a thorough PM on the pair of them.'

'Thanks, Declan, I appreciate that. When do you think you could do Jack's?'

'Happy to move things around and do him after Sharon's, if you're happy for me to do that.'

'I'd be very happy.'

'Leave it with me, it's no problem. What a day you guys are having, are you both okay?'

'We're good, just keen to get to the bottom of what is going on.'

Declan stood up. 'I'll go see what Susie is up to. I'll meet you in my primary office in ten minutes, give you a chance to get gowned up. Are the CSIs on their way?'

'I think so, they weren't at Jack's scene very long.'

Declan left them waiting in his office for Wendy and Joe to arrive.

. . .

Morgan walked into the mortuary and did a double-take. If she closed her eyes she'd think she was at a spa as the gentle music played in the background. Declan and Susie were ready to get going. Sharon Montgomery was still inside of the body bag she'd been sealed into yesterday. Wendy and Joe were whispering to themselves in the corner, and she had no doubt it would be about Jack. Declan clapped his hands together once, so loud the noise echoed around the tiled room as if someone had let a firework off. The bang made her start and she stared at him.

'Sorry, have I got your attention? I know this is a difficult day for you all and you all have a lot going on but are we okay to get started?'

Everyone nodded, taking their positions. When Sharon was laid out on the steel table and her clothes had been photographed and bagged up for evidence, it was hard to look at the wounds on her body, even harder to look at her partially decomposed face – there were even more wounds than Morgan had noticed.

Declan announced, 'Well, he was certainly an angry little man, thirty-three stab wounds. There was no need for that because there is very little blood, which tells me one of those wounds near to her heart killed her almost immediately. Her heart wasn't pumping when the majority of those were made, or there would have been a lot more.'

He pointed to Sharon's back which was dark purplish-red where all the blood had pooled, and pressed his gloved thumb into an area of the flesh. It caused a white circle that rapidly disappeared when he removed it. 'Liver mortis is fixed. She died in that position. She was lying down in the tent when she was attacked.'

He picked up her left hand to study it, then her right. 'There are no defence wounds. He took her completely by surprise, and I would say the first blow to her chest was fatal because if she had woken up to someone attacking her with a knife, she would have instinctively lifted her hands to protect herself and there are no wounds on them.'

Morgan felt a familiar bubbling sensation begin in her chest. She was furious that whoever had done this had not only killed Sharon immediately, but then carried on stabbing her. 'Overkill.' She said it out loud.

'This is someone who knew her maybe?' Ben whispered. 'Why would you be so angry with someone you didn't know? Why continue to stab her? I mean, if the first blow killed her why carry on when they could just get the hell out of there?'

Declan was measuring the wounds one by one. 'Or it is someone who is either very angry or very sick? Maybe they were enjoying themselves too much to stop.'

Morgan clenched her fingers then released them. She thought of Sharon's father, and Eddy – did either of them have the rage to do this? She doubted it. 'If that's the case, then we have a much bigger problem than we thought. If the bastard who did this did it for pleasure, he isn't going to stop. He's going to be chasing his next high. We need to issue a warning to women who may be considering going on solo camping trips in the Lake District.'

Ben stared at her. 'Bloody hell, that will cause huge problems, and it will cause a bit of a media frenzy. We need to clear it with the boss before we consider putting out a press release.'

Morgan didn't argue with Ben. She knew he was right. She was often impulsive and he would rather be cautious, but she knew this wasn't something she could decide. It was out of her hands for the time being.

'What if Jack did kill Sharon in a fit of jealous rage, then kill himself?' asked Ben to the room.

'Then hopefully we will find some lovely DNA to prove that and link him to the crime scene. Given the amount of blood at the scene, it's very likely we'll find traces on the killer's clothes or body. I can check Jack.' Declan was talking directly to Ben.

Morgan heard Jack's voice telling them last night that he'd been in Sharon's car, her house, been with Sharon in her bed – his DNA was going to be all over her, but that didn't make him a killer. Would her blood be on him?

TWENTY-SEVEN

Sammy had been told to go check the campsite and move the woman on who'd only paid for two nights and was still there last night, four nights in total. That meant he had to ask her to move or get her to pay for the last two nights. Man, he hated this kind of stuff. When he'd taken the job as groundsman, he hadn't realised it entailed booting people off their pitches when they overstayed. Thankfully it didn't happen often, but a couple of times was too many for him. He wasn't the confrontational type and never had been. If the job description had said part-time bouncer, he'd have run a mile and not applied.

As he parked next to her Suzuki jeep, he silently begged her to come out of the tent to see who was there. There was no sign of life. A couple camping on a pitch at the opposite end were walking past with their hiking boots, backpacks, and with Ordnance Survey maps around their necks.

He smiled at them. 'Morning.'

They nodded and both replied, 'Morning,' in London accents.

He paused, looking up at the tent, there was a funny smell,

but he wasn't sure where it was coming from. 'Hey, have you seen the woman whose car this is?'

They shook their heads and carried on walking. He watched them, thinking how rude they were, snotty southerners who only cared about themselves. Sammy let out a big sigh and shouted, 'Hello, are you in there?'

He was greeted by complete silence. He waited a minute in case she was asleep, but there was no sound of shuffling around, so he thought maybe she wasn't inside. She may have taken ill and left the tent, *what and walked herself home, you idiot?* He ignored the voice inside his mind. She may have called an ambulance, it was a possibility, or there could have been some kind of emergency. His shoulders dropped. What if she'd got lost walking and was stranded somewhere?

'I'm coming in, sorry if you're inside and I give you a heart attack. Hopefully you're not in there though, but my boss will kill me if I don't check on you.'

He stood on the ladder and unzipped the tent, pulling the flap wide open. He didn't quite know what he was looking at but the smell was enough to make his mouth fill with water as he felt his gut wrench.

He realised that the woman was dead. She had to be, people who were living and breathing did not smell this way. There was a sheet covering her, but he could clearly see something sticking out of her chest through it. He reached out to poke her in the arm and it was then that he let out a scream; she was stiff and cold. He fell backwards, forgetting he was on the ladder, and landed with a heavy thump against the side of his car. He didn't realise he was still screaming until the couple who hadn't got very far came running back to see what was wrong with him. He knew he should phone the police, he knew he should do something, but right now he could only keep screaming.

The woman calmly walked up to him, raised her hand and slapped him hard across the cheek. The screaming stopped and the sound of her hitting his flesh replaced it. He cupped a hand to his face and stared at her.

'You hit me?'

'You were screaming like a banshee.'

The guy she was with was staring into the tent. He didn't need to stand on the ladders as he was tall enough to peer in, and Sammy heard him say, 'Oh my God.'

He took out his phone and must have dialled 999, because Sammy heard him asking for the police and an ambulance. The woman who had turned her attention to what was inside the tent stood on the ladder, and he grabbed her arm, pulling her back.

'Don't, it's a crime scene.'

She glared at him, but he took no notice. He moved closer to the tent then and quickly turning on his phone, he began to snap photos of the 4x4, tent and the body inside.

Sammy who had regained his composure yelled, 'Hey, you better not do that.'

'Why not?'

'Give her some respect, man, what you going to do, post them all over Facebook for some sympathy likes?'

The guy shook his head. 'No, I'm a reporter, I'm doing my job.'

Sammy glared at him. He knew he didn't like him, what a jerk. Realising he should be taking charge, he stood up straight and in front of the guy.

'Stop it now. Get away from here, the police are on their way, and you'll get arrested for messing around with a crime scene.'

His partner grabbed his arm. 'Come on, Fin, don't be stupid.'

They walked a short distance away from the car.

'We're going back to our tent,' she called over her shoulder to him, and he was glad.

He rubbed his cheek, which was still smarting, and thought he better phone his boss and tell him the reason the woman in the roof tent had overstayed. He figured she had a pretty good excuse, although his boss was an arsehole and would probably still try and claim the money back from her family somehow.

Surely that would shock him enough to make him feel bad for the woman who'd been murdered? Or at least he hoped it would.

TWENTY-EIGHT

Ben, who was always the utmost professional when it came to attending post-mortems, had his phone switched off, and Morgan's was on silent. Wendy's began to ring just as Declan was finishing up Sharon Montgomery's internal examination.

'Sorry, so sorry. It's all been a bit hectic.'

Declan nodded. 'You're forgiven.'

The ringing stopped then began immediately.

'You want me to get that?' Ben asked.

Morgan had taken out her phone. She had that all-too-familiar feeling inside. Her stomach was already in knots as her internal sensors kicked in, a combination of dread and turmoil.

'I have three missed calls off Marc.'

Ben sighed. He had retrieved Wendy's phone and put it onto loudspeaker. 'Hello.'

'Who's this?'

Everyone knew Marc's voice with his soft Mancunian undertones.

'It's me. Ben. We're just finishing up Sharon Montgomery's PM. Wendy's all gloved up, what's up?'

'Christ on a bike, why are you all always so busy?'

Morgan rolled her eyes at Ben, who replied, 'You tell me? We don't do it to ourselves.'

'No, suppose not. Body at a campsite, found by the groundsman in another of those bloody roof tent things. I'm just arriving at the scene with Cain and Stan.'

Morgan felt a rush of hot bile rise up her throat, surely not another and so soon.

'When can you get here?'

'Declan's going to do Jack next.'

'He won't need you there for that one. I told you, it's pretty cut and dried with Jack. Poor lad must have had some kind of breakdown. I need you and Morgan here at the scene. Wendy too, if possible. I don't want to wait hours for a CSI to come from out west or north to cover when she's on duty and the best there is. Actually, I'm going to need Declan here, too. He's going to have to postpone Jack's PM until he's been to this scene.'

Morgan winked at Wendy, who grinned. She didn't dare look in Declan's direction – she knew he would be annoyed at Marc issuing his orders.

'Where are you?'

'Oh, yes. That would help, wouldn't it? Hang on, Cain will tell you.'

Cain's voice echoed around the room.

'It's a semi-wild camping site at the edge of Rydal Water; it's halfway up Loughrigg Fell. It only opened last year.'

'Is it on Google Maps? And I thought you were with Amy?' Ben asked.

Cain paused.

'Yeah, it should be, if not ring me when you get near and I'll come find you. Oh, and the boss man phoned and said he needed me. It was not optional.'

Morgan could hear the underlying anger in Cain's voice.

Declan finally spoke. 'Cain, tell your boss he needs to put in a formal request for me to attend the scene. I need authorisation from my end; he's not in charge of me.'

'*Absolutely, Declan.*'

Cain lowered his voice.

'*He's such an arse at times, I think he forgets he doesn't have authority over the entire world.*'

Declan smiled. 'Quite.'

Cain ended the call, and Morgan felt the bitter taste of fear in the back of her throat. Two women murdered in the space of a couple of days, and Jack's apparent suicide. It didn't sit right with her. It was beyond terrifying. She looked around the room which was in complete silence. She had to break it first.

'We need to put out a warning for female solo campers like now, Ben.'

Ben was nodding. 'I know, we will get that organised and approved, the press office can take care of it.'

'I don't care if it sparks a panic, and if HQ won't authorise it then I'll do it myself.' She stared him in the eyes, daring him to challenge her. He didn't, he was wise beyond his years, and she knew that he wouldn't stop her either. If she had to put her job at risk to help save another woman's life then she would do it in a heartbeat, even if it meant having to visit every single campsite in the Lake District to warn them personally.

She would bear the consequences later.

TWENTY-NINE

Morgan drove to the campsite whilst Ben was on the phone to Marc. She had a rough idea of where it was, and remembered reading an article about it whilst searching for Sharon Montgomery on Google. She wanted to find the killer before there were any more victims. When Ben finished his phone call, she couldn't help herself.

'If Jack killed Sharon, then killed himself, who killed this woman?'

'Morgan, I'm with you, okay? I'm not against you. I don't think Jack killed himself either.'

'Which means that the person who killed these two women, killed him. Why?'

Ben shrugged. 'I haven't had enough coffee for this.'

She was biting the corner of her bottom lip, concentrating so hard. 'His death takes him off the suspect list. So, did Jack know who the killer was? Is that why he was killed?'

'If Jack knew who the killer was, wouldn't he have told us last night? He was scared he was in trouble, that we'd find evidence to say he'd killed Sharon. He would have said he knew or suspected someone if he did.'

'Hm, good point. Okay, so the killer thought that Jack was the perfect decoy and killed him. But why would he then kill whoever this victim is when he'd found himself someone to take the blame? What if this victim has been dead longer? He could have killed her, then Sharon, realised Jack was the perfect person to lay the blame on then killed him.'

Ben was nodding. 'Makes sense, I suppose it depends on who was murdered first. Is this a good thing then?'

Morgan glanced at him, eyes wide. '*A good thing?* Three people are dead.'

'As in if he thinks by killing Jack we'll stop looking for the real killer, then it would mean there aren't going to be any more victims, because he's going to think he got away with it and needs to calm it down to avoid getting arrested.'

'Maybe not at the moment, but there will be.'

'Why will there be? If he's trying to pin it all on Jack, it wouldn't make sense for him to kill again and ruin all that planning.'

'You're forgetting one key thing.'

'And that is?'

'Killers like this can't stop once they get a taste for it. Well, some do or leave it years between kills until something sets them off again, I suppose. But two women killed close together? I think he's going to struggle to contain all his violent urges. I mean he might be able to, I'm no forensic psychologist and this is just my opinion, but I think he might move on and continue in a different part of the country. I don't think he's going to be able to put off killing again for long, which is why we have to issue a press release warning all solo campers there's a killer out there hunting them, because there are plenty more beautiful places to solo camp all over England, Scotland and Wales.'

'Morgan, that's terrifying. It sounds like the blurb for some new horror movie.'

She shrugged. 'It's true though, we can't bury our heads in

the sand. Maybe Sharon and this victim were already dead and there was nothing we could have done to prevent their murders, but we can try and stop him finding another victim.'

The police van at the bottom of the narrow road signalled they'd found the campsite; Scotty was leaning against it. He squinted, then waved them through, recognising them. Morgan waved back and carried on up the single track to reach the campsite that was shrouded by a copse of trees, making it impossible to see from the road.

'I guess the trees helped them get planning permission. You'd never know there was anything up here, would you?' said Ben.

'How did the killer know about it then?'

'Morgan, I told you I need coffee. You keep firing all these incredibly important questions at me and my brain feels as if it's fried. I'm struggling to string coherent sentences together at this point.'

'They're hypothetical. I have to say them out loud, so I remember them. I'm not actually expecting you to be able to answer them all. I'm not that mean.'

She turned the corner and saw the uniformed officer guarding the entrance gate. Behind him was a huge open field with a small 4x4 parked up, its roof tent engaged. At the opposite end was a tent next to a Mini Cooper. There was a man and woman loitering near to it, and she did a double glance at the guy, surely not? It couldn't be, but her heart was racing. She recognised him and wanted to turn around and drive back the way she'd come. It had been years, but she'd never forgotten the way he'd betrayed her. It still caused her a physical pain in her chest just thinking about it. Ben didn't give him a second glance, and she didn't know if she should say something or ignore it and pretend this wasn't happening.

Finley Palmer had grown his hair since the last time she'd seen him, he was still as handsome as hell, but he looked a lot more casual than when she'd met him. He was wearing head-to-toe North Face outdoor hiking gear. The woman he was with looked older than him, dressed as if she was ready for a yoga class.

Getting out of the car, Morgan didn't look in their direction, but she could feel Fin's eyes on her. She didn't give him any sense that she'd acknowledged him and began to get suited up.

Ben's voice carried on the wind as she heard him say, 'What the hell are those two people doing over there? This is a crime scene. Get them out of here.'

Cain pointed to Marc who was now in conversation with Fin. 'He said they could stay because we can't let them drive out of here in case it ruins any forensics.'

Cain glanced at Morgan, and she realised he knew exactly who Fin Palmer was. 'It's ridiculous because we wouldn't let any other reporters be so close to a live crime scene.'

Ben's head snapped in Cain's direction. 'What?'

'He's a reporter, not sure who for now because I haven't seen him for a couple of years, but I bet he still is.'

Cain's gaze fell onto Morgan, and she felt her cheeks begin to burn. Not sure why, as it was Fin who'd betrayed her by writing a story about her murderous biological father, Gary Marks, and practically accusing Morgan of being a chip off the old block. He'd not spared any gory little detail about her biological mother's murder and the fact that her father was the Riverside Rapist.

Ben was looking over at Fin and any moment now it was going to register who he was. He turned back to Morgan and Cain.

'Get him the fuck out of here. It's that guy who wrote all the crap about you, isn't it?'

'Don't make a scene, Ben, play it cool. Pretend you don't know it's him then he can't get off on it.'

Cain was smiling. 'With pleasure, boss. Morgan, do you want to assist or are you happy to watch?'

'I'll watch, thanks.'

Cain began to head over to where Marc was in conversation with Fin and the woman. He turned back to Morgan and winked at her. She turned away, preferring to focus on the victim. There was a guy hovering near to a battered old Skoda, his complexion pale as he tried not to stare at the tent, and she walked towards him.

'Hi, I'm Detective Morgan Brookes. Did you discover the body?'

He nodded. 'Yes, it gave me such a shock. I fell off the ladder. I didn't expect to see that.'

'What did you see? Do you want to sit in your car and talk me through it?'

'Yes, please. Then can I go? I don't think I'm much good to you hanging around here, and I don't want to be in the way or watch whatever is going to happen next. Sorry, I'm a bit of a wimp.'

She smiled at him. 'You're not a wimp; it's a horrible thing to see. I fell off one of those ladders yesterday morning when I did the same thing.'

'You did, oh my God. There's been more than this one?'

'Unfortunately, yes.'

He was shaking his head. 'Why?'

'I wish I knew. What's your name?'

'Samuel Cross, everyone calls me Sammy.'

'Can I get your date of birth and address, please, Sammy?'

He told her, and she scribbled it down in her battered old pocket notebook.

'You work here?'

'I'm the groundsman, maintenance and sometimes bouncer guy.'

Morgan looked at him. 'Bouncer? On a remote campsite with no clubhouse or bar on site.'

'Yeah, I hate it. That's what I was doing this morning. The lady in the tent had overstayed by two nights and not paid. My boss told me to either get the money off her or throw her off the site.'

'Does that happen often on campsites?'

'No idea, it's happened a couple of times, but people usually just pay up. I think because this one is so off the beaten track and has nobody working on site all the time, they think they can get away with it.'

She nodded. 'You parked up and then what?'

'I called out to her a couple of times, you know, to let her know I was there. It smelled bad. I think I knew the moment I got close and got a whiff of that smell something was very wrong, but you don't expect it, do you?'

'No, you don't.'

'Well, I stood on the ladder and told her I was opening her tent, unzipped it and realised something wasn't right. I couldn't see her, there was a sheet over her, but there was something sticking out of her chest. The smell was awful; I fell off the ladder and I began to scream, which was when those two came running back to see what was happening. That guy was taking photos, by the way. He said he's a reporter and I told him to stop, so you better check his phone.'

Morgan's fingers instinctively clenched into tight fists as she felt the rage begin to build inside of her. 'Just a moment.'

She got out of the car to see Cain and Marc going at it a little distance away from the couple and couldn't help it – she was striding towards Fin Palmer with an anger so black inside of her chest she couldn't see anything but his face and the desire to throw a punch that would smash his smarmy nose in.

'Morgan Brookes, how are you? It's been too long.'

'Give me your phone.'

He shook his head. 'Why would I do that?'

She held out her hand. 'I said give me your phone.'

'No.'

Morgan had to suck in a deep breath. 'I have been told that you took photos of a crime scene without permission, so you either hand your phone over or I'm arresting you for obstruction.'

The woman looked from Fin to her. 'What? You can't do that.'

'Yes, I can. Tampering with evidence and you're putting a murder investigation at jeopardy, so you either delete those photographs now or...'

'Or what?'

Ben was standing next to her. His voice was quiet and calm, but Morgan knew he'd realised who Fin was. 'I will arrest you; it's not a threat, it will be my next step, so you show me what photos you have of the crime scene and then you delete them. It's not an option.'

Marc who had joined asked, 'What is going on?' The confusion in his voice apparent.

Morgan answered, 'This is Finley Palmer, he's a journalist who likes to write sensational stories. The guy who found the body said he took photos of inside the tent, and he will no doubt use them in one of his factually incorrect articles.'

Marc straightened up. 'Phone now.' He had the palm of his hand outstretched, and Fin rolled his eyes, making a protest about how ridiculous this was before unlocking his iPhone and passing it to Marc, who opened the photos app and began scrolling through them. He shook his head. 'Nothing on it except pictures of the fells and lakes.'

Morgan knew that wasn't right, and she wanted to snatch the phone out of Marc's hand.

'Factually incorrect? I think you'll find my facts were spot on, Morgan, and like I said I haven't got any photos.'

Marc handed his phone back to him. 'If I see one photograph of this crime scene in a newspaper or online, I will come and arrest you. It's not a threat, it's the truth.'

Fin shrugged. 'Yeah, yeah.'

The rage inside of Morgan was at boiling point.

Ben looked at their car, then at them. 'Give my colleague your details and statements, then you pack up your stuff and you get off this crime scene.'

'You can't do that, we've paid for another night,' said the woman.

'Yes, we can. You're lucky I'm letting you pack your stuff because technically I can make you leave everything here in situ until we've finished processing the scene, which could take days.'

Fin reached out his hand and gently took hold of the woman's arm. He didn't speak, just turned away.

'Cain, can you get their statements, please?'

Cain was grinning. 'Yes, boss.'

Then Ben was guiding Morgan away from this corner of the campsite. He whispered in her ear, 'He's an arsehole.'

Morgan couldn't agree more, but she felt the tightness in her chest begin to loosen as her anger subsided. Her friends had her back, had come to her rescue and protected her from Fin Palmer, although she dared not think what crap he was going to write about them all after this little encounter. Of all the campsites in the Lake District, why the hell did he have to be at this one?

THIRTY

Morgan finished taking Sammy's statement.

'What should I do now?' he asked her, looking as miserable as she felt.

'Does your boss not want to come down and talk to us?'

He shrugged. 'Probably not, do you need him? He's lazy and never moves from the office unless it's to go get food.'

'I need to know everything about the victim he has on file, so it would be useful.'

'I should have said, sorry. She's called Lydia Williams; she booked in for two nights. Oh my God.'

'What?'

'Where's her dog? She put on the booking form that she was bringing her dog with her. Is it dead too? I can't if it is. I mean it's bad enough someone has done that to her, but if they killed her dog too that's fucking despicable. There's just no need man, no need.'

Morgan couldn't agree more. 'We won't know until the forensic pathologist has assessed the scene. I hope not. Could it have got loose and be running around the fell?'

'Well, possibly, but someone would have reported a lost

dog. Walkers and tourists will do anything for a lost dog or injured animal, shame they don't care the same about humans.'

Morgan took out her radio handset. 'Control, can you tell me if there have been any reports of a dog running loose in this area, or one that's been found?'

'Morgan, that's a definite no. I've been on shift the last couple of days and nothing has come in about a dog running loose in the area.'

'Thank you, can you add to the log that Lydia Williams was booked onto the campsite for two nights and had a pet dog with her?'

'Roger, breed, name of dog?'

'I don't know, sorry.'

'No worries, when you find out we'll add it on.'

She turned to Sammy. 'I'm going to need to speak to your boss at some point. Can you tell me if there is CCTV here?'

'No CCTV, but there are a couple of trail cams around the site, so he can check in and see who is doing what if he needs to, which is why he knew that Lydia Williams was still here. He must have looked at them this morning.'

'How would he do that?'

'I think he can do it remotely; I'll phone him now. Do you want to talk to him?'

'Yes, that's great.'

Sammy took out his phone and began conversing with the guy who had answered. She looked in the side mirror and saw Declan walking towards the Suzuki next to them.

Getting out she smiled at him.

'We really need to stop meeting this way, people are going to talk, Morgan.'

'Out of my control, sorry.'

She stood next to him whilst Wendy, who must have arrived a few minutes before him, was filming the scene with a body camera. Once she'd photographed it and was satisfied, she would let Declan approach it.

Ben joined them. 'It's remote, that's for sure.'

'I have good news. The owner has a couple of trail cams set up to watch the perimeter and keep tabs on who is coming and going.'

Ben turned to her. 'For real?'

She nodded, and he reached over and high-fived her. 'Halli bloody lujah! There is a god after all.'

'I never said they worked, or he's got any evidence before you get yourself too excited.'

'I'm not expecting them to, it's just wonderful to think there is the slither of a chance that they may have caught the killer at some point.'

'I have everything crossed for you both. Surely at some point you are going to get someone who is plain stupid and doesn't watch the crime channel twenty-four seven,' replied Declan.

'The victim is Lydia Williams. Who does the car PNC to?'

Ben nodded. 'Lydia Williams, four Kents Bank Close in Lancaster. Thirty-nine years old.'

'I wonder if she knew Sharon Montgomery? They clearly have the same interests, so she probably knows of her if she doesn't directly know her. I wouldn't be surprised if she followed Sharon on Instagram. If that's true then this is all connected somehow, that's my personal opinion, not my professional one. I'm just saying, it wouldn't be too big of a stretch to assume that.'

Ben smiled at her. 'Well, you're welcome to do a deep dive into that when we get back to the station.'

'Thanks, I will. Oh, Declan, she might have a dog inside the tent with her.'

Declan groaned. 'No, why did you go and say that, Morgan? I don't do dead animals, they break my heart.'

'Sorry, on her booking she noted she was bringing a dog with her, and we haven't seen one. Comms said they've had no reports of a dog being reported as running loose. I thought I'd better warn you in case you find one curled up next to her.'

'Morgan,' Declan's voice was pained.

She turned away to look at the open roof tent. 'I mean, I'm praying it isn't, that maybe she changed her mind and left it with a friend or put it into kennels.'

'You're not helping me at all.' Declan wagged a finger in her direction.

She heard voices behind her and noticed that Cain was watching Fin and the woman he was with like a hawk.

'Wendy, can you do me a favour, can you get some photos of those two over there?'

Wendy turned to her and began to snap pictures from different angles. 'Who are they?'

'Witnesses who didn't witness a thing. He's also a sneaky reporter who took photos and then denied it.'

'Take his phone off him, what a creep.'

Wendy wasn't wrong, he was a creep. 'Marc gave it back to him and said there was nothing on it.'

The couple had loaded their tent and belongings into the car and began to slowly drive towards them. Morgan had to fight off the urge to give Fin Palmer the finger. She didn't, she stared him out until they were out of the entrance to the campsite.

Wendy shook her head. 'Was that?'

Morgan nodded. 'It was, told you he was a creep.'

'Did Marc check her phone? They could have swapped them over. He's crafty, he'd have known you were going to ask to see it.'

Morgan let out a sigh. 'Probably not. I don't think Marc has the foresight to think that far ahead.' She was annoyed with herself for not suggesting it. She should have known he would do something like that. All Fin Palmer cared about was selling stories, and he didn't care who he had to upset to do it.

Cain strolled back towards them. 'I'm not being funny but is he not a suspect?'

'Who?' said Morgan, Wendy and Declan at the same time.

'Creepy reporter guy. He's so smarmy but what if he and that woman he's with did it together? Then had the audacity to hang around and watch the drama unfold. You're always saying killers often return to the scene of their crime. How about putting yourself directly into the middle of it? There's no bigger ego trip than that.'

'I don't know, I think he loves himself too much to risk anything like that and having to go to prison. Whatever it was it's our bloody bad luck that he just happened to be camping here at the same time there was a murder.'

Cain arched one eyebrow at her. 'Exactly my point.'

'Ahh, bollocks,' Ben announced, and everyone turned to look his way. 'We know where he is, we can go arrest him if we have to. Nothing would give me greater pleasure. Who wants to work on his locations and whereabouts the last few days to see if we can discard him as a suspect or draw him in?'

Morgan shook her head. She would very much love to gloat over Fin Palmer if he was in the cells, but she didn't want to have to talk to him more than needs be.

Cain held up his hand. 'I would like that very much, boss.'

'Good, I thought you might.'

Wendy stepped away from the car. 'All yours, Declan, and I didn't see a dog inside the tent, you'll be pleased to know.'

Declan placed his palms together in the prayer position and then walked towards the car with his heavy case in one hand.

THIRTY-ONE

Everyone was in the blue room ready for a briefing. Ben was there with two blue folders now on the desk in front of him. One for each victim. Task Force was still on drugs warrant at another empty shop in Barrow that had been turned into a cannabis factory. Morgan and Cain were sitting nursing mugs of coffee. Marc came rushing in, cheeks flushed, and Cain glanced at Morgan. She could read his thoughts without him having to say a word. They were both wondering why Marc was in such a flap, but nobody cared enough to ask him. Stan followed him in with a mug in one hand and a sheaf of papers in the other, looking the complete opposite. He was more chilled than any of them, and Morgan envied him a little.

She was still raging about Fin Palmer being a witness and at the scene – of all the people in the entire world it had to be him. On the drive back to the station, Ben had asked her if she was okay and she'd told him she was fine, it had been a shock seeing him again that was all. The reality was she was not fine, she was reliving the utter betrayal he'd put her through when he'd written that article about her early life and splashed it across the *News and Star* for the whole world to see. Not only that it had been picked up by the tabloids then splashed across those too the next day, and she hated him for that. The guy had the morals of an alley cat and given the choice she'd rather take on a four-legged, wild, biting, scratching, flea-riddled cat than him.

'What are we thinking as a collective about both scenes?' Marc was standing up staring at them.

'Same killer, same MO, same victim type, similar locations,' said Morgan.

He was nodding. 'Totally agree, are Sharon and Lydia connected in any way? Do we know if they're friends?'

Morgan had to try her best not to roll her eyes at him. 'Boss, we've come straight here from the scene, no one has had time to do any background checks or look into that yet. Lydia isn't on my initial list of Sharon's followers. And we haven't even spoken to the main witnesses from Sharon Montgomery's case. There's her best friend who is sleeping with her stepdad. They both need speaking to separately to see if their stories add up. We need to ask them about Jack too, to see if either of them knew about his relationship with Sharon.'

Marc sighed. 'Then we need to split into two teams, and I think I'm going to have to draft in more officers from South maybe, if they can spare them.'

Ben nodded. 'What about Will Ashworth or Gilly Mahaffy? Can we see if either of them is available? If we need help, I'd like it to be from detectives we know are capable and have an amazing track record. If they're busy, maybe they can send someone up.'

'I'll ring Will when we've finished here.'

Ben looked at Morgan. 'Morgan, you concentrate on Sharon Montgomery, you've already made a good start on her. If you and...' He paused then smiled. 'I was going to say Amy. How about if we borrow someone from section for now? Amber keeps asking if she can do an attachment with CID.'

Morgan felt her heart sink; Amber would be her last choice,

but maybe she was being mean. Cain was groaning; he didn't care who knew how he felt.

'If you bring Amber up here, do not put her with me. I cannot work with her. I'll take Stan over her any day. Sorry, Morgan, you're going to have to work with her. You won't take any of her crap and will get her told.'

Stan looked hurt. 'Thanks a lot, I get the feeling I'm only slightly preferable to this Amber and you guys don't even know me.'

Cain began to backtrack. 'I didn't mean it like that, mate, of course you're not, it's just difficult when you're new to an established team. We know each other inside out, know how to not get on each other's nerves, but you'll get used to us all.'

Ben turned to Morgan. 'Are you okay if we borrow Amber?'

She nodded. He'd already put her on Sharon's case so she didn't need to see Fin again. She couldn't really complain too much, and besides, she would tell Amber if she got too much.

Marc clapped his hands. 'Good, that's a start. I'll speak to Madds and see if he can spare her for a couple of weeks.'

Ben had brought up pictures of the crime scene on the Smart Board. 'Let's go over what needs doing with Lydia. We need to find out if she took her dog camping with her because that's either gone AWOL or the killer disposed of it. We literally know nothing about her except her address; Lancs police are going to do the death message to her family and sort out the ID. Cain, can you liaise with them to get all the info we need about her from them, place of work, friends, that kind of thing. Once we have that information we can go speak to them. Morgan, you and Amber, if she's free, can follow up on the interviews with Sharon's friend and stepdad. Do you think he's going to give you any bother? Because if he is we can swap and send Cain there.'

'He's nothing that I can't handle.'

Marc smiled at her. 'No, I guess he isn't. Are these murders connected then?'

Morgan's head snapped up from the piece of paper she was writing notes on, was he being serious? He looked as if he was and she couldn't stop what was about to come out of her mouth for love or money.

'Connected as in we have two women with identical situations, both on their own, both camping in roof tents, both have popular social media accounts and love solo adventuring, both found stabbed multiple times inside of their tents with a knife protruding from their chests. I mean, I don't know, boss, maybe it's two separate killers who just happened to be emulating each other, in this area at the same time. What are the chances?'

Ben was staring down at one of the folders in front of him, but she could see the sides of his mouth turning up the tiniest bit. Cain, on the other hand, was full-on sniggering out loud, not caring who could hear him.

'Yes, when you put it like that, I can see they're clearly connected, Morgan, it was more of a hypothetical question.'

'Good, because if you couldn't I would be extremely worried. Same MO for both murders. I think we seriously need someone to do a deep dive into their social media accounts. I think both of them knew the killer, knew of the killer or if they didn't their killer certainly knew about them.'

She did manage to stop herself from saying, *stop talking, stupid boss* out loud and instead nodded. Standing up she grabbed her sheet of paper. 'Are we done here? Because I want to go talk to Leah King.'

Ben nodded. 'Go find Amber.'

Morgan smiled at him, hoping he didn't have the knowledge to decipher that it meant *go fuck yourself, I'm going on my own.*

Although Ben hadn't been trying to make her mad, he was annoying her almost as much as Marc. He forgot she was a capable detective who didn't need babysitting every time she left the station, and she wasn't remotely worried about being in this killer's field of vision. Morgan wasn't and never had been or would be a solo adventurer who would go camping on her own. The one time she tried to take up running to beat Cain at a bet, she hurt her ankle so bad it still ached on rainy days and that was the end of her fitness spree. She wasn't the outdoor type. She was a mug of coffee, rainy weather, light a candle and read a book kind of gal and always would be.

THIRTY-TWO

Morgan slipped out of the station by the back door. She hadn't looked too hard to find Amber, preferring to go and speak with Leah on her own. Leah lived in a small flat above the crystal shop in Ambleside. Morgan had been relieved to have an excuse to leave all the guys behind. There was too much testosterone in the small office that was just not the same without Amy. She hoped that Ben would request that Gilly come work with them – rather a woman than another man, there were far too many of them already.

Ringing the intercom for the flat, she waited patiently for a reply. Eventually it crackled to life, the voice quiet, hesitant.

'Hello?'

'Hi, Leah, I'm Detective Brookes with the Rydal Falls police station. Can I talk to you about Sharon?'

Morgan knew by the long pause Leah was going to try and avoid it.

'Now isn't a good time.'

'I don't want to be rude, but I don't think there is ever going to be a good time to talk about Sharon's murder. It's always going to be painful, and I really need to get as much background information about her as possible.'

'*Why?*'

'It will help me to build up a personal profile of her. It could help to find her killer.'

Another pause, this one not quite as long. The blue door opened and a red-eyed, red-nosed woman, much taller than Morgan, was staring down at her. She looked up and down the street before opening the door wide enough for Morgan to step through. There was a tiny entrance with a steep flight of stairs leading up from it.

Leah pointed. 'Go up.'

Morgan did, not waiting to be asked again in case the woman changed her mind. The stairs led directly into the flat, which was bigger than Morgan had expected. A much bigger, very magnolia-coloured flat. Everything was cream including the sofa, cushions and curtains. Leah pointed to the sofa.

'Before you ask, yes, I am devastated. I know I was sleeping with her stepdad, but it's over now and he won't be coming back here again or into my life.'

Morgan wondered who had told Leah that the police knew about their relationship, had it been Sharon's mum or her slimy stepdad?

'That really isn't any of my business. I just need you to confirm if you were with Stefan the night she was killed.'

'I was for a little bit.'

'How long is a little bit?'

'An hour, two at the most.'

'He didn't stay here all night?' Morgan felt her shoulders stiffen as she sat straighter.

Leah lifted her little finger to her mouth and began to nibble at the nail, working it until the skin tore and a thin line of blood appeared.

'No, not all night. Oh, maybe I shouldn't have said that.'

'Is it the truth?'

'Yes, it is.'

'Then you definitely should have said it. I'm not here to try and blame anyone. I really want to find out what was going on in your friend's life. Was Sharon having problems with Stefan?'

'She wasn't until she found the pair of us together last week. They'd always got on great. I used to be so jealous that she had this super-cool, super-rich stepdad. Not jealous enough to kill her though.' Leah sniffed then and pulled a tissue out of her sleeve.

Morgan was perched on the edge of the sofa. She got the impression that Leah was definitely not as upset about her friend as she should be, and that she was being a little overly dramatic to make herself look more sympathetic.

'So, Sharon and Stefan were fine with each other until when?'

'Until she found me coming out of the shower in her mum's bedroom.'

'What happened, where was Stefan?'

'He was getting dressed. She dragged me into the hallway naked, well I had a towel wrapped around me and it fell off. I was so embarrassed. She didn't care; she dragged me out of the house into the drive with no clothes on. If the maid hadn't been home and felt sorry for me, I don't know what would have happened.'

'Did you speak to Sharon after this incident?'

'No, she wouldn't answer any of my calls or messages.'

'You must have been so angry with her for showing you up like that.'

'A little, I was sadder to be honest that I'd upset her.'

Or that you got caught, a voice whispered inside Morgan's head. 'Have you ever had arguments that have ended in violence in the past?'

She shook her head.

'Look I am or I was upset that she did that to me, but I didn't want to kill her over it. I get that she was pissed with me. I acted stupid and could have caused all sorts of problems for her mum. I feel terrible about what I did, but it wasn't all my fault. Stefan can be quite demanding when he wants something. He doesn't stop until he gets what he wants. I guess having money that isn't always spoken for and plenty of it makes you a little more adventurous. You're talking to the wrong person.'

'Who should I be talking to?'

'Stefan, he was furious with her.'

'Furious enough to murder her?'

Leah shrugged. 'Poor Sharon. After everything that happened with Eddy, she deserved so much better.'

'Sharon's YouTube channel was doing really well; she has a lot of followers on Instagram.'

'Yeah, she was doing well.'

'You don't sound so happy for your friend.'

'She made me look like some kind of prostitute in front of her stepdad; I was still annoyed with her then she went and got herself killed. Plus, she was making buckets of money even though she had a golden credit card off mummy, and she thought it was okay to ruin my life when I finally had the chance to be with someone who could make my life better.'

Morgan studied Leah, she didn't like her at all. She was selfish, motivated by money and an awful friend who had tried to split up Sharon's parents – and was a terrible actress too.

'Did Sharon ever mention to you if she was having problems with anyone through her social media accounts, any stalkers or creepy people?'

'There are always weirdos who message on Instagram and Facebook, it's full of them.'

'True, but was she particularly worried about anyone. Eddy?'

'Worried enough to tell me about them you mean? Eddy

had left her alone as far as I knew. She said he'd called around to see if they could start again, I mean talk about delusional, but I suppose he wanted a free ride as much as I did.'

Morgan nodded. 'Did Sharon tell you about the guy she was dating? Jack White?'

Leah shook her head. 'She was dating? No, she never said a word about him. I had no idea she was seeing someone, maybe that was the reason she was a bit distant. I'm going to be honest with you, Morgan, and it might make me seem as if I was the worst friend in the world, but I don't see the point in lying to you about anything, nothing I say is going to hurt Sharon anymore, is it?'

Morgan smiled at her, thinking, *I already know that you are the worst possible friend that Sharon could have had in the world. Who needs enemies when you have a friend ready to step in and ruin your life for free?*

'Go on.'

'Sharon and I, well we weren't close like we used to be. We were drawing apart, different lifestyles, different goals that kind of thing and she was so obsessed with making content for her YouTube channel.' Leah did air quotes to emphasise her point. 'She had started the process of pushing me away herself. She knew that we were no longer besties, and it hurt, it hurt a lot. I spent a lot of my time following her around and doing whatever she wanted to do to make her happy; we were always at her house. She rarely came to mine. She didn't want to slum it when she could have luxury, I get it, I really do, but I sacrificed a lot to make her happy. It's a shame when it was my turn to be happy that she didn't see it that way and had to make a whole big deal out of it.'

Morgan snapped her mouth shut, she knew her jaw had gone slack, and she was staring at Leah in a gormless manner that didn't do her any justice, but it was hard pretending not to be offended on behalf of Sharon at her so-called friend's lack of loyalty.

'Do you know a woman called Lydia Williams?'

Leah shook her head. 'I don't think so, why?'

'You don't follow her on social media?'

Leah paused, her eyes were watching Morgan's face intently.

'I don't know offhand; I'd have to search her name to see if I do. I mean I have a lot of friends and followers who I wouldn't know if I fell over them in the street. Everyone does, maybe not as many as Sharon though, but I have a fair few. Why are you asking me about her? Did she kill Sharon?'

'Not that I know of. She was found dead earlier today in similar circumstances to Sharon.'

Leah had the decency to let out a gasp, cupping a hand to her mouth, but Morgan wasn't convinced it was genuine and found herself looking at the knife block on the kitchen worktop behind the woman in front of her, to check if there were any knives missing, because right now she would have no problem arresting Leah on suspicion of murder. The only problem was she had no hard evidence, just a gut feeling deep inside of her that the woman sitting opposite her could quite easily have stabbed her friend to death and thought nothing of it.

THIRTY-THREE

Morgan left Leah, who had gone back to sniffling into a tissue as if to prove to Morgan she did have a heart inside of that block of ice surrounding her chest. In the car she quickly wrote down notes as the radio was quietly playing in the background.

Selfish, cold, admitted she wasn't close with Sharon, was angry about her spoiling her chance of a good life with Stefan's money. Couldn't say if she knew Lydia Williams, could have killed her to draw the attention away from Sharon. Greed and money are a good motivation for murder, so is revenge!

She let out a long, drawn-out sigh and sat back in the seat, closing her eyes for a moment. The song had stopped and was replaced by a voice on the radio that made her sit up straight, and she opened her eyes.

'You were unlucky enough to be on a campsite where a woman was murdered in cold blood, how did you feel when you realised what had happened?'

'Shocked, it's not the kind of thing that usually happens

when you go away for a long weekend camping with your new girlfriend.'

'You're no stranger to murders though, are you? As a crime reporter, you covered the string of murders that happened some years ago in this area that were carried out by a serving police officer at the time.'

Fin Palmer's voice was smooth and made her so angry she wanted to punch the radio to stop him talking.

'Yes, I did. That was pretty harrowing too, Dave, it never leaves you. Late at night when you try to sleep those images are there, replaying over and over again in your mind.'

'Arrggh.' Morgan slammed the palm of her hand against the button to turn his voice off. The bastard was repeating what she'd told him in confidence. He was playing games with her. She took out her radio and dialled Cain's collar number. He answered immediately.

'Where are you? The boss is pretty mad you snuck out without Amber.'

'Where I am isn't important, where are you? I thought you were going to speak to Palmer.'

'I am, we're having difficulties locating him.'

'I can tell you exactly where he is. He's on the bloody radio talking about the crime scene earlier. You need to get to the Radio Cumberland offices and shut him up. Where are you?'

'Christ.'

'Yes, exactly.'

'We're not far away, just turning onto that street. Do I need to arrest him?'

'You may as well seeing as how he can't keep his mouth closed.'

Cain ended the call, and she felt bad for being so mean to him. She turned the radio back on despite the blackness that was rising inside of her chest, wanting to hear Cain shut him down.

'Can you describe what you witnessed?'

'I don't think I can, Dave, it's an active investigation and the police won't want me discussing the finer details on air. However, I can tell you that, from the press release that was issued yesterday, I'd say this body was found in very similar circumstances.'

'Two bodies, in two days, both found in similar circumstances. Same killer, same MO?'

If Morgan didn't know any better, she could have closed her eyes and thought she was back in the blue room at the briefing an hour ago. The blackness inside of her was fizzing into a tidal wave of bright red. Palmer needed to shut up and now. He had no right discussing this live on air.

'Hey, who are you?'

Muffled voices. There was a scuffle in the room as a chair tipped over, and Fin's voice called out, *'I want a lawyer,'* before Fleetwood Mac began playing, 'You Can Go Your Own Way'.

Morgan wondered how much carnage Cain had just caused in that little studio, and her face cracked into a huge grin. Ben and Marc were going to be mortified when he got back to the station with Palmer, and she kind of wished she could be there to watch the drama unfold.

At least he was quiet for the time being. It was time to go and speak to Stefan Montgomery.

The gates to his large lakeside mansion were wide open, so she drove straight through them and parked next to the Porsche 4x4. It occurred to Morgan that the Porsche could probably have made it up the narrow coffin road to where Sharon's body had been found, if Stefan was a competent driver and wasn't afraid of scratching or dinting his car. As she got out of the small white car she took a slow walk around the Porsche to see if there was any damage. A few scratches, but nothing to shout about.

'I can assure you everything is in order. Do you want to run a PNC check to confirm that? Although you have no right on private property.' Stefan's voice was loud and cocky, and she glanced his way.

'No need, I was just admiring it. I like these cars, wouldn't mind one myself.'

'On your wages I think you might regret that purchase; the insurance alone and fuel costs a small fortune each month.'

The tiny red hairs on the back of Morgan's neck bristled. How did he know what her circumstances were? She could be richer than him, even though she had no idea of his net worth and clearly wasn't. She shrugged. 'That's good to know, it doesn't deter me from looking at one though, but thank you for your advice.'

Stefan was staring at her, but it didn't bother her, she was used to it.

'What do you want?'

'I need to speak to you about your alibi for the night Sharon was murdered.'

'Do I need a solicitor?'

'You tell me, do you?'

'No, because I didn't kill her. You better come inside unless you're taking me to the station on some made-up charges.'

'If I was here to arrest you, Mr Montgomery, there would be a team of armed police behind me. I just need to talk to you about what happened leading up to Sharon's murder, but if you'd prefer to come to the station to talk that's fine.'

He shook his head. 'No, I'd rather not.'

He turned and went back inside of his house, and she followed him. He led the way into a huge room that looked out onto the lake. The view was breathtaking. She could see right across to the round house on the other side of the water. There was someone out on a ride-on mower on the other side cutting the grass.

'This is beautiful, what a view.'

He nodded. 'It's nice, but you don't notice it when you see it day in day out, might as well be living in the city. It would be an easier commute that's for sure.'

Morgan didn't think she'd ever not pause for a moment to take it all in. 'Which city?'

'Manchester, my business is based there. I work from home a lot these days, hate driving to Manchester, the roads are awful.'

She nodded; they were awful. 'How are you both?'

He fixed his gaze onto her, his eyes boring into her it was so intense.

'What, like you're bothered?'

'I am, I'm truly sorry for your loss. I know how painful it is to lose someone close to you.'

'You do? Are you just saying that? Is that the corporate spiel they tell you in police school on how to address grieving parents?'

Morgan didn't like Stefan much more than Leah, but she did feel his pain. The problem with being an empath was she felt everyone's pain whether she wanted to or not.

'My dad was murdered a few years ago, and my mum was murdered in front of me when I was a toddler, so yes I know how much it hurts.'

'Oh, sorry. That must have been hard.' His tone had lost all the cockiness from seconds ago.

She nodded. 'Is the family liaison officer with Beth?'

'I have no idea. Beth is staying at Storrs Hall Hotel. She packed a case and left after we got back from the mortuary.'

'Oh dear.'

'Oh dear, is right. My entire life is a shit show of the highest degree. I feel as if it's all spiralled out of control and I don't like not being in control.'

'I've spoken to Leah.'

He had been staring out of the window but snapped his head around to stare at her.

'And what did she have to say about the mess she helped to create? Because I'm not taking all of the blame. Did she tell you she practically threw herself at me?'

'Not exactly.'

'No, I bet she didn't. We were drunk, she made the first move and me not being able to keep my own dick in my pants couldn't resist. I bet you think I'm a total creep, sleeping with my daughter's best friend, but it's not like they're teenagers; she's a consenting adult.'

'It has nothing to do with me. Leah said you weren't with her all night when we think Sharon was murdered, she also said she didn't see you much this past week because you told her you were busy.'

Morgan let that hang in the air, watching Stefan's face closely. He closed his eyes and began to slowly shake his head. When he finally opened them, he stared her straight in the eyes.

'No, I wasn't with her all night, but it didn't mean that I snuck off to murder my daughter. Is that what she was insinuating?'

'I couldn't tell you; she said that you were very angry with Sharon.'

'I think I need a lawyer; I don't think I should say anything else in case it incriminates me for something I didn't do. We're done here.'

He stood up and pointed to the door.

'If you have nothing to hide why the change in attitude? Where did you go when you left Leah?'

'Home to try and ease my guilty conscience, if you have to know. I realised that I was regretting the quick fumbles with Leah; they didn't mean anything to me. She was a bit of fun, and I wasn't going to mess things up with Beth. I love her more than anything, even though it's too late and I should have figured that out before I slept with Leah. That is all you're getting. If you want anything else then I'm not talking to you without legal advice.'

Morgan nodded. 'Thank you, that's okay. I can see myself out. One last thing, did you know Sharon was seeing a police officer called Jack?'

Stefan's eyes were wide; he looked as if he was frozen in time at this revelation. Morgan realised this was news to him; he looked genuinely shocked.

'No, I did not.' He shrugged. 'Did he kill her?'

'We're trying to find that out.'

'I bet he's not been arrested; you'll all cover it up because that's what you lot do. You take care of your own.'

Morgan shook her head. 'He's dead, so no we couldn't arrest him.'

Stefan sighed. 'How convenient.' Then turned his back on her to stare out of the window again.

Morgan left him there, hoping to find the maid on her way out.

THIRTY-FOUR

Fin Palmer did not go quietly. Cain was in his element tussling the prat out of the Radio Cumberland building, whereas Stan stood to one side looking decidedly uncomfortable at the unfolding situation. Dave the DJ was filming everything on his phone until Cain threatened to smash it on the floor and arrest him too.

'Get off me, I haven't done anything,' Palmer was yelling loudly to the small crowd that was forming outside of the building.

'Shut up, Palmer, you know you're not supposed to be chatting shit about an active investigation on a radio station.'

They were almost at the car and Stan ran to throw open the door. Cain pushed Palmer inside and slammed the door shut on him. Once they were in the car, Palmer stopped struggling and changed his demeanour as he sat very still.

'You're such a show-off, you know that, don't you?'

Palmer was checking his reflection in the rear-view mirror and smoothing his hair down that had got a little mussed in the tussle. 'It's called showmanship, a good story needs a little drama.'

'A good story? These are innocent women who have been brutally murdered in cold blood.'

'Yes, it's very sad, but what can I do about that? They're already dead, it's too late for them.'

Stan looked at Cain who nodded. 'He is an arsehole.'

'Yes, Stan, he is.'

'So what are you doing with me? I'm sure you have better things to be doing with your time than this?'

'Taking you to cool off in the cells for a bit, mate, give you a chance to reflect on your appalling behaviour.'

'Is Morgan around?'

'No, she's busy chasing a killer and you're lucky it wasn't her who came to get you because she'd have punched you square between the eyes like you deserve.'

'Pity, I was hoping to get to speak to her. We have some unfinished business. I'd like to take her out for a drink.'

'Shut up, Palmer, you actually make me feel physically sick.'

They drove to the station in silence.

———

Cain booked Palmer in and left him with the detention officer, who was gushing all over him, clearly thinking he was a bit of a catch. Ben was standing at the top of the stairs waiting for them.

'Did you hear that?' Cain asked.

He nodded. 'What did you arrest him for?'

'Perverting the cause of justice, being a class one arsehole wasn't a good enough reason.'

Ben's laughter echoed down the corridor. 'Good work, Cain. Have you heard from Morgan?'

'She is the reason Palmer is in the cells; she heard his interview and radioed me.'

'She did? Good. She's okay then?'

Cain nodded. 'She's fine. You know I don't blame her for not looking for Amber.'

'Why is that?' Amber's voice was loud in his ear from behind him.

Ben grimaced. Cain turned around to look at her. 'Because you're crap at brewing up.'

Amber looked confused. 'Really, well you didn't complain when I was providing you with more biscuits than the McVitie's factory could make in one shift.'

Cain shrugged. 'Fair point.'

Ben stepped between them. 'Amber is happy to be working with us. Did you two speak to anyone from Lancs about Lydia Williams?'

'Not yet, we ended up chasing smarmy Palmer down. Can we leave him as long as possible, like just until we have to let him go and let him stew awhile?'

'Fine by me, unless the boss intervenes.'

Cain rolled his eyes because they both knew fine well Marc wouldn't want Palmer languishing in a cell longer than he needed to. He wouldn't want him writing anything detrimental about the department that would cause a stir with headquarters, especially not with PSD already being involved.

Amber left them and walked into the office to sit at Amy's desk. Cain followed her in, finding it highly offensive that she was so brazenly making herself at home.

'That's Amy's desk.'

Amber dead-eyed him. 'And? She's gone off to have a baby, Cain, I doubt she's going to be needing it for quite some time.'

He turned away from her, gritting his teeth. She really grated on his last nerve without even trying.

Marc rushed through the door looking more stressed than Cain had seen him in some time.

'Tell me you had a good reason to bring the reporter in?'

'He was talking about the crime scene live on the radio.'

'What about freedom of speech?'

'What about it? Not to be blunt, boss, but he's a dick and he was saying things that might compromise the investigation.'

Marc let out a sigh. 'Can we get rid of him? Let him go with a warning or a slap on the hand? We don't need any bad publicity.'

Ben arched one eyebrow in Cain's direction as if to say I told you so, and Cain shook his head.

'If you want me to do that right now, I can. I don't see what harm it will do to leave him there for a couple of hours though.'

'Just get him out of here, Cain. You're going to open up a can of worms that we won't be able to contain if he starts a campaign against this department. We have enough to be dealing with.'

Cain stood up. 'Yes, boss.'

He was trying to keep his cool, but he was losing it. Marc was too much of a jobsworth at times. He did everything exactly by the book and sometimes it didn't pay off.

THIRTY-FIVE

Morgan was about to get into her car when she saw the maid coming out of the barn and waved at her. The woman had a basket full of laundry, and she walked towards her.

'How are you? I guess things have been very stressful around here.'

She shrugged. 'It's so sad. I feel terrible about Sharon, and now Beth has left and Stefan is on his own and they're grieving without each other, making it even harder.'

'How long have you worked for the Montgomerys?'

'Too long, fifteen years.'

'Do you not like it?'

'Oh, yes. Sorry, that sounded wrong. I do, I love it. It's not too hard and the pay is wonderful compared to what the girls get cleaning in the big hotels these days. What I mean is I feel old I've been here that long.'

Morgan smiled at her. 'How old are you, if you don't mind me asking?'

'Forty next month.'

'You're still a teenager.'

'Ha! Tell that to my knees.'

'Sorry, I didn't catch your surname?'

'Marie Jones.'

'How were things before the incident with Stefan and Leah?'

'As in was this the first time he'd brought other women here?'

'Yes.'

'There have been a few over the years, nobody serious. Quick affairs that fizzled out before they'd begun.'

'Why do you think that was?'

'He's an idiot, he's a man which doesn't help, and a man with money is even worse. He gets bored, some bimbo throws herself at him, his ego won't let him say no and then afterwards he always regrets it because he loves Beth deeply.'

'Wow, you know a lot.'

Marie shrugged. 'I see a lot, sometimes I feel like slapping him across the face and telling him to wake up. Beth is a good woman, kind, she doesn't deserve to be disrespected that way.'

'But you don't say anything?'

'I'm the maid, it's not my job to do marriage counselling. It's just hard watching it going on and if I'm honest it's tiring. That last time when Sharon caught her friend with her dad, I was kind of relieved because I knew she would do something about it.'

'Was Stefan mad with her?'

Marie nodded. 'Furious that he'd been caught red-handed, ashamed maybe.'

'Mad enough to kill her?'

'No, he's not a violent man. In all the arguments over the years – and there have been some real good ones – he's never, ever lifted a hand to either Beth or Sharon.'

'How well do you know Leah King?'

'Enough to know she's a little gold digger who was happy enough to break up their marriage and hurt her best friend in the process. Horrible girl, I used to catch her stealing Sharon's things, make-up, clothes, shoes, handbags. She'd say she was borrowing them, yet she never returned them, and I think Sharon let her get away with it because she was embarrassed that she had all of that stuff and Leah didn't. If you ask me friends don't steal from you. I wouldn't trust her in a charity shop if you get what I'm saying.'

'Did you ever see Sharon's boyfriend?'

Marie's eyes opened wide, and she shook her head. 'She was dating? Oh, wow, that's something I didn't know. Poor guy must be devastated.'

'He's dead.'

Marie's jaw dropped open, her eyes opening even wider. 'What? How?'

'It looks like suicide.'

Marie dropped the basket of clean bedding she'd been holding and leaned against the side of the car. 'Oh God, that's terrible.'

'Yes, he's a colleague of mine so it's all been a bit of an awful shock.'

'So much death, so much pointless death.'

Morgan nodded, never had truer words been spoken.

'Did Beth or Stefan know Sharon was dating?'

Marie bent to retrieve the basket off the ground, and when she straightened up, she looked Morgan in the eyes.

'Did Leah know about Sharon's boyfriend? She was jealous of everything Sharon did.'

Morgan shrugged, noting that Marie hadn't answered her question and had sidestepped it like a professional criminal. 'I asked her but she denied it, said she had no idea.'

'I'm not telling you how to do your job, Detective, but I think Leah is not the innocent little girl she portrays. She's a cunning, selfish thief who I would imagine has no qualms about going after what she wants and taking care of whoever tried to stop her. I bet she was furious with Sharon after that incident. I can't see Leah letting that go without any kind of repercussions.'

Morgan agreed, the more she heard about Leah King, the more she disliked her, but was there a connection between Leah and Lydia Williams? Female serial killers were rare, but they did exist. She knew she needed to take a look at the CCTV from the campsite to see if it showed anyone wandering around, possibly with Lydia's dog in tow. She was going to have to find out and fast because if Leah was the killer, who was to say she didn't already have another victim in her sights.

THIRTY-SIX

Morgan googled the head office for the campsite and was surprised to see it was on a farm not too far away. For a moment she wondered if the farm was owned by Joss, the farmer who'd discovered Sharon's body. It wouldn't sit well with her if it was.

When she arrived at the farm, she found it wasn't the same and felt her shoulders drop a micromillimetre with relief. Joss had seemed like a nice guy, if he was connected to both murders it would have meant he'd be coming in for questioning. Driving into the yard through the open gate, she saw Sammy, who'd found Lydia's body, coming out of a static caravan and waved at him. He didn't look surprised to see her and waved back.

'Hey, can I take a look at the trail cam footage? Have you had time to review it?'

She hoped he said yes because if he said no, she would be furious with him. His head bobbed up and down.

'Yeah, I told my boss to ring you but he's mid-argument with his wife, so, you know, priorities.'

This made her smile despite the graveness of the situation. 'Can you show it to me? Did you see anything?'

'A couple of deer, a fox, gazillion rabbits and a dog sniffing around the trail where the rabbits had been running around.'

'Lydia's dog?'

He shrugged. 'Has to be, it was happy enough mooching around so it was definitely alive. It headed some way down the fell, out of sight of the camera, but the weird thing is its tail was wagging as if it was excited.'

'That is weird. Why would its tail be wagging when its owner had just been killed? Unless it knew the killer?'

Sammy's head snapped up to stare at her. 'You think it was someone she knew? Wouldn't they have taken the dog? That's sick, man, I mean I don't get it anyway but to leave her dog on its own out here.' He was shaking his head. 'I sent the footage to the email address you gave me. Is that okay?'

'Perfect, thank you, Sammy.'

Raised voices came from inside the caravan.

'I'll leave you to it unless you think I need to intervene.'

He shook his head. 'They both have big mouths, but they never get violent and they're both as bad as each other so don't worry about it. I hope you catch the sick bastard who did this. I don't think I'll ever close my eyes again without seeing the inside of that tent screaming at me.'

Morgan gave him a sad smile of commiseration and thought *me too, Sammy, me too.*

Morgan went straight into Ben's office, barely acknowledging Stan or Amber as she strode past the desks they were sitting behind. It didn't feel the same that was for sure. She was hoping that Stan would end up with Amber, and she and Cain could team up. So fired up with her theory about Leah, she didn't knock on the door and walked straight in.

Ben looked up from his computer. 'Well, hello you.'

'The dog was alive and well, it's on the trail cam footage

heading away from the campsite, tail wagging and everything. Unfortunately, there was nothing to show the killer though. I have a theory.'

'Let's hear it because I'll take anything.'

She smiled at him; he was grinning at her with that cheeky smile that never failed to make her heart do a little double jump. The rough stubble on his jaw only added to his charm.

'What if Leah King killed Sharon, realised that Jack figured it out so killed him too, then killed Lydia Williams to make it look like a serial killer.'

'That's a lot of what ifs, even more than mine earlier.'

She shrugged. 'It's the best I have.'

'What's her motive?'

'Revenge, greed, anger that Sharon caught her sleeping with her stepdad and cut her off out of her life, therefore cutting off the free ride that she'd enjoyed all these years. I spoke to the maid, and she said that Leah was a thief, always taking things without asking.'

'Being a thief and lacking in morals doesn't necessarily make her a killer though.'

Morgan sat down on the chair opposite him and sighed. 'No, but she's a good suspect. We need to work on the assumption that she could have killed Sharon and Lydia.'

'How did she kill Jack? I mean he would have been a dead weight, how on earth did she get him up to the tree branch to hang him?'

'I didn't say it was a hundred per cent fool proof, did I?'

Ben laughed. 'It's an interesting concept and yes, you're right, we need to consider her involvement with Sharon's murder. I just don't know about Lydia and Jack.'

'If we consider her for Sharon's murder then she has to be responsible for Lydia's, they're identical MOs. Maybe Jack really did take his own life out of guilt or grief, stress about Amy having a baby he never wanted, problems at work. It could all have got on top of him, and Sharon's murder was the last straw.'

Ben was nodding. 'Yes, you're right about the women. Let's say we push Jack to one side at the moment. What do we need to do or what are you thinking we should do? Oh, and I thought you'd want to know Palmer is in custody, or he was. Marc told Cain to release him.'

Morgan was leaning over Ben's desk her elbows resting on it. 'Did he now? That's a shame. You should have heard him talking crap on the radio, it was shameless. I'm glad Cain locked him up, and why did Marc wimp out? That's just typical.'

'I didn't wimp out; I'm just trying to keep this department off the radar whilst we have so much going on.'

Neither of them realised that Marc had stepped into the room. 'I know you have beef with him, Morgan, but we still have to do things by the book.'

'I don't have beef with him. He has no morals and doesn't care about any of the victims or their families; all he cares about is writing stories that sensationalise their murders.'

'Whatever, it's sorted. Some journalists thrive off it, we can't police them all. What were you both talking about that had you so engrossed with each other anyway or is that a private matter?'

Morgan had to stop herself from sticking her fingers down her throat and pretending to vomit all over Ben's desk.

'No, sir. We were talking about Leah King being a possible suspect for both murders.'

He nodded. 'The friend who was sleeping with the stepdad?'

'Yes.'

'Have we got enough to bring her in?'

Ben answered for them both. 'Not really, we could do with some forensics.'

His phone began to ring, and he picked it up. 'Matthews.'

'It's me.'

'Declan, what have you got because we're clutching at straws.'

'I have something very interesting for you as a matter of fact. The rope around Jack's neck looked familiar to me, not that I've used that kind of rope before, but the colour and texture that kind of thing. To cut to the chase, I found a couple of strands of blue fibres stuck to the chest wound on Sharon Montgomery. I also found a single fibre that was identical to the ones retrieved from Sharon on Lydia Williams's neck wound.'

'And?'

'When I compared all three samples under the microscope, they are identical to each other. I mean they need to be confirmed forensically but whoever killed Lydia and Sharon came into contact with the rope that was around Jack's neck.'

Ben whistled. 'The knives used to kill both victims, could they have been used to cut the rope around Jack's neck?'

'That is for you to figure out. I'm just giving you a heads up on my findings. It's clear to me that the same person came into contact with the rope and all three bodies.'

'Thanks, Declan.'

'Anytime, let me know how you get on.'

The line went dead, and Ben fixed his gaze on Morgan. 'All three crime scenes are linked to each other. Declan has found the same fibres on both bodies that match up to the rope around Jack's neck.'

'What the actual—' Marc stopped himself from completing the sentence.

Morgan was looking at Ben who said, 'So, either Jack killed both women and then himself or someone killed all three of them.'

Morgan asked, 'Why would Jack kill them? He had no motive, he's only been going out with Sharon for a couple of months, so it doesn't make sense. I mean that's a big leap, killing Sharon in a fit of rage maybe, but he would have killed her at home, wouldn't he? There would be evidence all over her house and we found nothing. What would he gain from waiting until she was camping then finding her and killing her in her tent? That would prove it was premeditated and I'm sorry, but I don't buy it. The arguments he had with Amy and that time he got into a fight with Cain were all the same kind of stressors, and he didn't try to kill either of them – he just lost his temper and wanted to strike out at someone.'

Marc turned to leave. 'Who knows what he was thinking? We're never going to know and to me it looks as if we already have our killer. I don't see the point in wasting any more time. It's obvious Jack White killed Sharon whether it was in a fit of rage and then maybe he thought he'd cover it up by killing Lydia, realised that he'd only made things a hundred times worse and then killed himself. It's the only explanation. Now I'm going to have to speak with HQ to see how we approach this because it's going to cause public outrage.'

Morgan didn't agree with him, not one little bit, but continuing to openly disagree with him wasn't going to work in her favour at all. He'd made up his mind that Jack had done this. Even though Jack wasn't the good guy she'd once thought, she knew he wouldn't kill two women and then take his own life, it didn't make sense to her. She was going to have to prove he was innocent all on her own.

THIRTY-SEVEN

Amy hadn't stopped crying since Cain had been to break the news to her about Jack. She had fallen out of love with him when he'd turned so angry with her because she was pregnant. She had never expected him to behave that way in a million years, shocked maybe because they hadn't ever discussed having kids. It wasn't something either of them were bothered about. Nobody had been more surprised than she was when she realised that she wanted this baby regardless of Jack's feelings. She'd always thought that he might eventually come around to the idea, and when she'd seen him on the doorstep, she had hoped his visit yesterday had been some kind of truce. It turned out he'd come to her because he was in trouble, and it had nothing to do with her or the baby which was Jack all over. She had worried he might do this by the state he was in, but had she really, truly thought that he would? Either way it didn't matter, she hadn't been able to stop him and now...

A fresh wave of tears poured down her already red and swollen cheeks, and, as if to add insult to injury, an intense pain in her lower back that radiated to the front of her stomach took her breath away and she doubled over sucking in a deep breath. It was like the worst kind of cramp and backache all rolled into one, and she cried out.

'No.' Her eyes squeezed shut as she waited for it to subside and realised that this might be more serious than a Braxton Hicks contraction, which would just be her luck. She didn't have time to go into labour right now, not when she was consumed with grief and guilt.

When she could straighten up, she began to gather her things together just in case this was happening. She pottered around unplugging her phone charger and shoved it into her hospital bag. Then even though she wasn't hungry, she made herself a sandwich because she needed some kind of energy if she was going to push a baby out. Her stomach was churning, and she thought she might be sick.

Cain was going to kill her. They would be up to their necks in the investigations and wouldn't be able to spare him to go to the hospital with her. Amy decided that if she had to go, she would go on her own. She wasn't the only woman in the world to have to give birth without a birthing partner. It happened all the time, she would just have to suck it up and get on with it.

Another wave of cramps hit her, and she squeezed her eyes shut, breathing deeply until it passed.

She looked at the clock. She hadn't timed it but that felt as if the last one had been less than ten minutes ago. She dialled the maternity unit at Kendal hospital for some advice. It would take her twenty, maybe thirty minutes to get there and that was even if she could get a taxi because lately there was a shortage of drivers and it had been taking forever. Eyeing up her car keys she wondered if she could drive herself and pull over if a contraction came, then she realised that was totally stupid and dangerous. This baby had already lost one parent. What if she crashed and it was born with her in a coma? *Stop it, Amy, stop thinking weird thoughts.* She shouted the words out loud and dialled the only local taxi number she knew.

The contractions were coming a lot faster than she'd ever anticipated. On all the documentaries she'd watched and books she'd read they were supposed to happen slowly over a long period of time and gradually increase in intensity. She wondered if the grief and sadness she was feeling over Jack had speeded things up.

The taxi driver had parked outside of the A&E department on double yellows with his hazards on and ran inside to get help. She guessed he didn't want her giving birth on his backseat, and to be fair to him neither did she.

As she was heaved out of the car and into a wheelchair by two nurses, she wished she'd phoned Cain; she didn't want to be on her own anymore. He would make it all better. His stupid jokes would help to keep her mind off the pain even if she did want to throttle him and tell him to shut up.

She was taken straight into one of the birthing suites. The maternity unit hadn't long reopened and she stared longingly at the small pool in the corner. She was so hot, she wanted to strip off and get into it and submerge herself fully in freezing cold water.

The nurse was asking her questions that she couldn't answer, then she was being helped out of her clothes and into a hospital gown so the midwife could examine her, a blood pressure cuff cinching the skin on her upper arm as it tightened.

Once she was on the bed she asked for her phone, which was given to her, and she caved in, phoning Cain and leaving him a gasping voicemail, telling him where she was and if he wasn't busy could he come see her.

She let out a low groan as another contraction hit her before she'd even ended the call and thought that he would never let her live this one down.

Whether she was ready or not, in a few hours her entire life was going to change. She couldn't stop it now, things were in motion that were out of her control. Then she closed her eyes and tried to breathe deeply through the pain that took away all her conscious thoughts.

THIRTY-EIGHT

Yolanda Crystal didn't read the news, she didn't watch it either and when urgent local alerts flashed up on her phone, she quickly swiped them away. She wasn't interested full stop in the goings on in the crazy world around her. All she cared about was her own inner peace and that of her followers. She was taking over the world one yoga class at a time. She loved being able to solo travel and record her classes in the most beautiful of places.

The Lake District never failed to inspire her. She was planning an evening new moon vlog deep into Grizedale Forest, where she was going to set up her little campsite on her own. There was a small access road that was mainly used by farmers and cyclists. If she drove carefully, she knew there were a couple of places she could pull off the road and set up camp out of view of anyone passing by, so she wouldn't get chased away. It was Sharon who'd inspired her on her own journey of self-discovery, and she hoped to meet up with her one day to tell her this. She was loving the freedom this life afforded her, and the following she had gathered was just the sweetest apart from the odd weirdos that left strange comments, but she ignored those.

Logging on to do one last check before she left the world of the internet behind, she saw a message from one of her newest followers, Fairy Rose.

> Love your content, would be great to do a collab with you some time. If you're ever in the Grizedale Forest/Hawkshead area give me a shout.

She clicked on the profile to see a woman with pink hair grinning back at her, yoga pants and crop top on, sitting in the lotus position with a view of a forest behind her that looked very much like the Grizedale she remembered from her trips there as a kid with her parents. They would fill the Vauxhall Zafira of a weekend, her two sisters and two brothers, and off they'd go with a ginormous carrier bag of crisps and sandwiches for a walk through the woods and a picnic. At the time she'd hated those family day trips out, but she knew now that her mum and dad had only been doing their best with what little they had, and she looked back on them with nostalgia. Especially now she didn't see much of her family. She was the only one without kids, the others were in relationships and lived locally, but she'd moved away to live in the city. Realising what she was missing, she was in the process of moving back to Barrow-in-Furness to be nearer everyone. It was funny how as she found herself getting older, she just wanted a quiet, peaceful life, and her family around her.

She wasn't an expert on the forest, but she knew that area pretty good. Maybe she would contact Fairy Rose. It might be nice to do a collab. She sighed when she saw that Fairy Rose only had three hundred followers – damn, that wasn't exactly going to get her many extra likes on her YouTube channel – but everyone had to start someplace. She sent her a quick message.

Hi, actually I'm heading that way soon. If I can get a signal
when I've set up camp, I'll message you, maybe you could
come meet me and we could record the new moon session
together.

She smiled at her phone screen; she might as well call
herself Saint Yolanda. Still, it was nice to be supportive of
others, and it would make her look good if she was seen to be
giving a newbie a helping hand. All publicity was good, as long
as it didn't cause a scandal. So many influencers were getting
cancelled because of stupid comments they'd made. She wasn't
going to make that mistake. She was the queen of neutrality and
made sure she never said anything to cause a stir, be offensive or
give anyone a reason to give her any grief. If she wanted to truly
make a living from her YouTube channel, then she would do
anything. There was no way she could go back to a corporate
job now she'd tasted the freedom this lifestyle afforded her, and
she wanted more. Maybe one day she could set up her own little
yoga studio, but for now she was grateful she could do what she
was doing with no stress and a calmness in her life she'd never
known could exist.

THIRTY-NINE

He'd been thinking that things were complicated, a lot more complicated than he'd anticipated. Then he'd heard the radio news reporter make the boldest statement he had ever heard. The guy who sounded as shocked as he was said that the police were not looking for anyone in relation to the two murders. What the hell did that even mean? He pushed back in his chair, stretching his arms above his head, realising that it meant he had a get out of jail free card, one that had been handed to him with a huge fucking grin on his face and at no cost to him whatsoever. He should cut loose now, stay quiet, keep out of the way and go about his business like he usually did. The chance of some jumped-up copper falling for what he intended was too much for even him to think about. There had to be some catch. It was too perfect. His foot kept tapping against the floor, a nervous tick he'd had since school that he tried to control. When he got nervous or excited it was hard to contain it, even when he placed his hands on his thigh to stop it.

Staring down at Yolanda's Instagram account for the tenth time today, he knew he should stop this madness that was consuming him, but how did you stop something that was like a sickness inside of you, growing and getting stronger each day until it completely took over? That was the battle raging inside of him right now.

Did he admit defeat and walk away whilst he had this most perfect opportunity, that never, ever happened. Or did he finish his little spree with the beautiful Yolanda Crystal? There was no way that was her real name either. The thought made him more excited than he wanted to admit. What was exciting over doing the right thing? It was everything, the buzz of adrenaline that ran through his veins at the thought of hunting her to her remote camping place and having some fun with her. Maybe this time she wouldn't be found as quickly as the previous two, and he'd be able to see if her body mummified in the right conditions. It would be nice to be able to keep checking on her progress before it was discovered and someone reported her missing. Although he couldn't guarantee she would find the ideal secluded place to record her New Moon vlog that she'd posted about yesterday on her Instagram account. Was there anywhere that was completely remote when there were fell walkers, farmers, campers, mountain bikers and God knows what else kind of extreme sport some people liked to torture themselves with?

The door opened and in walked one of his colleagues, mugs of coffee in hands. He smiled as they passed him one. Today was getting more interesting by the hour.

He was staring at the picture of Yolanda he'd screen-shotted from her YouTube channel as he wondered what he was going to do.

Was he going to take this golden opportunity and not spoil everything?

Or was he going to have some fun?

He would let his instinct guide him; it was in fate's hands whether she lived or died, and it was in fate's hands whether he got away with the murders or was captured and held account-able. He didn't think the cops had a clue what they were doing, and to be fair to them he could see why – he'd done a pretty good job of throwing a spanner in the works. Risky killing a copper, but worth it for the distractions it alone was causing.

FORTY

Morgan went to find Cain. He would listen to her. He was at the brew station rifling through a cupboard and she knew he was looking for biscuits. Grabbing his elbow, she pushed him along the corridor to the stationery cupboard and into it, shutting the door behind them.

'Steady on, Morgan, I'm spoken for, although I might be tempted if you can provide me with something to eat.'

Morgan slapped his arm. Then whispered, 'Cain, I do not want sex and sorry, I haven't got anything worth eating.'

'Then what are we doing in here?'

She lifted a finger to her lips to shush him. 'Talk quiet, Marc's around.'

Cain was squinting at her, a look of total confusion on his face. 'Can we pretend I have no idea what's happening, and you explain it to me?'

She smiled at him. 'Sorry, I have to talk to someone and you're my only option.'

He rolled his eyes. 'Gee, thanks, Morgan. I'm your last resort.'

She lightly slapped him again.

'Ouch, that's police brutality.'

'Marc is about to announce that Jack killed Sharon and Lydia then himself. He's convinced he is responsible. He's talking to HQ now about releasing a statement to the press.'

'He can't do that; he hasn't investigated it.'

'I know, but he's got it in his head, and you know how stubborn he is.'

'What did Ben say?'

'Not a lot, I think he feels as if his hands are tied.'

'You don't think it was Jack? Be nice and tidy if it was though, wouldn't it?'

'No, I don't think it was Jack. It doesn't make sense and before you say he might have lost it, I've considered that and if he'd lost it, wouldn't he have killed Amy because of all the stress over the baby? I mean thank God he didn't, but you know what I mean.'

Cain nodded. 'Yeah, I guess so.'

'We have to prove Jack was killed too.'

'How are we going to do that? Has Declan finished his PM yet?'

'I'm going to phone Declan now and speak to him about it in more depth. I also think we need to issue a press release to any women who may be considering going solo camping, because I think the killer is still out there and I don't think they're going to stop now they've got a taste for it.'

'Why wouldn't they stop if it's all neatly tied up and someone else is going to get the blame? And how are you going to issue a press release without getting in trouble when Marc is about to say that there's no cause for concern, we have it all under control and are not looking for anyone else in connection to the two murders? Do you know anyone who would do that off the record?'

Morgan sighed. 'Fin Palmer would, I think.'

'The same Fin Palmer I arrested a couple of hours ago?' Cain looked incredulous at her suggestion.

'I don't know who else. He's a creep and I hate him with a passion, but he can't resist a story.'

'Morgan, this is so fucked up. We're going to get in so much trouble if we do this.'

'Then you know nothing about it, pretend this conversation didn't happen. I just need his address from you, or his phone number.'

He nodded. 'It's on the custody paperwork; I can go get it for you.'

'Thank you, when the shit hits the fan, I won't mention you, okay? And don't go and drag yourself into it because that's not what I want. I'm happy to take the fallout. If it means we get to save someone's life, it's worth everything.'

'Including your career? You'll get suspended at best.'

'I really don't care. I can't stand by and watch them blame Jack when they're guessing and not focusing on the cold, hard facts.'

Morgan leaned forward and wrapped her arms around Cain who hugged her back even harder. 'You're my fearless leader, Brookes, and I wouldn't have it any other way. Should I come see Palmer with you?'

She squeezed him, grinning. 'No, I better go alone. I don't want you involved any more than you already are, and besides, I doubt he'll talk in front of you after earlier. Thank you, Cain.'

Cain put his hand on the doorknob then turned to her. 'Are you doing this so you don't have to work with Amber?'

Morgan shrugged, and he shook his head, a smile on his lips. 'You're a chancer, Brookes.'

Then he stepped out into the corridor and straight to the lift, to go back down to custody to get Palmer's contact details for her.

FORTY-ONE

Cain met Morgan in the corridor and slipped her a pale-yellow Post-it note that she pushed into her pocket. They looked as if they'd just done some kind of illegal drug deal, but she didn't care. She ran down the stairs to the rear yard, grabbing a set of keys to a car off the whiteboard. Once she was out of the car park she drove to The Coffee Pot, her favourite café. It was sandwiched on the main street between a Thai restaurant and a newsagent. The outside had been painted sage green and a new sign put up; it looked good after its refresh.

Inside, Jade, the owner, on the other hand, looked as if she could do with a refresh, bless her. She had dark roots that made her usual honey blonde hair look messy, and it was tied back in a low ponytail. Jade's pretty blue eyes had lost all their sparkle. Even though she was wearing a new apron that matched the outside of the shop and the new logo, she looked exhausted. It made Morgan's heart ache so bad for her. Jade had lost her daughter to another maniac a year ago.

'Hey, Jade, how are things?'

She smiled at Morgan. 'I'm muddling along, how are you?'

'Busy and in desperate need of caffeine.'

'Then you came to the right place. Are you sitting down for five because if you are I'll bring it over to you.'

'I am.' Morgan double clicked her phone to use Apple Pay, and Jade waved her away.

'Shoo, go take a seat.'

She felt her cheeks burn a little at Jade's kindness, but didn't argue with her. Jade always insisted on giving her free coffee as a thank you for finding her daughter's killer, even though Morgan would never dream of expecting her to.

She sat down and checked her phone to see if Palmer had replied to her message.

Be there in ten minutes.

She sucked in a breath and exhaled deeply, wondering what on earth she was doing meeting the guy she despised the most on the entire planet.

Jade placed a latte and a cheese savoury baguette on the table in front of her.

'No arguments, I bet you haven't been eating properly. I saw the news, those poor women. What is the world coming to?'

'It's getting scarier every day. I bet it brought it all back to you, you must miss Melody so much.'

Jade nodded. 'I just feel as if there is something permanently missing, which there is, but you know what I mean. The flat is so quiet. I miss her mess, her make-up all over the bathroom; I miss her blaring Taylor Swift at full volume all hours of the day and night. I can't bear to listen to her music now because I just cry.'

'Oh, bless you, I can't even begin to imagine how hard it is for you.'

'It's just she was so young, she had her whole life ahead of her. I wish it had been me; I would give anything to swap places with her.'

Morgan stood up and pulled Jade in for a hug, rocking her back and forth to soothe her. Jade hugged her back ferociously. The bell above the door jangled and in walked Fin Palmer, who looked at the two women and arched an eyebrow, which made Morgan want to punch him and he hadn't even spoken yet.

Jade pulled away. 'Thanks, Morgan, I needed that more than you know.'

She turned to Fin. 'Can I get you a drink?'

'Tap water, please.'

Jade left them to it, and Morgan watched as he sat down opposite her, staring into her eyes.

'What's this about? A public apology for getting me arrested? Because I know fine well it was your fault.'

'Nothing to do with me, but thanks for coming.'

Jade placed the glass of water on the table.

'You got yourself into that mess. Why were you on the radio in the first place? That was your doing, so don't blame me.'

'How are you, Morgan? It's been a long time, and I miss you.'

She doubted he was being sincere, but she was willing to play along with him to get what she wanted. 'I'm tired of chasing killers, if you want to know the truth.'

'I imagine you are, maybe if you weren't so good at it every person with the desire to murder wouldn't take it as a direct challenge for you to catch them.' He was smiling, thinking he was being amusing.

How had she fallen for this guy? Actually, she knew exactly how – he could turn on the charm when he needed to. He had done that with her, turning it all the way up. When she'd first met him, she was knee-deep in a murder case and feeling out of her depth, overwhelmed and just needed someone to talk to. He had swept into her life when she was at her lowest. She'd let him until she realised exactly what kind of a man he was when he'd printed that bullcrap story about her biological family and exposed every dark secret she hadn't known she'd had before she'd even had the time to process it. Morgan was so thankful that Ben was nothing like him.

'I just do my job, that's all.'

'It's more than just doing your job, how about an exclusive interview with you? The whole world would love to know more about the elusive, super detective, Morgan Brookes.'

She shook her head. 'And bring even more lunatics to Rydal Falls and into my life, it would be like an open invitation. No, thank you.'

'Then why am I here?'

She took a long sip of her latte, debating if she should say what she was going to because there was no going back once she did.

'I need a favour from you.'

Fin sat back, a genuine look of surprise on his face.

'What kind of favour?'

'I need your word that all of this I'm going to tell you is off the record, except for what I want you to write.'

'That's quite some demand.'

'If you don't keep it off the record then this conversation is over, Fin. I haven't got time to waste with you. I'll find someone else who will keep it off the record.'

She knew she had thrown him because he looked thoroughly confused. He took a sip of the tap water and grimaced, making her smile. Jade was as perceptive as Morgan and had given him warm water and no ice.

'I will keep your name out of it, I can say a trusted source, but tell me, is this going to get me arrested again? Because I've had quite enough of your police station for one day.'

'I don't think so, I mean I can't guarantee it, but you have freedom of speech, you're making a public safety announcement.'

'Then why did they arrest me before?'

'You were talking about a live investigation; this is going to be an assumption on the case that the police may be making or have overlooked.'

She had him, his eyes were wide, glazed with excitement and anticipation at what she was about to tell him.

'Misconduct? The public love that, they think the police are inept anyway. Well, most of them, maybe not you.'

'Not intentionally, more an overlooking of things that could compromise the safety of women, but none of it is malicious, there is no ulterior motive, no hate crime against women. It's more the fact that they're pushed to their limits and possibly not thinking straight.'

'Your department?'

Morgan paused, was she getting them into a whole new level of trouble they didn't need?

'Not specifically, we always have and always will put the safety of the public first.'

'Then who?'

A queasiness in her stomach made her wish she hadn't started this.

'Nobody.'

Fin threw his arms up in exasperation. 'You have to give me something; this is all just riddles.'

'I think that the suspect may still be at large, and I think they could kill again. I want you to issue a warning to all women who partake in solo camping, hiking, anything outdoorsy where they are on their own. I want to ensure they are on high alert just in case.'

Fin's phone began to ring. 'Excuse me.'

She listened to his one-sided conversation and knew what it was about. He ended the call and looked at her. 'There's been a press release stating that they're not looking for anyone in connection with the two murders; they believe they have the suspect and will share more when they have the details.'

Morgan shook her head then stopped what she was doing, remembering who the guy sitting opposite her was and what he was capable of.

'You don't agree at all?'

'I don't know, Fin, I just have this gut feeling that we could be missing something.'

'Look, let's call a truce. I'm sorry, I was an absolute idiot when I wrote that story about you. I regret it, I don't feel bad about most of my articles but that one really made me question what I was doing with my life, but once it was in print there was no going back.'

She didn't know if he was being honest or just trying to get her on his side. She shrugged.

'It hurt a lot, I was only just finding out things I hadn't known about myself, and I trusted you.'

He had the decency to look embarrassed and lowered his head. 'I know and I really am sorry. Let me help you, I'll write an article about how I think there's more to this than the police have said. I was there at a crime scene and saw how bad it was, so I will say it's all my opinion so you don't get into any trouble; but I'll also say that until we have more evidence from the police that they have the right perpetrator, then all women should be careful. I'll issue the warning. How does that sound?'

'You're not going to name me in it at all?'

He shook his head. 'No, I owe you this one, Morgan. By the way, who do they have in mind or who have they got in custody if they're so certain it's stopped? Why the big secret, it has to be someone in the force or local government maybe?'

'If I tell you this, it is not to go into print. I need you to promise me, Fin.'

'I won't say a word, pinkie promise. Well not until I hear it officially.'

'One of our officers was found dead near to the first crime scene yesterday.'

His mouth dropped so wide open she could see his tonsils at the back of his throat. He lowered his voice. 'And they think he did it? Holy shit.'

'I'm not saying that, and I don't believe it, that's all I can say. You can't print that part. You'd better not.'

'I won't, but the shit is going to hit the fan when this gets out. Can you keep me updated, let me know when I can break it?'

'I'll do my best.'

'Thanks, Morgan. If this means the killer could still be out there, are you not worried given your past run-ins with mad men?'

'Not really, I don't think I'm this killer's type. I'm not outdoorsy, I don't like camping, I have nothing to offer him that he gets off on.'

Fin smiled at her. 'Good, I'm glad. I worry about you. I'm glad we've called a truce.'

Morgan smiled back, not sure if she was at truce level with Fin Palmer, but she'd see by what he put in tomorrow's paper whether he was going to do the right thing for once or feed her to the wolves. Either way it was done now. She'd just have to take whatever fallout was coming her way and deal with it.

As long as Ben didn't hate her too much, she could live with herself if it meant it potentially saved someone's life.

FORTY-TWO

Back in the car Morgan phoned Declan, but it went straight to voicemail. No sooner had she hung up than her phone rang, and she answered it to hear his smooth voice with the gentlest of Irish lilts.

'*What do I owe the pleasure, Morgan?*'

'Hey, thanks for ringing back. I know you must be so busy. I wondered if you had any results for Jack?'

'*Did you get the update about the rope fibres?*'

'Yes.'

'*I'm not a hundred per cent sure this is a suicide.*'

Morgan had to stop herself from shouting yes and punching the air.

'Why?'

'*The rope didn't break the little hyoid bone in Jack's neck. It's more likely that he suffocated. This does happen occasionally, but it's messy when that happens, a lot of struggling, clawing at the rope to loosen it because the person is literally slowly choking themselves to death. It's not nice at all, well no death is nice, but this is a horrible way to go. I see none of that. What I do see is a deep red groove just below where the hyoid bone is. If I had to hazard a guess, I would say that someone much taller than him looped the rope around his neck and strangled him, cutting off his air supply. But they're strong, there was no hesitation. It's possible he may even have been under the influence of drugs or alcohol, but I'm going to need the tox results back for confirmation.'*

'Have you told Ben this?'

'Left him a voicemail to phone me back. You are welcome to tell him.'

'Marc thinks Jack is responsible for the two murders and has issued a press release hinting that the killer has been apprehended and stopped.'

'Mary, mother of God, why has he done that without all of the facts?'

'I literally have no clue. I think he wants it to be Jack, and it would be a good result if it was.'

'But?'

'But, it doesn't sit right with me.'

'Well, it doesn't sit right with me either. What a mess.'

Morgan smiled despite the gravity of the whole situation. It was Declan's voice – he always managed to cheer her up. 'Thank you, speak soon.'

'Tell that brute Ben it's quiz night tomorrow in case he's forgotten.'

Morgan laughed. 'I will. Honestly though, I don't see why you don't just go for a drink instead and put yourselves out of the whole always coming last misery.'

'Ah, I can tell you why. We have an image to upkeep, it's not every team that manages to come last week in week out. We can't let that slip.'

'You know for a bunch of intelligent guys you would think you'd have this quiz thing nailed. How's Theo by the way?'

'Doing much better all things considered. He's still not over what Gordon did. I don't think that will ever get any easier for

him, but he's back at work and even plucked up the courage to choose the photos for the Women's group calendar. I admire his courage greatly.'

Morgan was laughing. 'Poor Theo, he's been through so much.'

'Yes, he has. I told him they could make him a saint, but he said not with our quiz team reputation. It reflected too badly on him for that. Got to go, bye.'

He hung up, and Morgan was still giggling to herself. She really didn't know where to go from here. Her phone rang again, and this time it was an unknown number.

'Hello.'

'Hi, is this Morgan?'

'Yes.'

'I'm Helen, a midwife at Helm Chase Maternity Unit. We have your friend Amy with us, she's in labour and trying to get hold of Cain but he's not answering his phone.'

'Oh my gosh, is she okay? Please tell her I'll get hold of him right now.'

'She's doing okay, but I don't want him to miss the birth which is progressing quite fast.'

'Give her my love. I'll go find Cain.'

'Thank you.'

Morgan pulled out her radio from the side pocket and dialled Cain's collar number. It crackled to life.

'Have you been sacked yet, Brookes?'

'Amy's in labour. She's managed to get herself to the maternity unit but the midwife who phoned said labour is progressing quickly.'

'Oh.'

'Yes, oh. Tell Ben you have to leave. Don't make her go through this on her own, not after the tragic news about Jack.'

'I won't, I wouldn't.'

There was a long pause then he whispered. *'Morgan, I'm scared, what if I pass out or am no use to her whatsoever.'*

'You will be amazing; all you have to do is let her squeeze the shit out of your hand and maybe don't look down there if you think you're going to pass out. You can do this, Cain, she needs you.'

'I can do this, yes, I can. Thanks.'

'Let me know as soon—' But he'd gone, the radio chatter broke the silence in the car.

Morgan hoped Amy was okay. What a day this was turning into.

FORTY-THREE

Sitting in the car, Morgan checked the log for Lydia, to get a contact number for whoever was dealing with Lydia Williams's death notification. They had hardly any background information on her. She smiled to see the name of a detective she knew and had spoken to several times before.

As her phone began to ring, she heard the soft voice of Alison Reynolds answer. *'Reynolds.'*

'Alison, it's Morgan Brookes.'

'Morgan, long time no speak. Which technically is a good thing, right?'

Morgan laughed. 'Technically it is. I'm phoning about Lydia Williams, have you managed to get any background information on her yet? Things are a bit messed up here, there's so much going on.'

'Ah, yes. Bless you, I saw the news about your colleague. Well, hopefully I can tick some boxes for you. Apparently, she was a bit of a recluse. I spoke with her younger sister. Both parents are dead, which I suppose is a blessing, she has an older sister, but they were estranged. They don't have to endure the horror of finding out their daughter was murdered. Her younger

sister lives in York and is on her way here, but she said that Lydia had no partner that she was aware of, loved camping in that roof tent thing. She'd not long bought it and adored her dog Barney more than she did people. She'd worked in an office in Lancaster city centre but had handed in her resignation the Friday before she went camping. Her sister said she told her that the boss was a creep.'

'Oh that's interesting about the boss, and I get that, I prefer our cat Kevin to most people. Lydia sounds like my kind of woman, bless her.'

'Her sister asked about Barney. Have you located him yet?'

'No, there was no sign of the dog at the crime scene. Whether he ran off and is out on the fells, and I haven't heard any reports that he has, but it's a bit strange that he's disappeared off the face of the earth.'

'Unless whoever killed Lydia, killed Barney too.'

'I did think that, but wouldn't we have found the dog's body?'

'I wish I could answer that for you, maybe he didn't want the shame of killing a dog. Isn't it funny how us humans are dispensable, yet dogs and cats aren't?'

'Yeah, some humans are the scourge of the earth though animals are just cute, innocent things. Thanks, Alison, I'll let you know as soon as we find Barney.'

'Take care, Morgan, that would be great.'

Stan and Amber were out when Morgan returned to the station. Ben was pacing up and down the office.

'Where have you been, I was worried.'

'Enquiries.'

'Oh, you're okay then, a message now and again would be a comfort. Come up with anything useful?'

She shook her head; she hated lying to him, but she wasn't

going to drag him or Cain into her dealings with Palmer and make things awkward for them both.

'Amy's in labour, not surprised really after the last twenty-four hours.'

Ben's eyebrows raised as she asked him, 'Has Cain gone to be with her?'

'Yes, he was so pale I thought he'd painted his face white with greasepaint.'

Morgan smiled. 'Bless him, he's worried.'

'Nervous too, I'm on pins and it's nothing to do with me. How long does this labour thing last?'

'Anybody's guess, the midwife did say it was progressing fast though, so hopefully for the pair of them it won't take too long. Marc issued the statement then?' She tried to keep her voice calm, neutral and not accusatory because she knew it was out of Ben's control what Marc and the powers that be above them decided.

'Yeah, too soon If you ask me.'

'Hey, I spoke to Declan. He needs to speak to you too about Jack.'

'I've already spoken to him.'

'And?'

'And I think our first instincts were spot on. I don't think he took his own life. So, give me some suspects for this, Morgan. How tall is that Leah you went to speak to, and is she strong?'

'Unfortunately, she's about two inches taller than me. Jack wasn't overly big, but he was nearer to your height than mine. I think she'd struggle to strangle him, move his body and everything else. Don't get me wrong, I think she's good for it and she's an awful friend, but it's the height thing.'

'What if she had an accomplice?'

'That would work if they were taller than her.'

'Okay, so what about...' Ben was standing in front of the

board reading through the list of names under Sharon Montgomery's photograph. 'Stefan Montgomery, how tall is he?'

'Taller than Leah and Jack for sure, but we hardly know anything about Lydia Williams. I spoke with Alison Reynolds from Lancs CID before. She said Lydia has a younger sister who is on her way here, also has an older one she doesn't speak to, no parents, doted on her dog, kept to herself and loved camping. We need to speak to her boss, find out more about her life. We need to go through her social media like we did with Sharon, find if anyone on the list of interesting commenters match with those on Lydia's social media.'

'Yes, we should. Great idea, then we can speak to her colleagues too. Somebody has got to know something.' He leaned over and brushed his lips against her cheek. 'Let's get out of here before Stan comes back with Amber and Marc in tow.'

'Where are they?'

'Marc is busy with the Chief Super, and I sent the other two out to do some CCTV enquiries around Sharon's house, just in case someone has evidence that Jack did not leave when he said he did or that there isn't some creep hanging around stalking her.'

'Thank God, I was worried you were going with the Jack is guilty theory.'

He shook his head. 'No, I didn't want to openly argue with Marc in front of the team, especially when we have two newbies, but I told him he was way out of his comfort zone.'

He grabbed her hand and dragged her towards the door; out in the corridor they let go of each other and Morgan walked single file behind Ben, wondering if she should tell him about her meeting with Fin Palmer. She'd never kept anything from him in the past, but she didn't want him to get into trouble either. As long as Fin kept his word then he would never need to know. Although this made her feel a little uncomfortable, she knew it wasn't like she was doing it for herself. It was to warn other women there was a real possibility that danger was still lurking out there, watching and waiting for them to put themselves in a difficult situation.

Lydia Williams worked in an office building opposite Lancaster Town Hall. Her role was customer service and data entry officer, and Morgan had no idea what that meant, but she was going to find out. There was a video doorbell camera on the door. Ben straightened his tie before pressing the button and announcing who they were. The door clicked open, and they walked in to where a receptionist was staring at them.

'We're here to talk to Lydia Williams's colleagues.' Ben smiled at her; she wasn't remotely interested.

She pointed upstairs. 'First floor, lift's broken, you'll have to walk up those stairs at the end of the corridor.'

Morgan asked, 'Did you know Lydia?'

'Not really, I mean I know her face, but I didn't speak to her or anything. There's a lot of people work in this building. I haven't got the time to talk to them all.'

Morgan nodded, turned and followed Ben to the stairs, where she whispered, 'What a charming woman.'

Ben stifled the laughter, cupping a hand over his mouth. They reached the first floor to an open-plan office filled with desks and lots of people. Nobody looked as if they were devastated at the news one of their colleagues had been murdered. They were all typing furiously on computer keyboards or were on the phone, except for one woman who was staring into space, her eyes a little red.

Morgan walked over to her and introduced herself.

'Did you know that Lydia Williams has been killed?'

The woman nodded. 'Justin announced it at the team briefing this morning then carried on talking about what we needed to do as if it was a minor inconvenience and she'd just called in sick. Everyone was so shocked. He didn't give us time to talk about it or ask questions, which just proves what a crap place this is to work. I'm out of here as soon as I find something else.'

'Were you friends with Lydia?'

'Kind of, we weren't best friends, but we chatted to each other about stuff and took our breaks at the same time.'

Morgan looked around at everyone. The noise was deafening. 'Did she have any good friends here?'

'No, we all get paid to work not to socialise.'

'Who says that?' asked Ben.

The woman whose lanyard read *Karen* pointed to an office on the other side of the room.

'Justin, our boss and fearless leader.'

'You don't like Justin?'

Karen looked around before lowering her voice. 'Nobody likes Justin.'

'Ah, I see, how was he with Lydia? Did she get on okay with her work or was she having any problems with anyone?'

'The only problems she had was with him, he's a creep. Married and always trying it on with every woman or teenager that comes to work here.'

'What kind of problems was Lydia having?'

'He always got her to stay behind on a Friday when everyone else was rushing to get home; he would call her into his office.'

'Did Lydia ever tell you why?'

Karen shook her head. 'No, well, she insinuated he was hitting on her like the creep he is.'

'Did he ask her to stay behind last Friday?'

Karen nodded. 'She texted me to say she'd quit and would see me around, that he is a total loser and to keep out of his way.' Then she lowered her head as a guy came out of the office door and headed straight towards them.

'Can I help you?'

'Detectives Matthews and Brookes, can we speak to you about Lydia Williams?'

He glared at Karen who still hadn't lifted her gaze in his direction. His shoulders stiffening, he nodded, then pointed in the direction of his office. 'Of course, officers.'

They followed him into the large room that overlooked the city square. He pointed to chairs.

'What can I do for you?'

'We're here about Lydia Williams.'

'Yes, it's terrible news.'

He didn't look as if he was overly upset by it, Morgan thought, then she asked, 'Were you and Lydia close?'

He shook his head. 'Not particularly, I'm not close to any of my staff. That's not my job, I'm here to make sure they do their work and meet the targets.'

'So, you weren't friends or seeing each other?'

Justin's face was turning pinker by the minute, and he was beginning to squirm.

'No, what gave you that idea?' He was staring in Karen's direction.

Ben intervened. 'We're just trying to find out if Lydia had any problems at work, any other staff members that didn't get along with her, any issues with anyone overstepping their boundaries. That kind of thing.'

Justin was beaming now; his cheeks were so red, Morgan thought if she held out the palms of her hands, she'd feel the heat emanating from them.

'Lydia was very quiet; she didn't have any friends here. She did her work and went home, leaving her job behind.'

'What does that mean? Don't all of us do that when we leave our place of work? I know I do.' Morgan had her fingers crossed because that was the biggest lie she'd ever told, but he didn't need to know that she could never switch off when she went home and was always thinking about the current case she was working.

'Well, yes. Some of us are a little more dedicated to our jobs though. I work lots of extra hours, late evenings, weekends if I have to.'

Morgan said, 'Karen mentioned that you often asked Lydia if she'd stay behind on a Friday when everyone else was leaving. Why was that?'

Justin was openly glaring in Karen's direction now.

Ben coughed into his fist and asked, 'Could you tell us why?'

Justin looked awkwardly at Morgan.

'If I review the footage from last Friday, will I find out you were the last person to see her before she died?'

Justin snapped his head back in Ben's direction. 'I liked her okay, I flirted a little with her and she flirted back. I wanted to get to know her, but she wasn't really into me, so nothing happened.'

'Were you okay with this? You seem to me like a guy who is used to getting what he wants.' Ben winked at him, and Morgan knew he was trying to play into Justin's ego, but it made her skin crawl all the same.

'Of course, I'm not some total creep. She didn't want to have a bit of fun or go for drinks, that was completely her choice.'

'And your wife wouldn't have minded you going out late on a Friday evening with one of your employees?' Morgan couldn't stop herself and knew she was goading him, but he was a sleazeball.

'Well, of course she would.' He was getting flustered now.

'So, why did Lydia text Karen to say she'd quit her job because you were a total creep?'

Justin's expression was one of pure fury. 'How dare she say that. I did nothing wrong. I just asked her for a drink after work; it wasn't anything I wouldn't do to any of my team members.'

'Ah, yes. I believe you like to hit on all the female team members, especially the younger women. Do you make a habit of this, Justin? I mean how many sexual harassment cases have been filed against you in the last twelve—' She didn't get time to finish her sentence because Justin flew across the desk fists curled, spittle spraying out of his lips as he launched himself towards her.

Ben stepped in-between them and did some kind of jujitsu move that the personal safety trainers up at HQ would have given him a standing ovation for. Justin's arm was twisted at such an angle and he was flipped onto his back and on the floor with Ben straddling him so he couldn't move.

Morgan pulled a pair of cuffs out of her pocket and snapped them on his wrists whilst Ben read the guy his rights. The whole incident took less than two minutes. They pulled Justin up to stand with the entire office now standing up behind their desks and watching with grins on their faces. Whilst Ben marched Justin out past them all to the exit, Morgan couldn't resist.

'I think you guys can grab an early finish.'

Everyone began to clap and cheer. Morgan waved at them all as she followed Ben out towards the lift. She radioed for a van to meet them and transport Justin to custody because there was no way they could take him in the back of the small Focus they were driving. He might try and attack them again.

Well, that hadn't gone how they'd expected, but at least they had a good suspect in custody. He'd proved he had the rage to stab Lydia multiple times. The question was, did he know or have reason to kill Sharon or Jack? If he was innocent, why had he reacted to their questions with such violence?

FORTY-FOUR

Lancashire police had sent a van for Justin because the police station was literally two minutes away from the office building. The two officers had searched his pockets before putting him in the van. The echo of the doors slamming shut had given Morgan a deep sense of satisfaction, knowing that Justin was inside and he wasn't going quietly. He was thumping against the side of the van with either his fist or his head. It didn't matter to her; she didn't care one little bit. One of the officers was already in the van, the other came to talk to them.

'Do you want him detained in our cells or are you taking him back with you? It doesn't matter to us either way, although we're a bit full. It's been like a shoplifting convention this morning. All the usual suspects were out in force, Lush and Primark were hammered. It's a shame they're so crap at it really. I honestly don't know why they bother when they can't even walk in a straight line.'

Ben smiled at her. 'Ah, I remember those days too well. Would it be a bother to you if you escorted him to Rydal Falls for us to interview him there?'

She grinned back at him. 'Absolutely not, I'd love a scenic

drive to the Lakes. Make a change from these gridlocked streets of hell.'

Morgan was smiling. 'The scenery is beautiful; the workload is horrendous.'

'Ah, yes. I heard about the two murders and the suicide of one of your own. It's been a tough few days for you all.'

'It's been busy.'

'We'll get him taken to yours then, and booked in. After that, do you need anything from us?'

'Depending upon what comes out in interview, we might need his house searching, but we'll liaise with your control room and see who is best to conduct that. If you can just get him booked in, we would deeply appreciate it.'

'No problem, I'm Lisa by the way and you're... let me guess. Morgan, I know because I've seen you on social media. Are you Morgan's boss Ben?'

Ben looked mildly worried that Lisa knew who they were. Morgan laughed.

'Infamous for all the wrong reasons, it sucks.'

'I bet it does. We won't hang around for you to get there, if that's okay, once we've booked him in. Our sarge will be having a heart attack that we're having to take a van out of the area.'

Ben snapped out of the daze he was in and nodded. 'That's amazing, we really appreciate it.'

'Cool, nice meeting you.'

More thumping and shouting came from inside of the cage. Lisa smiled. 'He's going to have a headache by the time we reach Rydal Falls.'

Morgan thought that was good. It was the least he deserved. They watched the van drive away before going back to their car.

'That turned out a bit different to what I was expecting.' Ben was already getting into the passenger seat. 'Can you drive? I have a headache.'

'Are you okay? Do you need some paracetamol or to go home?' Morgan asked.

'What I need is a day off with you lying in my arms and not a single thought about murder investigations, and if you ask me, you need that too.'

'Oh, I do. It sounds like heaven, coffee and toast in bed, wild hot sex and nothing to do but admire how handsome you are.'

'Flattery will get you everywhere, and a couple of painkillers. Seriously, do you think we've made a mistake here?'

'How, he was going to attack me?' Morgan replied. 'Why is he so angry? On the surface it looks as if he's hiding something. It's not going to hurt to formally interview him. Why are you doubting yourself?'

'It's the whole Jack thing; it really doesn't fit.'

'No, it doesn't. I want to spend some time trying to see if Jack knew Lydia Williams, if that's okay. I think we're missing something on their social media accounts. I think the killer has been using them to monitor what both victims were up to. They were both very active on there, so it makes sense that he's been stalking them that way; and I don't want to burst the slimeball Justin bubble, but if he's not been on there or doesn't follow them, I don't hold out much hope for him as the killer. A creep and an arsehole yes, no doubt about that. I'll take a look at his accounts and see if he links to either of the other victims, too.'

Ben let out a groan. 'I'm getting too old for this. I must have spent twenty years working shed break-ins, burglaries, domestics, and the occasional murder but they were few and far between. I wish things would go back to that slow flowing non too serious cases so we can both catch a break.'

Morgan reached out and squeezed his fingers gently. 'I wonder how Amy is getting on? Are we still going to look into Stefan Montgomery too?'

'We need a team of ten, maybe twelve to follow up on all these enquiries. Especially now that Cain isn't here to help.

Right now, I think it's important for you to look at all the victims' social media accounts, to see if you can find anything that links them. Are you friends with Jack on any of them?'

'I think so, I don't really use it to be honest, but I accept friend requests and followers if I know them personally, so it's likely.'

'Good, that would make it easier for you. When we get back to the station let's get you set up in an empty office, away from everyone so you can concentrate.'

'What about Justin?'

'Stan and Amber can interview him; I'll give them a list of key questions I need answers to. We need to speak to his wife too and see if she can alibi him for the nights of the murders.'

'Ben, I need to tell you something.' Morgan couldn't keep it in any longer.

He turned his head to look at her. 'What?' The look of concern in his eyes made her feel terrible.

'I had a meeting with Fin Palmer earlier, well I was at The Coffee Pot and he came there.'

'What do you mean a meeting? Did you bump into him by chance? If he's following you...' Ben shook his head. 'I swear to God, I'll strangle him with my bare hands.'

'No, I asked him to meet me there.'

'Why? What the hell for?'

'I wanted him to run a story about the murders, I'm sorry. I should have asked you, but I wanted something putting out there that there may still be a killer in the area. I asked him to write it up, so it didn't look as if it came from the police, and he promised he'd write it from his perspective.'

'And you believe that he'll do that? Christ, Morgan, what were you thinking? The guy threw you out to the wolves once, to sell papers. Don't you think he's going to have a field day with this? You walked right into his open arms, how could you be so stupid?'

She'd known he was going to be mad at her, but she hadn't realised it would hurt so much. 'I'm not sorry, well I am for not telling you sooner. I didn't want you to be involved and that's the only reason why, but I'm not sorry if he prints something that makes other female solo campers stop and take notice. The way Marc put it, there is nothing to be concerned about, it's like those two murders were a little glitch that he's single-handedly put a stop to, and that in my opinion was far more irresponsible than what I've said.'

Ben shook his head and turned to look out of the passenger window. He couldn't look her in the eyes. If she'd felt queasy before, right now she wanted to pull over and vomit all over the grass verge.

'I can't, Morgan, please. I don't know what to say, just leave it okay?'

The rest of the drive back to Rydal Falls was uncomfortable and now she was regretting ever thinking about speaking to Fin Palmer. Her life as she knew it could be over if he betrayed her again. Tears pricked at the corner of her eyes as she stroked the bare ring finger. She had known Ben would be angry, so she wasn't sure why she was feeling so bad. It hadn't stopped her from doing what she'd done, and she just had to hope that for once in his life Fin might do the right thing.

FORTY-FIVE

Two detectives from Professional Standards were sitting in the office when Ben and Morgan walked in. She didn't know them, but Ben nodded at them both and she didn't miss how his shoulders had stiffened, his whole posture had.

'Mike, Dan, how's it going?'

Morgan smiled at them, retrieved her laptop bag from the floor underneath her desk and left them to it. Regardless of the mess she'd made of things, she was going to find an empty office and do what Ben had said she could, at least until he'd calmed down.

She went up to the third floor, as there were a few empty offices up here that had once housed the coroner and his assistant. Morgan went into one and tried the window to see if it opened because the dust in there was thicker than her fingertip. Relieved that it did, she went to the toilet and grabbed a handful of toilet roll to wipe the desk and chair down. When it was as clean as she could get it without a hoover or duster, she sat down and opened her laptop. Leaning over, she closed the door, blocking out the rest of the world.

She wanted to concentrate and try and quell the sickness

that was rolling around inside of her stomach, as if she was on the Windermere ferry in a bad storm. If Fin did quote her as speaking out against her superiors, those two from Professional Standards would be carting her off to interview the moment the story dropped and yes, she had known this was the most probable outcome and had gone with it. So, why was she regretting that now?

Logging on to her Instagram account, she brought up Sharon's and Lydia's profiles. Taking out a notepad, she wrote down their names, then added Stefan's, Leah's, Beth's, Justin's. She realised they knew nothing about Lydia apart from that Justin was her boss and he was a total loser; Beth hadn't been spoken to either not since they'd found Sharon's body. Morgan phoned Caroline, the FLO.

'Hey, it's me, Morgan. How's things? Are you with Beth at the moment? Does she know about Lydia Williams?'

'No, I'm not with her and she's doing surprisingly well and told me she'd ring me if she needed me. I informed her about Lydia when Ben notified me. What's up?'

'Has she said anything about Stefan or Leah, anything about Sharon?'

'She's been very quiet, the only person she kept talking about was the maid. I can't remember her name offhand.'

'Marie?'

'Yes, her.'

'What's she been saying about her?'

'That she's a lifesaver, she should have listened to her subtle hints about Stefan and his flirting. How she misses her more than her husband because she was a friend more than the woman who took care of things.'

'What about Sharon?'

'Lots of tears, not much talking about her daughter though. I'm not going to lie, Morgan, I kind of think she's more upset at

not seeing this Marie than she is about her daughter's death and her husband's infidelity.'

'That's odd.'

'Yeah, I thought so too. Who knows? Maybe they're a lot closer than we realise. I was wondering if they were in a relationship.'

'Maybe, I could do with talking to Beth.'

'Well, she's at Storrs Hall Hotel, living it large. Booked herself into a suite, been eating room service. I wouldn't want to pay the bill for that when she leaves.'

'Hm, how tall do you think Beth is?'

'Taller than me that's for sure and I'm five foot ten.'

'Have you seen much of Marie?'

'Nope, just a couple of times.'

'Is she taller than you?'

'Only slightly. Why are you bothered about how tall they are?'

'Declan and I think that Jack didn't kill himself, that he could have been strangled and his body was staged, but it would need to have been someone taller than Jack.'

'Well Jack wasn't that tall, what was he, about five six maybe five seven at the most.'

'Thanks, Caroline.'

'Anytime.'

Morgan hung up and stared at the notebook on the desk, adding Marie Jones's name next to Beth's. If they were a couple or secretly dating, why would they want to kill Sharon and Lydia, even Jack? What was the reason for any of it? Revenge, greed, jealousy?

Morgan typed Marie's name into Instagram and scrolled through a list of accounts to find one where the bio picture looked a little like her. Clicking on her name, she realised this glamorous woman staring back at her with her softly waved hair falling over her shoulders and make-up to die for was in fact

Marie Jones. She was stunning, nothing like the Marie she had spoken to, although she guessed there wasn't much point going to work looking that good when she was cleaning up someone else's mess.

She clicked on the follower tab and scrolled down.

Morgan dropped her pen.

Marie was following Lydia Williams, Jack White, Sharon Montgomery – and all three of them followed her back. It was too much of a coincidence. Or was it? She quickly did the same for Jack, who followed Sharon, but not Lydia. Her mind was spinning.

FORTY-SIX

'Have you seen this?' Marc had stormed into the office waving a sheet of paper in the air, but noticing the two PSD officers sitting there he dropped his hand to his side.

'Ben, I need a word.'

Ben knew the moment Morgan had told him about talking to Fin Palmer there was going to be a shit storm coming their way, though it had happened much sooner than he'd imagined and now he didn't know how he was going to be able to protect her when there were already two PSD officers looking into them after being the last people to speak to Jack. Ben had given them his statement, and then they had asked to speak to Morgan, and he'd told them she'd be back soon. He had just been about to go and find her when Marc had barged in like a bull in a china shop.

He followed Marc to his office, closing the door behind him so nobody could listen in.

'What's the problem, boss?'

Marc thrust the paper his way. It was a printout from a local news website.

Police May Have Given Misleading Information to the Public Regarding the Two Murders

Ben felt as if he was going to vomit all over Marc's desk. He looked up at him.

'Read the rest of it.'

He scanned the short article.

Is there anything to worry about after two women were found murdered in the space of 48 hours? According to the statement given by Rydal Falls police there isn't, they have a suspect. However, after this reporter was first at one of the crime scenes, I think they are being a little premature with the assumption there will be no more murders. I witnessed firsthand the horror of what happened to the victim who has been named as Lydia Williams, 39 years old from Lancaster, and I still cannot get the image out of my head.

I would like to believe that the police have this under control, but I'm sceptical especially as they have released no further information to back up these claims. In my opinion I ask any lone, female, solo athletes, campers, vloggers, tourists, walkers not to go out into the Lake District alone. Not to publish your locations on social media or your itineraries until we have had clear evidence from the police that the killer has been caught.

Fin Palmer

Exhaling a long, slow breath he thanked Fin for not dropping Morgan into it from a great height, because there would be nothing Ben could have done to stop the fallout if this was quoted as coming from her.

'How bloody dare he,' exclaimed Marc. 'Why is he saying this after the statement we released?'

Ben's knees felt as if they were going to give way, the stress and pressure was too much, and he was exhausted. He dropped into a chair, motioning for Marc to sit down too. Marc copied him.

'Look, Marc, I can't say I blame him. You're not going to like what I'm about to say but that press release you issued earlier, I think it was too soon to presume there was going to be no more murders. Have you read Jack's post-mortem report or spoken to Declan about it?'

'No, I've been in meetings.'

'Well, Declan believes Jack was murdered, that he didn't hang himself. Identical fibres from the rope used to strangle Jack were found at both Sharon's and Lydia's crime scenes. I think it's a good thing that he's issued this warning. Do you want any more women's deaths on your hands?'

'On my hands? The first two aren't on my hands, Ben. It's not as if I could have prevented those. They had already happened.'

'No, but if someone else goes out camping thinking it's safe to do so because of that earlier press release, then their blood would be, and I don't want to live with that kind of guilt on my conscience.'

Marc was staring at him, and then he buried his head in his hands on top of the desk.

'In the words of Stan, what a shit show.'

Ben couldn't disagree.

'What do we do about Palmer?'

'Nothing, leave him to it. He hasn't done anything wrong; he's allowed his opinions. If we go after him again, it's going to make everything a hundred times worse. He'll make it his personal vendetta to make us look like fools.'

'Do you ever wish you could rewind time and start again?

Start the day fresh knowing you could change stuff that had happened for a better result.'

Ben nodded. 'Every, single day, boss.'

Marc's eyes narrowed, and Ben knew he was trying to figure out what he meant.

'Your wife's death?'

'Yes, that was the biggest shit show of my life and what I wouldn't give to go back to that day and change it. Not work late, go home on time, show her the attention she so desperately needed. Only I can't and all I can do is try to make sure I never make those same mistakes again, with anyone.'

'I'm sorry, for what it's worth. I don't know if I've ever told you that.'

'Thanks.'

'If Jack isn't responsible then who is? Have we got any leads that are worth following up on?'

'Morgan is trying her best to find connections between the three victims.'

'Good, do you think she will?'

'At this point she better had, or we're all screwed. I need to go find her.'

'What do we do about this?'

'Nothing, ignore it. Like I said, it's Palmer's personal opinion. If we challenge it, we're only making it worse.'

Ben stood up. 'Have you heard that Amy's in labour? Cain's gone to be with her.'

Marc was shaking his head. 'Poor Amy, what a day she's having but at least she's going to have a beautiful baby to show for all of this pain when it's over. They always say that when one life ends another begins.'

Ben smiled at him, wondering if Marc was going soft in his old age or whether the last few days had worn him down as much as it had Ben.

FORTY-SEVEN

Morgan heard the footsteps walking along the deserted corridor and opened the door. She knew it was Ben. He was the only person who would figure out where she was. He stepped into the room, closing the door behind him.

'Palmer released a statement. You'll be pleased to know he doesn't mention you. You're off the hook.'

Although this news was a huge relief to her that Fin hadn't screwed her over again, she was a little annoyed with Ben's attitude.

'Marc came into the office guns blazing only to shut up when he saw PSD sitting there. We've had a little chat, and he agrees that it was probably a wise thing to do and the best course of action is to leave Palmer well alone. How are you getting along?'

'Pretty good, I've found one person up to now that is linked to all three victims. Marie Jones is Insta friends with them.'

'Should I know Marie Jones?'

Morgan turned her laptop screen so he could see her profile picture. He shook his head.

'Imagine her with her hair in a bun, no make-up on and wearing a uniform.'

Ben bent closer to take a better look. 'The maid?'

'Yes.'

'You think she did it?'

'I don't know, but I've cross-checked all the victims against each other. Jack wasn't following Lydia, and I don't think he knew her. I think if we could get some CCTV footage of Jack leaving Amy's house, it could show Maria giving him a lift or at least talking to him. There must be houses with cameras along the way.'

'We watched him leave Amy's house remember?'

'What about the rest of the way home? He would know Marie if he was dating Sharon, I'm sure he would. He was walking, he wasn't in a car, so if she saw him and offered him a lift that would make perfect sense.'

'I suppose so, but how is she strong enough to do that? And what about Sharon, why kill her?'

'I think Marie and Beth have a thing going on. According to Caroline, Beth is besotted with Marie. What if Marie thought that by killing Sharon and trying to blame Stefan, that would clear the way for her to have Beth and that beautiful home all to herself.'

'Why Jack?'

'Jack saw something only he probably didn't realise it at the time because he was in a funk about Amy.'

'She was taking care of loose ends. But why Lydia?'

'To make it look like there's a serial killer and throw us so far off her trail, and it almost worked, didn't it? I think poor Lydia was just a pawn in their game.'

'Okay, wild theory but plausible. Completely plausible. I'll find some PCSOs to do the door knocking and look for video footage of Jack. Do we have enough to bring this Marie in for questioning?'

'Not really, this is my theory and there's no forensic evidence to support it, unless we search her house and find the same blue rope she used to strangle Jack with. There were fibres at the other two crime scenes, maybe she used the knives that killed them to cut up pieces of rope? Or maybe if we searched Stefan's house we'd find some there because she might have planted it to make him look guilty.'

'That's more like it, especially if we go with the train of thought that she's trying to get rid of everyone so she can be with Beth. I'll see if we can get a search warrant for the Montgomerys' house first. I think she would try and set him up if she wanted everyone out of the way, don't you?'

Morgan nodded. 'Yes, if there's nothing there, we can search her home then. I don't think you can arrest her until we've found something though. We don't want her to know we're looking at her, so make her think we're after Stefan.'

'Gotcha. I'll go get the search warrant and tell Marc we might have something.'

He leaned down and brushed his lips against the top of her head. 'Good work, Brookes, as always.'

She smiled at him and felt some of the knots in her shoulders begin to untie. They needed a break and hopefully this was it.

FORTY-EIGHT

It took an hour to assemble a team to go to the Montgomery home. Morgan had asked Caroline to find out Marie Jones's address and had been stunned to find out she lived in a one-bedroom apartment above the garage that she had seen her coming out of on a previous visit. Stan, Amber and Marc had gone in the van with two task force officers. Ben and Morgan were following behind. Morgan kept checking her phone and sighing. She'd messaged Cain thirty minutes ago to find out how things were going, but he hadn't even read it, and she realised that he must be too busy to not even look at his phone. She hoped he hadn't fainted. Amy would never let him live it down.

'Any news?' Ben asked.

'Nothing, I feel so nervous for her, and so bad about the last few days.'

'If I'm honest with you, I don't think she'll even be thinking much about Jack at this point. She's going to be so consumed with pain and hopefully some good drugs to help ease the pain.'

'Maybe not, but I can't stop thinking that in a different life he wouldn't have left her. If he hadn't left her and they were still together he'd be with her right now, holding her hand not lying in a body bag inside Declan's mortuary, leaving her to do this on her own.'

'Wow, that's deep and scary and she's not on her own, she has Cain.'

'Yeah, that's what I'm worried about, Cain not being able to handle it. It's true though, his life completely changed course, didn't it? And now look how it's ended. It's so sad and pointless.'

'Not if he didn't kill himself.'

'Well, no, but if he hadn't been involved with Sharon Montgomery, I don't think he'd be dead right now.'

They rounded the corner to see two police vans and an unmarked car all waiting in the lay-by not too far away from the Montgomery house. The plan was Morgan and Ben would go first and gain entry then they'd follow through. Morgan had the warrant in her hand ready to give to Stefan. It included any outbuildings, which technically covered the garage and Marie's living quarters.

Morgan buzzed the intercom, and the gates swung open without anyone asking them who they were. She glanced at Ben, but he drove through and she said, 'Good to go,' into the radio so the others could follow them through.

Marie was standing on the doorstep, and Morgan jumped out of the car, walking briskly towards her before Ben had even turned the engine off.

'What's all this?'

'Is Stefan home?'

Marie shook her head. 'Not sure where he is.'

'I guess you're in charge then?'

'I suppose I am whilst the Montgomerys aren't here. Why?'

Morgan handed her the warrant. 'We have a search warrant for the house and outbuildings.'

'I don't understand, why do you need this? What are you

searching for? I'm going to have to speak to Stefan first. I can't let you in to trample all over the place.'

Ben had joined Morgan. 'You ring Stefan, but this is a legal document giving us permission to come inside. I'm afraid you can't stop us.'

If Marie was feigning innocence, she was doing a very good job because her eyes were flitting from Morgan to Ben to the officers who were all getting out of the vans and car behind them.

'Okay, I'm not sure what this is about though. Can you at least explain that to me?'

'We believe that Stefan may be involved in the deaths of three people, and the search warrant gives us legal permission to enter this house and look for any evidence.'

Marie let out a gasp. 'What? Three people? Have you gone mad?'

'I wish we had. You need to step to one side now, Marie, just let them do their job okay, we'll be as fast as we can and cause minimal mess.'

Morgan turned to Ben. 'I'll take the garage.'

Ben nodded. 'We'll take the house.'

'Is the garage open?' she asked Marie, who nodded at her.

Snapping on a pair of blue gloves, Morgan headed towards the large outbuilding. Marie didn't even argue with her or mention that she lived above it. The woman was standing to one side as the team filed past her, seven officers including Ben. Finally realising that things were getting serious, she pulled a phone out of her pocket and rang someone, Morgan assumed either Stefan or Beth, to tell them what was happening.

———

The garage was surprisingly empty. In one corner was a stack of gardening equipment, a ride-on mower, assorted tools, everything you could possibly need to look after a garden this size. Morgan remembered that Beth took care of everything. Stefan said she wouldn't take any help because she liked to keep fit that way. She paused, gardening was hard work, it took a lot of strength to be able to bend and weed. There were some trug buckets under the workbench, and she tugged them out one at a time. There was brown jute twine, green twine, plastic twine, every kind of twine you could dream of but there was no blue rope. At the far end of the garage was a locked door next to two industrial-sized washing machines and a dryer. There was also a huge clothes maid with bedding drying on it.

Morgan tried the door handle. It was locked. She spied a toolbox at the far end, tucked right back under the workbench, but as she bent to drag it out someone threw themselves at her.

Morgan was knocked to the ground, all of the wind gushing out of her as she hit the concrete with a loud thwack. Whoever had pushed her was strong. Morgan lay on her side, disorientated on the floor as her arms were tugged behind her. She tried to fight the person off, but they were kneeling close to her neck, a thigh either side stopping her from turning her head, and sitting on her shoulder blades.

A voice whispered, 'Shhh.'

As she opened her mouth to scream, a dirty rag was stuffed inside, making her gag so much she was almost sick. A wave of sickness rolled over her as she felt herself being dragged towards a trapdoor in the floor that she'd never noticed seconds ago, near to the ride-on lawn mower.

She'd never seen it. She had no idea who was dragging her, their face was covered by a black mask, and she wondered if she was hallucinating...

Had she knocked herself on the head?

Then she was bundled down into a hole that wasn't very big. She fell about three feet into the bottom of the pit, which was thankfully cushioned by something, so her landing was soft, but she hit her head against the wall on her way down and blacked out – not hearing the door above her slam shut, the old piece of matting being thrown over the floor and the mower being moved across it.

FORTY-NINE

Ben was searching Stefan's office when his phone buzzed. He read the text and frowned.

Nothing in garage. Got to go to the hospital Amy is in a bad way. Xxx

He straightened up and read the message again. Dialling Morgan's number, it went straight to voicemail, and he realised the service wasn't great as his signal went from one to zero bars of service. He texted her back.

Okay, let me know what's happening when you get there. I can't spare two of you at this moment, Morgan. One of you will have to come back as soon as you know how she is. Xx

He went to the door to see the plain car had gone. Worried now about Amy, he wondered if he should ring the hospital, but they wouldn't tell him anything – he wasn't family. He carried on, even though he was more than a little bit perturbed that Morgan had taken off without even coming to speak to him first.

Clearly she was still annoyed with the way he'd been with her earlier but what was he supposed to do? Ignore the fact that she'd met Fin Palmer behind his back? He trusted Morgan but he didn't trust Palmer. He was a weasel.

'Anything?' Marc was leaning against the doorway.

'Nothing, for a house this size it has very little stuff in it. I was hoping we'd find some rope that matched the one at Jack's crime scene.'

'I guess they follow the Marie Kondo way of living.'

Ben turned to look at him. 'What does that even mean?'

'She's big on getting rid of clutter and streamlining your life, had a bestselling book about it.'

'Oh, right. Never heard of her. By the way, Amy's not good. Morgan had to go. She got a call from the hospital.'

'Really, that's bad news. What's Morgan going to do that Cain can't?'

Ben shrugged. He didn't actually know, that was a valid question.

'Did she find anything?'

'Said the garage was clear.'

'Damn it.'

Loud footsteps and shouting from the hallway outside filled the air.

'Who said you could come in here and what are you doing in my house?'

Stefan was back and sounded furious. Marc side-eyed Ben and they both headed towards his voice. He was red-faced and shaking, shouting at Amber.

'Where's Marie? Who let you bastards into my house?'

Ben stepped between Stefan and Amber. 'We have a search warrant; this is all legal.'

'The fuck it is. What's your cause? Why are you here invading my privacy? Marie.'

He yelled her name so loud it echoed around the house.

Marie appeared at the end of the hallway, her face red. She looked as if she was about to burst into tears at any moment.

'I couldn't stop them; they have paperwork.'

She rushed towards Stefan holding out the warrant for him, and he snatched it out of her hands so violently that she quickly stepped away from him. He read it, then tore it in two and threw the pieces onto the floor.

'Get the fuck out.'

Ben shook his head. 'No, we are here legally and if you cause any trouble, I'm going to have to arrest you for obstructing the course of justice, and I really don't want to do that, Stefan. Let's just be calm about this, the quicker we get done the faster we can leave you in peace.'

Stefan sucked in a deep breath as if trying to control his temper, but his knuckles were clenched hard. Out of nowhere he threw a punch at Ben and smacked him in the face, hitting him hard on the right eye socket. Ben stumbled back as the two task force officers who were standing halfway down the stairs rushed at Stefan, who began throwing punches at anyone and everyone.

Ben saw the red dots of the taser line up on Stefan's chest through his left eye, which was open, his right one had swollen shut, and before he could shout no to whoever had their taser centred on Stefan's chest, he heard the static buzz as the barbs were released. They hit the target dead centre and Stefan let out a shocked scream as he fell to the floor twitching.

'Holy crap,' Marc shouted, and Ben turned to see Amber standing there holding a taser that was attached to the task force officer's belt.

She shrugged. 'Wasn't going to stand by and watch you all get battered.'

Ben's eye was smarting and he didn't know whether to clap or yell at her to get out of the house. Marc was staring at Stefan who was still twitching, then turned to Ben who was clutching his eye and muttered, 'What a clusterfuck.'

Ben wasn't used to hearing his boss swear. He had to stifle the laughter that was threatening to explode because it really was a clusterfuck. Instead, he said, 'Somebody call an ambulance for Mr Montgomery.'

And then he sat down on the bottom step and wondered what the hell had just happened.

Marie was staring down at her boss in horror; she looked at Ben. 'Is he going to be okay? I mean he doesn't look okay. Let me get you some ice.'

'He'll be fine, in bit.'

Then she rushed towards the kitchen area. When she came back with a tea towel filled with ice, he thanked her and pressed it against his aching eye. It wasn't the first time he'd taken a punch in the line of duty and wouldn't be the last, but it had taken him by surprise which annoyed him more than being punched. He'd let his guard down big-time. What else had he let slip because he wasn't paying attention?

Stefan was taken away in an ambulance, and Amber went, too, keeping an eye on him. Ben declined medical treatment but did agree to let Marc drive him back to the station. They left everyone else behind to finish the search.

Back at the station, Ben went straight to the toilet to look at the damage to his eye. The ice had helped a lot. It was purple and black, still swollen shut but it wasn't cut or bleeding. That had been a good punch. When he went into the empty office, he sat down and sighed.

Marc came in with two mugs of tea and put one on the desk in front of Ben.

'Good for shock, stuck a couple of sugars in it for you.'

'Thanks. I'm okay, that will teach me to let my guard down.'

Marc was bending over him staring at his eyes. 'Yep, he got you good. What the hell do you think is going to happen now?'

'Not a lot if we don't find any evidence at the Montgomerys' house then we're back at square one, no killer in custody and three dead bodies in the mortuary. Let's hope they don't decide to make it four whilst we're running around like headless chickens with no idea what's going on.'

'Have you heard from Morgan or Cain? Do you think we should phone the hospital?'

Ben took out his phone, he had no new messages. 'I don't know what to do, boss, they're not going to discuss Amy with either of us.'

'Surely one of those two can give us an update. I feel as if I'm walking on eggshells waiting.'

Ben lifted his phone, snapped a picture of his eye and sent it to Morgan and Cain.

You missed all the fun, how is Amy? Let me know ASAP.

'Do you need to go home, Ben? Sorry, I should have asked you earlier, it was just a bit much, you know.'

'No, I'm fine. I can see out of my left eye so it's all good, and besides, we're already two, no three detectives short, so I don't think me feeling sorry for myself is going to help anyone.'

Marc nodded. 'Thanks, I appreciate that.'

The door opened and in walked Stan holding an evidence bag with a length of blue rope inside of it. Marc jumped up and clapped him on the back.

'Where did you find that?'

Stan was grinning at him. 'You'll never believe it, we searched the entire house and garage, then I realised we'd missed the maid's living quarters above the garage, so I got her to let us in and this was coiled up in a drawer hidden underneath some newspapers.'

'Well done, thank God you did. Where's the maid now?'

'Waiting to be booked into custody. I didn't think you'd want me to leave her free to roam around. I tried ringing you, boss, to ask if it was okay but there wasn't much signal.'

Marc took out his phone and saw he had a missed call off an unknown number.

'Well done and yeah, it all got a bit mental, didn't it.'

Ben smiled at Stan. 'Seriously, well done. That was a lucky find.'

Stan shrugged. 'Was a bit of a fluke if you ask me, but I'll take it if it means we have the killer behind bars and hard, forensic evidence to prove it.'

For the first time in days, Ben felt the tightness in between his shoulders begin to loosen itself and they dropped an inch lower than they'd been five minutes ago. Now all they needed was an update about Amy and some good news that she was fine and the baby was doing well.

FIFTY

Morgan opened her eyes and groaned. She couldn't see a thing in the murky blackness. Where the hell was she?

One minute she'd been searching for evidence inside the garage and... Christ, who had attacked her whilst there was a house full of police officers? Who had the audacity to throw her in some pit that wasn't even big enough for her to turn around in? Her shoulders were aching, and her hands were numb, and she realised it was because she was lying on them. Could she lose her hands if she didn't get off them? Trying her best to shuffle to the side to release some of the pressure on them, she managed to turn slightly.

Her face was pressed up against the rough concrete side. She wasn't exactly claustrophobic, but the fact that she couldn't breathe properly with the gag shoved into her mouth wasn't helping. Straining hard against the tie wraps, she tried to break them, but they were too strong. She'd watched a video on Instagram last year, where some guy was teaching you how to free yourself if you ever got into this situation. *Great, Morgan, you didn't even retain the information.*

Where was her phone? She realised that she couldn't feel it

in either of her pockets, but she still had the blue nitrile search gloves on her hands and they felt slick... if she worked at those tie wraps she might be able to slip her hands through them and free herself. She still had no idea who had pushed her down here and done this to her, but they were going to be sorry when she got out. Why hadn't Ben noticed she was missing? She strained to listen for any noise above her, but it was deathly silent. She tried shouting, the muffled noises were pathetic, and it suddenly dawned on her she didn't know how much air she had. What if this pit was airtight? A bubble of panic filled her chest, and she wanted to scream and cry, but she didn't. Instead, she tried to sit herself up. Maybe she could lift the trapdoor above her or at least bang on it to get someone's attention. It wasn't much, but it was better than nothing. Surely, they had realised she was missing.

Slowly rocking from side to side to get herself onto her front, she figured if she was able to get onto her knees, she might be able to raise herself up enough to push the door open.

Footsteps echoed off the concrete floor above her as someone was walking around, and she tried to yell the best that she could. It was pointless. The sound was so quiet she realised that whatever this place was it had been soundproofed. Whoever was up there wouldn't hear her and she might end up starving herself of what little oxygen there may be left.

She listened to where they were going and wondered if it was Marie. Had Morgan been right? Was the woman a killer? She could add kidnapping and police assault to her long list of charges if she was.

FIFTY-ONE

Amy's hands were slick with perspiration. She had been manoeuvred by the midwife with Cain's help and was now on all fours. Cain was kneeling next to her wiping her brow with a damp facecloth.

'When the next contraction comes, I want you to bear down and push with everything you have, Amy, you're almost there.'

The midwife smiled at Cain who was trying to hold off the panic attack that was threatening to take over. This was much worse than even he'd imagined, and he wished it was over for Amy's sake. He didn't know how much pain one woman could take. Amy was tough, he knew she was a lot tougher than him, he'd have curled up in a ball and cried for them to cut it out of him.

She looked at him, fear and desperation in her eyes, and he smiled at her.

'Almost there, you're doing amazing, I'm so proud of you.'

She was leaning on her elbows, his hand clenched tightly in hers. She began to groan as another brutal contraction began to pulse through her tired and aching body. She gripped Cain's hand tight, gritted her teeth and pushed with everything she had.

'Well done, Amy, the baby's head's out, breathe and with the next one push as hard as you can.'

Cain was tempted to look and see the head but not sure if he should. Unable to stop himself, he looked down to see the small head that had a mound of jet-black hair, covered in white grease and bloody slime.

'Oh my God, it's got hair. I thought it would be bald or ginger.'

Amy smiled at him. 'A lot of hair?'

He nodded.

She closed her eyes as another contraction came, and she bore down, gritting her teeth and pushed the baby all of the way out.

The midwife deftly caught it into her arms and passed it to her nursing assistant to clean up. Amy's whole body sank onto the bed. She was turned over and the baby passed to her. Her face bright red, her hair plastered to her skin, she cried with relief when she held her baby.

'Congratulations, Mum, you have a gorgeous, healthy baby girl.'

'A girl?'

Cain couldn't stop staring.

He nodded. 'A girl, a miniature Amy, oh God help us.'

Amy grinned, and Cain realised how exhausted she must be because she would normally have slapped him for that kind of remark.

'Amy, you did amazing. I mean look at you, that's an actual baby, it's breathing and everything.'

'Thank you, I couldn't have done it without you.'

The midwife helped to get the baby onto her breast to feed, and Cain didn't look away; he realised it was the most beautiful, natural thing on earth and he was so proud to have been here to witness all of it.

'Should I let everyone know?'

She nodded. 'I'm going to call her Ava Rose after my nan.'

'That's a beautiful name. I'll just step outside and ring Morgan. She'll tell everyone; they were on pins for you.'

Cain couldn't stop grinning. He felt as if he was floating on air, what a ride that was.

Walking around until he had a good signal, he rang Morgan, but it went straight to voicemail, which he hadn't expected because she knew he'd be ringing her with an update. Next, he tried Ben who answered immediately.

'It's a girl, Ava Rose, not sure how heavy she is but Amy did great. Mother and daughter are doing brilliant. She's just breast-feeding her now.'

'*Thank God for that, I've been so worried about her. Tell her huge congratulations. I can't wait to meet her and well done.*'

'Why were you worried?'

'*Well, I wasn't until Morgan sent that message that Amy was in a bad way and she was on her way to the hospital.*'

'Morgan's not here and Amy was never in a bad way. I mean she was in a lot of pain like, but she was never in any danger. The midwife had it all under control.'

The line went dead, and Cain looked at his phone. What a weird thing to say, why had Morgan said that?

'Do you want to cut the cord?' The midwife had poked her head out of the room and was smiling at him.

He pushed his phone into his pocket and headed back towards the room, not sure what was going on.

As he got inside, he looked at Amy and Ava and shook his head.

'I'm good for the cord cutting, I think that might tip me over the edge but thanks for asking.'

He sat next to Amy, unable to shift the uncomfortable feeling that had settled in the pit of his stomach.

FIFTY-TWO

Ben ended the call, the all-too-familiar feeling of panic rising in his chest that made it hard to breathe properly. He flew out of his office not quite sure where he was going, but he startled Stan who jumped off the seat of his chair.

'Have you heard from Morgan?'

Stan shook his head. Ben was dialling her number, but it went to voicemail. He ran to Marc's office. 'Morgan is missing.'

'What, how?'

'I don't know. She sent a message saying she had to go see Amy because she wasn't doing very well, but I've just spoken to Cain. Amy is fine, had a baby girl, and Morgan has never been to the hospital, nobody messaged her to go there. I need to speak to Marie now because the last I knew she was in that garage searching.'

He ran out of the office, and Marc picked up the phone. 'Ma'am, we have a situation. Detective Brookes is missing. Yes, you heard right, Morgan hasn't been seen or heard from for two hours. Last sighting of her was at Stefan Montgomery's house. No, I don't know if she left there. I'm assuming she did because the search team came back without her or without mentioning that she was still there. Thank you.'

Marc hung up and ran after Ben who was already in the custody suite. A detention officer was opening the door of cell nine, where Marie was sitting on a blue plastic mattress in a grey sweatshirt and grey joggers.

She stared up at Ben, her eyes glassy.

'Where is Morgan?'

'Who?'

'You know who.'

Marie shook her head, then a small smile crept across her lips. 'You're missing a detective? That's pretty careless. Where did you lose her?'

Ben rushed in and crouched down in front of her. 'In the garage, she was in the garage last. What did you do?'

'I didn't do anything. I was in the house the entire time, you saw me. I brought you ice for your eye. Did it help?'

Ben stood up and turned to Marc. 'I want all patrols back to the Montgomery house now, she must still be there.'

Marie was watching them. 'Tick tock, her clock might be running out.'

He whipped around. 'What does that mean? Tell me where she is.'

'I don't know, but good luck finding her, things have a way of going missing in that godforsaken house that don't always get found.'

Ben didn't agree with violence against women, had dealt with more than his fair share of wife beaters, but he had an urge to slap Marie across the cheek and wipe the stupid grin off her face.

He rushed back up to the office to where Stan was sitting looking confused.

'When you searched Marie's flat, did you see Morgan?'

'No, there was nobody there. It was empty.'

'It can't have been, she had to have been there.'

Stan shook his head. 'She wasn't there, I swear she wasn't. I had to go through the garage to get up to the flat and it was empty.'

'They must have CCTV, get hold of Beth Montgomery now, please, go find her and drive her back to her house if you must, but meet me there. I'm going to search the garage again.'

Ben didn't wait for other officers to help him. The control room should have already sent a patrol to the house. He didn't wait for Marc either. He didn't know where he was as per usual and didn't care one little bit. All he cared about was finding Morgan before anything happened to her.

———

Morgan tried to remember what the guy on the video had said. This was life or death. She could die down here if she ran out of air. Was it bite the tie wraps and pull as tight as she could? She wriggled until she had her hands near to her mouth, and it took her a couple of attempts to bite hold of the end of the tie wrap and grip it in her teeth, but it kept slipping because of the saliva. It was so hard with the gag in her mouth, then she realised if she bent her head a little bit more, she could push her fingers in her mouth. At first, she pushed the material further back, making herself retch before managing to hook a finger into a piece of the cotton and drag it out.

The relief when she could breathe was better than anything she ever knew existed. She sucked in greedy gulps of air with tears rolling down her cheeks.

Not wasting any time, she pulled the end of the tie wrap as tight as it would go with her teeth, then shuffled and moved around until her hands were above her head. She didn't know if this was going to work, the YouTuber was in a living room that was the size of this entire garage with lots of room to manoeuvre and she could barely move. What did he do? He whipped his hands down in front of his body and the tie wrap just burst open.

Counting to three she pushed her hands as far back as she could get them above her head then she brought them down over her head. As her hands moved lower, the pressure or whatever it was burst the tight plastic wide open, and she cried with the relief.

It bloody worked, well I never.

This needed to be shown in schools when they had public safety lessons or life lessons, whatever they called them, because in Rydal Falls there was more chance of being killed by a psychopath than there was of dying of a drug overdose or a car crash. Which was crazy, but true.

Taking a moment to slow her breathing down to normal and think, she lay back and wondered what she was going to do. She wasn't a hundred per cent sure what was happening, but Morgan knew one thing: she was getting out of here alive. After pushing and hammering against the trapdoor, she realised it must be bolted from above, but she wasn't giving in.

She felt around in her pocket and realised she had no phone, no keys, nothing to protect herself with except the bits of broken tie wrap that were pretty sharp. She felt all of the pieces to find the one with the most jagged edge. When she came face to face with whoever had thrown her into this pit like a sack of shit, she would be ready to poke their bloody eyes out with their own plastic ties. And she wouldn't feel one ounce of regret about it.

FIFTY-THREE

The footsteps came back into the garage, and Morgan realised they were louder this time. Whoever it was had a heel on the bottom of their shoes or boots that made it echo around the open space. She wondered if it was Marie; it sounded like a woman walking around up there. Opening her mouth to shout, she stopped herself, pausing a moment to make sure she was ready to fight. She managed to get herself onto all fours so she could spring up the moment the door was opened. Her head was a bit fuzzy, but she could worry about that when she was out of here. Sucking in a deep breath she began to shout. 'Help, help me.' Over and over again.

The footsteps hurried towards where she was which proved to her that whoever it was they knew about this pit.

'Hello, is someone down there?'

'Yes, let me out. Please.'

Morgan thought she recognised Beth Montgomery's voice and prayed it was her and not Marie. The sound of stuff being dragged around above her filled her with hope.

'Hang on, I just have to move this blasted lawn mower.'

Then the sound of the rug being dragged away and a bolt being worked free was like music to Morgan's ears. The door was thrown open, and the light that filtered down hurt Morgan's eyes. She lifted her hand across them to shelter them from the brightness.

'Morgan, how did you get in there? Did you fall in? Here, let me help you up.'

Beth reached down and gave her hand to Morgan, who clutched hold of it tight. She felt Beth yank her up and she clambered out of the pit. Onto her hands and knees.

'Oh my, you're bleeding. Your head is cut. We need to get you to the hospital.'

'I'm okay, give me your phone, please. I need to ring my boss.'

Beth nodded and patted her designer jeans for her phone. 'Oh, crap, it's in the house, let's get you inside and you can ring him there. I don't know what's happened, but it looks as if a bomb has exploded. There's broken glass in the hallway and everywhere is a mess, and I can't find Marie or Stefan. Has he done something to Marie? Did he kill Sharon? What the hell is happening?' Those last words were a strangled cry of fear and angst that made Morgan feel terrible for Beth.

Morgan didn't know what had gone on either but if there were no officers around clearly everyone had gone back to the station, and she wondered how long she'd been unconscious.

Beth hooked her arm through hers and helped her across the landscaped courtyard up the steps and into the house. She was right, it was a mess in here. The crunching of the glass from the broken hall table under her boots as she walked over it towards the kitchen an indication that all had not gone as planned when Ben and the team had searched the house.

Beth sat her on one of the high stools at the breakfast bar.

'I have a first aid kit, let me clean you up.'

'Thanks, I'm okay. I've had worse. Can you get your phone for me, Beth? They're going to be looking for me, and my partner is going to be beside himself with worry.'

'Of course, it's in the office charging. I'll go grab it. Here.'

She took a huge green plastic box out of a cupboard and passed it to Morgan, who opened it and began to rip open some packets of gauze to press against the cut on the back of her head. When she lifted the first pads away and saw the deep red blood that was covering it, she felt a little queasy. She hadn't even realised she'd hurt her head, but she'd hit it off the wall as she fell into that awful pit in the garage. Lowering her head onto her arms, she sucked in some deep breaths of air. There was no way after all of that was she passing out on Beth's kitchen floor. It wasn't happening, not now, not ever.

'Here you go, Morgan.'

Beth's voice sounded so far away. She lifted her head off her arms unable to turn to look at Beth because of the wave of sickness that was hanging over her like a dark cloud. She waited for her to come closer.

'If you want it, you have to come get it.'

Beth's voice was different; it had lost all its gentleness and was cold. Morgan straightened up. She shivered as a chill ran down the entire length of her spine. Forcing herself to turn around, she saw Beth leaning against the kitchen doorway with an iPhone in one hand and a shiny steel chef's knife in the other.

'What are you doing, Beth?'

'What are you doing, Morgan?' She mimicked her with a gleeful look in her eyes.

Morgan looked around for a weapon to defend herself with – that was the biggest, sharpest knife she had ever seen. There was a knife rack on the wall above the huge range cooker, but it was too far for Morgan to reach before Beth had buried the one she was holding into her chest or neck. The only thing she had to hand was the first aid box with what was probably the world's bluntest pair of safety scissors inside of it.

'I don't understand.'

'You don't need to, it's none of your business.'

'But Sharon was your daughter.'

Beth shrugged. 'Semantics she was a pain in the backside. Fawning over Stefan like he was her lover and not her stepdad, it made me sick to the stomach watching them. Do you know why she was so angry with Leah when she caught them together?'

Morgan shrugged.

'I'll tell you why, she was jealous of them.'

'But that's sick, she had a boyfriend. She wasn't in love with Stefan.'

'Excuse me, did you know her? No, you did not so don't go telling me that I'm delusional and it was all in my head. I've heard it too many times from that shrink who kept telling me it wasn't real.'

Morgan realised that nice, seemingly quiet Beth was most likely a ticking time bomb that had been building up to these murders for years.

'What about Lydia Williams? Did you think she was sleeping with Stefan or wanted to?'

'No, don't be absurd. They didn't know each other.'

'Then why?'

'She fit the profile, I mean I wanted it to look like there was a crazy, sick serial killer on the loose. She had to go.'

'What did you do with Lydia's dog?'

Beth tilted her head. 'It ran away; obviously I would never harm an innocent animal.'

Morgan felt as if she'd stepped into an alternate universe, this was so fucked up.

'Jack White, why kill him?'

'Jack was a convenient scapegoat, and he didn't love Sharon. She certainly didn't love him, not when she was pining over Stefan. He was a minor distraction in her wicked games.'

'Why me?'

'You were a huge mistake. I don't know what I was thinking except you were about to find all of Sharon's camera equipment in that toolbox you were about to search, and I know I was reckless and stupid but I did what I did. Look I chipped my nails when I tackled you and dragged you to that bloody pit. Three hours that manicure took because the stupid cow was gossiping to the nail tech next to her about her cheating boyfriend, and that's all I have left to show for it.'

She held up her hand and sure enough she was missing two nails on her right hand, and the others were scraped and chipped.

'Beth, listen to me, it's over. You can't kill me and get away with it. My colleagues will be onto you, they know I'm here and are on the way.'

'I know that, silly, I'm not a total flake. I'm going to be a good girl and let you take me to the station. I've been feeling a bit funny. I don't think my meds are working properly.'

Morgan noticed her take a step closer, towards her, the knife still clenched in her fingers. The contrast of those Barbie pink nails clasped around a steel blade that she was willing to use to kill her wasn't lost on Morgan, who gripped hold of the first aid box handle and slowly turned all the way to face Beth.

'You're not going to let me take you in, are you?'

Beth was giggling. 'Honestly, what do you think? You have a fifty per cent chance of getting it right.'

Morgan didn't know if this was going to work. She lunged for Beth, swinging the plastic box as hard as she could at her head at the same time as Beth thrust the knife towards Morgan. The knife caught the box and fell to the floor with a clatter; Morgan kicked it away from them as Beth launched herself at her, screeching like a wild woman. She took Morgan to the floor and the pair of them were fighting. Morgan managed to throw her off and swung her leg back so her Doc Marten boot connected with Beth's midriff, knocking the wind out of her. Beth was sucking in air, and Morgan didn't stop. She raised her foot again to stamp on Beth's head when she heard Ben's voice as he rushed towards her.

'Morgan don't, it's over.'

She felt him grab hold of her, wrapping his arms around her and dragging her to safety away from Beth who was reaching for the knife.

'I wouldn't do that if I was you, put your hands above your head.' Amber's voice was calm as she aimed her taser at Beth's chest in the exact position she'd aimed at her husband's two hours earlier.

Beth stopped what she was doing and began to giggle. 'Well, this was fun, wasn't it?'

Lunging for the knife, she grabbed it with both hands and drew it straight across her neck. As she kneeled on the floor the knife clattered to the ground, and she stared into Morgan's eyes as the blood began to spurt out of the huge cut.

As if realising what she'd done, she grabbed her neck with both hands to try and stem the blood.

Marc ran in with four officers and cried out, 'Holy hell, get a medic here now.'

He ran to the cooker, grabbing a tea towel from the rail then was kneeling next to Beth, wrapping it tightly around her neck to try and stem the bleeding. She opened her mouth, and an air bubble of blood popped over her lips.

Morgan watched in horror as Amber dropped the taser and grabbed another towel to wrap around the woman who was bleeding out in front of them.

They knew it was too late, the paramedics would never get here in time to save Beth's life.

The puddle of blood was spreading too fast all over the sparkling white Italian marble tiles, and they watched helpless as the light faded from Beth's eyes, leaving her staring up at the ceiling as she took her last gasp of breath.

FIFTY-FOUR

Morgan, who had needed some fresh air, was sitting outside on the stone steps to pull herself together. The Montgomerys' beautiful glass and slate lakeside mansion behind her, she closed her eyes. She felt the cool breeze that came off the lake revive her enough to stop feeling faint. The sun was setting fast, dipping behind the mountains in the background, and she knew once it had disappeared that the air would become chilly. She was cold to the bone with the horrors she had just witnessed. It was going to take time for her already full mind to process the last couple of hours. As the ambulance pulled into the drive she felt a tiny flicker of relief to see Nick, her favourite paramedic, behind the wheel. He took one look at her and shook his head as he climbed out of the truck.

'Morgan Brookes, what a surprise. I thought it was too good that you'd settled down and had managed not to get yourself injured for a while. I was hoping you were over this kind of thing.'

She grinned at him. 'What can I say, I tried, I really did.'

He carried his kit towards her, shaking his head. 'You clearly didn't try hard enough, let me take a look at that.' His gloved fingers were gentle as they moved her hair to get a better look at the wound. Snapping open the bag, he took out some gauze and bottles of something she couldn't read from the angle he was holding her head.

'Ouch, that stings.'

Nick was cleaning her head wound, that had thankfully stopped bleeding, with some wound wash. 'Hospital.'

'No.'

'Thought not, that's why I have my special Morgan Brookes kit with me.'

'You do?'

'Yes, I always have it with me in case you can't keep yourself out of trouble. I'll have your head glued back together in no time.'

'Thanks, Nick.'

'You don't need to thank me. I'd much rather be sorting you out than the woman on the floor in the kitchen who my friend is running a line on.'

'Yeah, you got the better end of this job.'

Ben, Marc and the officers were dealing with the carnage of the scene inside the kitchen. Amber was leaning against the hall wall watching them.

'Am I going to need one of your special kits if I take a job working with them?' She pointed to Morgan.

Nick shook his head. 'I don't think so, they're reserved for Detective Brookes.'

Morgan smiled at her. 'Not if you have your taser on you at all times. How come you have it anyway?'

'I told Madds I wasn't working with you lot without it. He agreed and let me bring it out. Good job I did, although I never got the chance to use it on her, but I would have in a heartbeat. You missed all the fun earlier when her husband punched Ben and I tasered him; he dropped to the floor like a rock.'

'Yeah, thank you, it sounds like it's been nonstop action. Welcome to the team, Amber.'

Amber smirked at her, and Morgan grinned back.

Ben came to see how they were getting on. 'Are you taking her in?'

Nick shook his head. 'No, she's the stubbornest patient I ever did treat. There, you're good to go, Morgan.' He'd finished taping gauze over the wound. 'I better see if Trev needs a hand. You know the score, any dizziness, fainting or blank spells you get straight to A&E.'

'I will.'

Nick snapped his case shut and stood up.

Ben smiled at Amber. 'Scene guard for me whilst I get her out of here?'

Amber rolled her eyes. 'Seriously?'

'Deadly.'

She shook her head. 'Might as well be back on response, at least I'd have my body armour.'

Ben linked an arm through Morgan's. 'Come on, Wendy has left some evidence bags in the office. You're going to get changed and then we're going to visit Ava Rose.'

'Ava Rose?'

He smiled at her. 'Amy's baby, she's a healthy eight pounds and five ounces, named after her nan, and Cain never passed out at any point during labour. She wants you to be the first person to see her so you know there is more to life than this.' He pointed in the direction of the kitchen where Beth's body was cooling on the floor.

Morgan was smiling. 'A girl, Ava Rose. I love it.'

Once she'd changed, Ben took her out to a waiting van and helped her inside. She couldn't understand how Beth had murdered her own daughter with so much rage. Clearly Beth wasn't a well woman, but still, it made Morgan shudder. She wondered if Sharon had seen her mum's eyes just before she killed her. Had Beth killed Lydia's dog too? She needed to know and would ask her as soon as she could interview her.

As they buzzed the doors to the maternity unit, Morgan whispered, 'I feel sick, do I look okay? I don't want to scare the baby, although you don't look much better, that's one hell of a black eye.'

Ben kissed her cheek. 'You look okay. I'm not going to lie, you've definitely looked better.'

She elbowed him in the ribs. 'Cheeky.'

'What can I say, you love me really and let me tell you, I love you a million times more than you could ever love me, so don't even argue the point.'

'I'm not going to, I'll take that.'

The door clicked and they walked towards the nurse's station, not quite reaching it before they heard Cain shout, 'In here.'

They turned to go into the room, where Cain greeted them at the door.

'Holy shit, Morgan, what did you do this time? And, Ben, that looks good on you. You look like a hard case fresh out of prison. Did you hit him, Morgan?'

Ben glared at him.

'Sorry, sorry. Glad you're both okay. You can fill us in, I need to know ASAP.'

Morgan stepped past him to see Amy sitting up in bed, her baby cradled to her chest and with a smile on her face that gave Morgan so much hope. She rushed over and hugged her gently, peering down at the baby. 'Oh my, she's adorable, Amy. Look at her hair.'

'I know, I thought she'd be bald. I never expected that. Do you want to hold her?'

Morgan shook her head. 'I don't know how to, I've never held a baby.'

'Neither did I until three hours ago. Cain is the expert, he'll pass her to you. Take a seat.'

Morgan looked to the chair and sat down on it. Cain gently took the baby from Amy and positioned her into Morgan's arms. She stared down at her perfect little fingers and toes; her nose was wrinkled, and she had the cutest face she'd ever seen for a baby.

'Oh, Amy, she's perfect.'

Amy grinned. 'She looks good in your arms.'

Morgan looked at Ben who had tears in his eyes that he was blotting with his shirt sleeve.

He smiled. 'Amy, she's perfect. Congratulations, you did amazing.'

'Thanks, boss.'

'Amy, I'm not your boss when you're not at work. I'm your friend.'

'Thanks, Ben.'

Cain was beaming as he looked around the room at his friends. 'Well then now we've all realised how wonderful babies are, who is going to tell me what the fuck happened to Morgan's head, again, and who punched you?'

'Cain,' said Ben and Amy at the same time.

Morgan laughed. 'It's a long story, not now. Let's not spoil this with talk of violence.'

Cain shrugged. 'Okay, but you better fill me in later.'

'I will, I promise.' Morgan reached down and stroked Ava Rose's cheek with her finger. It felt like a peach, all soft and fuzzy.

She sighed, this had been exactly what she needed, and she was so grateful she had friends to make her realise that life wasn't all bad, that not all people were evil.

Ava opened her eyes and looked at Morgan for the briefest of moments, releasing a rush of love so strong she knew she would always be there for her, Amy, Cain and Ben no matter what. They were a team, and she wouldn't let anything tear them apart. Between them they would look after this precious little girl, and she would want for nothing. Looking down at her, Morgan realised that her life did have meaning and it filled her heart with so much love.

EPILOGUE

Yolanda had messaged her new friend, Fairy Rose, earlier. There had been no reply, but she'd shared her location with her and she hoped she could find her. The trail she'd hiked along to set up camp had taken her longer than she'd realised. She had taken hours to get her tent, equipment and camera in the right position to try and capture the new moon as it rose in the sky. It was getting dark, and she was going to have to start recording soon before she lost all daylight. She heard branches snap in the distance and paused what she was doing. Nobody was out here except her; nobody knew where she was except for Fairy Rose who was probably walking towards her and making the noise. As she positioned herself on her yoga mat she called out.

'Hey, Fairy, I'm about to start, so if you wouldn't mind waiting until I've finished recording the intro then you can set up your mats and stuff.'

There was no reply, and Yolanda paused. Maybe it was a fox or a badger. Whatever it was, she didn't have time, she was running out of light. She used the tiny remote to set her camera recording.

'Hey guys, I made it. Isn't this something else? This area is stunningly beautiful. The moon is slowly rising, and the birds are still singing. It's the perfect place to do a little new moon yoga ritual and get those affirmations written down. I prefer to call them my new moon wishes. There's something far more magical about fairy wishes, isn't there? Talking of Fairies, I have someone I want you to meet soon; Fairy Rose is going to be doing this new moon.'

Yolanda stopped talking. Looking down, she saw a dark bloom of red spreading across the front of her white yoga bra. Then an intense pain as the knife that had been plunged straight through her back into her chest was tugged out and pushed in again with far more force. A small gurgle escaped her lips, and she screamed once before toppling to the side on her brand-new white mat.

Her killer watched from behind, impressed they had managed to sneak up on her so stealthily. She was dead before she hit the mat. They nodded to themselves then walked over to the camera, switching it off before dragging her body into the small two-man tent that Yolanda had put up less than an hour ago. They pulled the mat into the tent, collected the camera equipment and walked back along the trail the way they'd come, stopping on the main path to untie the dog that was panting with excitement to see them.

Bending down to pat its head, they kept hold of its lead and walked all the way back to the secluded car park where they'd left the car. Nothing was going to stop them now, especially now they knew how good watching a person die could be, and this one was even better. It had all been captured on film for them to watch over and over again in the comfort of their own home. They sighed as they patted the dog's head that was sitting next to them in the passenger seat of the car, wondering how long it would be before another influencer decided to tell the world what they were doing and where they were doing it. They would be watching and waiting, ready to make their next move.

They were always watching; it was what they did best.

A LETTER FROM HELEN

I want to say a huge thank you for choosing to read *Gone in the Night*. If you did enjoy it, and want to keep up to date with all my latest releases, just sign up at the following link. Your email address will never be shared and you can unsubscribe at any time.

www.bookouture.com/helen-phifer

I hope you're not too mad at the cliff-hanger ending, but I wanted this book to be different. This far into the series I thought you might enjoy a little bit of an I'm not going to forgive Phifer for that moment 😜 . Fin Palmer was as much of a surprise to me when he turned up as to you and I love it when that happens. I had no idea he was going to rear his ugly head again after all this time, but he did, and we coped. Writing is truly a magical process, I always say I have no idea where the words come from, but I am so grateful that they do.

I hope you loved *Gone in the Night* and if you did I would be very grateful if you could write a review. I'd love to hear what you think, and it makes such a difference helping new readers to discover one of my books for the first time.

I love hearing from my readers – you can get in touch on my social media or my website.

Thanks,
Helen

KEEP IN TOUCH WITH HELEN

www.helenphifer.com

facebook.com/Helenphifer1

x.com/helenphifer1

ACKNOWLEDGEMENTS

As always, the biggest thank you goes to my wonderful, amazing editor, Jennifer Hunt. Thank you for loving this book as much as the others and for your kind words of encouragement. Those little comment boxes are so lovely and never fail to make me smile, not to mention the relief that it's not a load of old rubbish. Thank you, Jennifer. Xxx

A special thank you to Jan Currie for her brilliant copy editing, I really appreciate all of your hard work Jan. Another huge thank you to Shirley Khan for her amazing proofreading skills.

A massive thank you to the whole team Bookouture for everything you do to publish these stories, you're all amazing and I can't thank you enough for continually making my dreams come true. Xx

A huge thank you to my wonderful readers who have been on this journey from the beginning. Your support and words of encouragement mean the world to me; I love you all. Thank you also to the new readers who may have picked up this book and wondered what you got yourselves into. I hope you enjoyed it and will go on to read the rest of the series; there is a lot going on in Morgan's life.

A massive thank you to all the brilliant book bloggers out there, you are worth your weight in gold, and I appreciate every single one of you.

I never set out to kill social media influencers. I'm obsessed with quite a few YouTubers myself at the moment, but only in a good way, and I want to give a little shout out to some of my favourites. If I get any downtime, you'll find me watching vlogs mainly on Salem because I left my heart there on my first visit in 2023. I also love true crime and horror locations. So, thank you to the amazing @Pumpkinandgray @grimmlifecollective @ThatSalemGirl @50statesofmadness64 for the endless hours of entertainment. You guys rock, I mean that from the bottom of my heart, keep doing what you're doing because it's so good.

A huge thank you to my amazing friend Paul O'Neill for not telling me he's had enough of these stories and always dropping everything to do my final read through for me.

As always, much love to my gorgeous family and friends. I couldn't do this without your support; it means the world to me. A big thank you to book club too, you make Mondays so much more fun.

All my love,

Helen xx

PUBLISHING TEAM

Turning a manuscript into a book requires the efforts of many people. The publishing team at Bookouture would like to acknowledge everyone who contributed to this publication.

Audio
Alba Proko
Sinead O'Connor
Melissa Tran

Commercial
Lauren Morrissette
Hannah Richmond
Imogen Allport

Cover design
The Brewster Project

Data and analysis
Mark Alder
Mohamed Bussuri

Editorial
Jennifer Hunt
Charlotte Hegley

RAISING READERS
Books Build Bright Futures

Dear Reader,

We'd love your attention for one more page to tell you about the crisis in children's reading, and what we can all do.

Studies have shown that reading for fun is the **single biggest predictor of a child's future life chances** – more than family circumstance, parents' educational background or income. It improves academic results, mental health, wealth, communication skills, ambition and happiness.

The number of children reading for fun is in rapid decline. Young people have a lot of competition for their time, and a worryingly high number do not have a single book at home.

Hachette works extensively with schools, libraries and literacy charities, but here are some ways we can all raise more readers:

- Reading to children for just 10 minutes a day makes a difference
- Don't give up if children aren't regular readers – there will be books for them!

- Visit bookshops and libraries to get recommendations
- Encourage them to listen to audiobooks
- Support school libraries
- Give books as gifts

There's a lot more information about how to encourage children to read on our websites: **www.RaisingReaders.co.uk** and **www.JoinRaisingReaders.com**.

Thank you for reading.

hachette
UK

Printed in Dunstable, United Kingdom